BREAKING THE GIRL AND EAGER TO PLEASE
Two Erotic Novels of Submission

ALSO BY KIM CORUM

Playtime
99 Martinis: Uncensored
Heartbreaker
Breaking the Girl
The Other Woman
Now She's Gone
Eager to Please
Dead Sexy: Two Tales of Vampire Erotica
Sex Scenes: Erotica Excerpts from the Novels of Kim Corum
Take Your Shirt Off: A Novel of Hollywood

BREAKING THE GIRL AND EAGER TO PLEASE
Two Erotic Novels of Submission

KIM CORUM

Abernathy and Monroe

For You

This edition published in 2009 by Abernathy and Monroe.

Breaking the Girl copyright © 2003 by Kim Corum
Eager to Please copyright © 2004 by Kim Corum

Paperback ISBN-13: 978-0-9841957-0-1
Paperback ISBN-10: 0-9841957-0-X

First published by New Tradition Books in 2003 and 2004.

Published by Abernathy and Monroe.

eBook ISBN–13: 978-0-9841957-1-8
eBook ISBN–10: 0-9841957-1-8

Breaking the Girl

a story of submission

Don't try this at home.

"Please," I said. "Just let me—"

"No," he hissed and pulled my hand away from between my legs. "Not yet."

"Please," I begged. "Please just let me touch it!"

"No," he mumbled, then, "No, Kristine, not until I say!"

That didn't stop me from trying.

The belt cracked against my ass. It drove a ferocious welt into my skin and burned like fire. I moaned.

"Please," I begged. "Please, please, *please*!"

"No."

It's always the same with us. Always the same with me. I always do this. I always beg to get it done and over with before the show has even really begun. I just can't wait. That's my problem—impatience.

"I can do it this once," I said, my voice rising to fever pitch. "Then I can do it again and—"

"Shh. Be quiet."

I stopped talking, begging, pleading. Plotting. I wasn't going to win him over. It was his way or no way. And I knew that. So it was his way.

He bent down in front of me, taking my head between his hands. I couldn't see him. My eyes were covered by a silk scarf, the one we used on special occasions, like a birthday or an anniversary. We celebrated at least once a week, regardless.

He rubbed my face and kissed me. My mouth opened and welcomed his tongue, sucked on it, loved its soft edges. My tongue drew circles on his, arousing a soft moan from his lips that came from deep down inside. I kissed him, hoping to soften him so he would allow me to touch myself and get the torture over and done with. But he knew what he was doing. He was withholding so the pleasure—the orgasm—would be doubled, tripled even. So it would be so intense I would shake and shiver and moan and groan and dance and sing. And beg for another.

I ground against the bed, moving my hips up and down. I was *this* close. This close and I needed to do it. Actually, my body just did it on its own; I just followed it and allowed it to search out the spot.

The belt came down hard again, halting me. A scream erupted from my lips. It was one of those I couldn't stop. I wailed until my throat was dry and my voice cracked. Another whack, another hoarse scream, this one less intense.

He put a gag in my mouth.

This time, I couldn't take it anymore. This time was different from the last. The last time had gone on half the night. The last time we tried this was yesterday. I couldn't wait like I had then. No. No. No! I had to have it now. *Give it to me!*

I couldn't utter a word and charm him into doing what I wanted. I couldn't bat my eyes and make him feel guilty. I was totally helpless, which was what he liked best.

Then he got behind me and I felt him glide his cock into me. Ahhh! YES! YES! The end was near. I was exhausted. But soon I'd be released. Freed. Unchained. And it'd be worth it, all of it.

As he began to fuck me, he said, "Tomorrow, we're going to try something different."

I cocked my head to the side and listened, hanging on his every word.

"Tomorrow, I'm going to tie you up."

Tie me up, tie me down, beat me, switch me, hold me tight, love me forever.

It never occurred to me to say, *This isn't natural.* Well, it did. Once. And I immediately dismissed the thought.

First of all, just let me say, I wasn't that kind of girl. I didn't like submission or domination and sex was just plain sex and though I had good sex, it never really ever went beyond the meat and potatoes variety. Me on top. Him—whoever he might be at that moment—on top. Cowgirl—facing *and* reverse. I tried anal once and only once and that was enough. (I only did it 'cause I was drunk and the guy would not leave me alone.) Doggie. The 69. The basic stuff no one actually sat down and taught you but you figured out on your own. Because, well, it *is* second nature. Sex, I mean.

But to have someone tie me up? No. To have someone blindfold me? Nuh uh. That just wasn't my bag. I just wasn't that kind of "tie me up, tie me down, beat me, switch me, hold me tight, love me forever" kind of girl. And if a guy tried to pull something like that, I was out the door. Goodbye, asshole. It just wasn't me. I was *not* that kind of girl.

He was that kind of guy. Which made me that kind of girl.

"You love it," he said once. "You love it when I'm in control of you, when you don't have a choice in what's going to happen to you or to your body. Tell me you love it."

"I love it."

And I did. I won't sit here and deny that. Let me rephrase it, though. *I loved doing it with him*. He was special to me. Special because he knew how to push my buttons, get me going and take me over the edge to that never-never land of multiple orgasms that left me weak, fragile and begging for more.

Oh, and I begged. I begged for it all. I wanted it all. Once I started doing it, once I got over that roadblock, over that initial fear, there were no boundaries left. No restrictions and certainly no limitations.

And there was no conclusion in sight. All I saw, all I thought of, was him and what he was going to do next. I wasn't a slave. I was a willing participant.

In the end, I knew what he was doing. He was beating me down, taking control of my body, my mind and my soul. Then he'd rebuild it, brick by brick, using his words of love to re-master me until I stood anew in his eyes, in the image he had created for me, of me.

Ain't love a bitch?

Maybe I should start at the beginning.

Let me just say that when I first saw him, I didn't see sparks. I didn't have an immediate attraction to him. Sure, he was handsome in that aloof, businessman kind of way. I liked his smile. But it didn't go beyond that. It didn't go beyond because he was a customer and I didn't go there with customers. I was a stripper. In New Orleans.

He kinda reminded me of Gatsby. That's the image I had of him all along. I'd always had a fondness for literary characters and I believed Gatsby to be far and above the best. He was so romantic, yet so vulnerable. Frank was romantic. He was not vulnerable. Obviously, I was. Like Gatsby, he watched from the sidelines before he made his initial move and after he made it, I was captivated.

I hadn't even planned on staying in New Orleans. I had gone to Mardi Gras with my friend, Chelsea. I'd just gotten dumped and was still reeling from the break-up when she offered a temporary solution to my blues: Mardi Gras. She'd even paid the way. She had just divorced her super-rich husband and could afford it. The girl was rolling in dough, which she was hell-bent on spending. She was afraid he'd try to take it back. She said, "If it's not there, he can't get his slimy little paws on it."

Mardi Gras was the best party. I danced with strangers all night long in the French Quarter, flashed my boobs for beads, drank way too many hurricanes and threw up in Jackson Square. I loved it. Every bit. That Mardi Gras was one of the best times I've ever had.

On our last night there, we were walking by Tempest, the stripclub. The bouncer in the doorway stopped us and offered us free admittance. Why not? We went in, sat down a few feet from the stage and giggled like schoolgirls. The girl who was onstage got pretty pissed off at us.

She yelled, "If you think you can do better, get your asses up here and do it!"

Never one to back down from a challenge, Chelsea jumped up there, dragging me with her, and proceeded to strip. At first I was horrified, but then I looked around. The place was packed and everyone was egging us on. So Chelsea and I did our "girl/girl" routine we pull on guys in bars—so they'll buy us drinks—and gave everyone a little show. The stripper even joined in. Soon we had our own threesome and after it was over, Chelsea and I were fifty bucks richer.

It was a blast, pure and simple, it was a blast. The manager gave us a free drink and the other strippers sat at our table and began to tell us how much money we could make doing what we'd just done.

It seemed like a good idea at the time. So, yeah. It just kinda worked out like that.

Chelsea and I extended our visit. But after two weeks, she was bored and ready to go back home. But I wasn't, mainly because I have never been one to turn down money. Especially not that kind of money and I was raking it in. Besides, stripping off my clothes every night made me feel like I had some measure of power. To have the complete undivided attention from those men—and women—gave me a thrill. To know they were hot for me made me feel special. I slowly became the most uninhibited person I knew. And once you do it and get over the initial hang-up, it's no big deal.

So why not make some money while you're at it?

Chelsea went back home to our little town of Castile, Tennessee and I set up residence in the Quarter with one of the other strippers, Jackie. She and I soon became best friends. We'd leave the stripclub about two in the morning then hit the clubs, dance till dawn then go out for breakfast, back to the apartment where we'd crash, get up around seven that night, shower and go to it again.

This went on for about six months.

I don't really know what got into me to start acting this way, but for the first time in my life, I was free—free to do whatever I wanted. I had no obligations. I was a free agent. I was thirty-two going on nineteen, though I didn't tell anyone my "real" age and had to lie about it to get the job. I looked younger than I was and, luckily, my breasts still pointed to the ceiling instead of down at the floor. I sure as hell didn't get the job because of my dancing ability.

It was so nice to be like that. It was so nice just to be *me* for once. I'd always done what was expected of me before: Graduate high school, go to college, flunk out, get a menial job, marry my boyfriend, divorce him, go to bars and try to find another one to take his place, fail miserably and wake up with some Neanderthal. The same stuff we all do, rotating our time between work, drink and sex.

Now I was doing what I wanted, when I wanted and was making more money than I could have ever imagined making. I was having the time of my life.

I never knew my life could change so drastically in such a short span of time. It was like once I let go of the past, and of all the things holding me back, I freed myself to all these different experiences. I not only let go of a crappy job, I let go of a crappy life. And once I let go, everything just opened up. It was like a metamorphosis of sorts.

Then he came into my life. He. Him. That man, that guy. That one person. The only one I would allow to do the things he did to me.

Once he was there, I could not for the life of me push him away. He stuck to me like super glue and nothing could tear him away. He became a permanent fixture, someone that I could never imagined living without once he was in. And there was no before after he came into my life. Before disappeared. It disappeared because it didn't matter anymore.

I could stop here and say things like, *Well, if I had called in sick that night, none of this would have happened. If I had gone home when mom called and asked me to, I would have never met him. If I had let one of the other girls give him a private dance, we would have never hooked up.* But he didn't want one of the other girls. He wanted me.

But I'm not going to say any of that. I don't regret meeting him. And I don't really regret the things that happened between us. Regrets are for fools. They do nothing but allow people to wallow in their own guilt, give a name to the misery they feel and give it a reason to ruin their lives.

I won't do that. It's not worth it.

Besides, I did enjoy myself. Tremendously. As with the stripping, being involved in a relationship like that is something I could never have imagined for myself. It just wasn't my thing. But once it happened, it just seemed natural, like second nature.

Love can change your mind about all sorts of things and drag your heart along with it. It can convince you that there is no way you could ever live without this person who is as sublime as a sunrise and as transcendent as dusk. It can change your mind to include something as subversive as this story I'm going to tell.

His name was Frank.

Just Frank. His last name really doesn't matter. It was Smith or Jones or Gallagher or... Hell. Just pick one. They're really all the same. I didn't know that much about him. I would press him for information that I felt I needed to know, but he'd never tell me anything. He'd say it didn't matter. It did, of course. It did, at first. After a while, no, it didn't matter.

He didn't want to know anything about me. He didn't care to know about my childhood (single parent home), my siblings (one older sister, Caroline, one younger brother, Paul), how I did in school (straight "C" student—I hated it), about my divorce (hellacious—the fucker would just not let me go), or why my last boyfriend broke up with me (I asked him to and to my utter surprise and delight, he did). He didn't care that I always cheated in relationships and that's why I couldn't "keep a man," as my mother would say.

The thing is, I never wanted a man, let alone enough to "keep" one and I only cheated to get men out of my life, to drive them away. To me, men were useful on two fronts: 1) To fix stuff; and 2) To fuck.

Honestly, I just didn't want to be tied down. I was afraid if I was tied down, I'd miss out on something.

Sure, when I'd get dumped, or do the actual dumping, I'd act all heartbroken and eat the obligatory ice cream and do the obligatory soul searching, but within a few weeks, just before the pity I was getting from everyone was about to run out, I'd perk up and move on. So, yeah, I never really attached myself to anyone. Not really. Not until him anyway. And I wanted him with every cell in my body. I wanted him to love me, like I loved him. I don't know if he ever did. He said he did, but who could tell? I think he did, but there was always some measure of doubt hanging around my head.

That's a lie. I knew he loved me. There was never any doubt after the first time he told me.

I never knew I'd want someone so much. So much that he would become my obsession, my force of life. So much that I would—literally—let him walk all over me. And enjoy every second of it.

Private show.

As I've said, I didn't feel an immediate attraction to Frank. He was just another customer who had requested a private show in the backroom. His request would help pay my rent.

I was working a table of college boys—I mean cheap asses—when the manager, Tom, came over and jerked his head to the side. I looked over. And there he was.

"So?" I asked.

"He'd like a private show," he whispered in my ear.

I eyed the man. He looked extremely elegant in his expensive suit. He even had on cufflinks. Gold ones.

"Come on, Kristy," he said and held out his hand.

"Excuse me, boys," I said and smiled at them. "I'll be right back."

Tom led me over to him. I studied him as we approached his table, wondering what was up with him. He studied me as well. His look was more than a little disconcerting; it was plain weird. He looked at me in a way that made me feel strange, as if he didn't own me, but it would only be a matter of time before he would. I didn't like that look. I didn't like it when men assumed I was a cheap whore, even if I did work as a stripper. I didn't like it. I didn't like it one bit.

He was handsome, beyond handsome, really. Old movie star handsome, like Rudolph Valentino handsome. Elegant. He could have stepped out of a silent picture with a highball glass in one hand and stunningly beautiful woman on the other. And he wouldn't have looked out of place.

His manners were even elegant. The way he smiled, only slightly, as we approached him. The way he cocked his head to the side and drank in my body, which was clad in a tight, aquamarine tank dress. He studied the way my breasts were trying to burst out of the top of my dress. The way my feminine curves jutted this way and that. He seemed especially pleased at my dark hair, which was pulled back into a ponytail. My face perfected with makeup, bringing out the blue in my eyes. My full red lips made even redder by lipstick.

He didn't so much as take me in as suck me in. I don't think he missed anything. He definitely liked what he saw. And as I stared at him, the feeling was mutual. His eyes were this intense shade of blue. They were so blue, they looked fake. I'd never seen eyes like that on anyone.

We stopped in front of him. He smiled—or tried to—up at us and nodded his appreciation.

"Come with us," Tom said and he followed us to the backroom which was so dark I could barely see anything until my eyes adjusted. There were several other strippers working in there. I waved to Jackie. She studied the man, raised one eyebrow, then got back to work.

He sat down on a sofa. Tom left us. I smiled and began to dance in front of him, tugging at the top of my dress.

"No," he said and stopped me.

"Excuse me?"

He shook his head. "Give me a minute. I want to look at you."

What the hell? Look at me? Good grief. I frowned at him and decided he was an asshole. Some guys were. Most just let you do your thing, paid you and went on their way. Others had to get their "money's worth." I figured him for one of those. But I didn't put up with that. When I was working, time was money. And he was wasting mine.

"Sorry," I said softly and began to move again. "House rules."

He seemed momentarily stunned by my forwardness. He blinked twice at me, but I didn't stop. I had a job to do and he wasn't going to get in my way.

I moved to the side, rubbing my breasts with one hand. He watched me and settled back into the couch.

"Do you have panties on?" he asked.

I nodded and rubbed my legs.

"Take them off."

I stared at him, almost appalled. Didn't he know that I ran the show? I almost gave up and told him to leave, but then I thought I'd already done about half the show, so why not finish?

I didn't say a word but did as I was told. I bent over and, taking my time, wriggled out of them, moving my hips as I did so and then kicked them to the side. I looked up at him. He nodded and seemed slightly impressed by the little show. I smiled at him and straddled him, rubbing my naked crotch up against his and moaned in his ear, then nibbled on it a little. I tugged my dress down and my breasts popped out. He stared down at them, seemingly pleased, and raised one eyebrow when I fingered my nipple. I felt his hand on my ass. I removed it and handed it back to him.

"You can't touch," I said and stopped moving.

He nodded.

I pressed up against him, rubbing my breasts in his face and my crotch against his. I suddenly realized I was wet. I usually didn't get wet because I looked at this as a job. But I was. Wet. I was turned on. And I was getting his expensive suit dirty.

That made me want to laugh. Whatever would he tell the dry cleaner? Hell, he'd just get his maid to do it. He wouldn't give a shit what she told him.

He muttered something.

"What?" I asked and looked him in the eye. "I couldn't hear you."

"You're very beautiful."

I smiled. I heard this all the time from my customers. But it seemed different coming from him. I wanted to believe he actually thought it and wasn't just using a line on me.

"Thank you," I said.

He nodded and seemed uncomfortable.

I rubbed a little more. Oh, shit. If I kept at this, I wouldn't stop. I'd keep rubbing until I got my groove on, then I wouldn't be able to help myself and I'd come. And I'd never done that before. I'd never wanted to before now. I got an idea. Might include a big tip. Guys loved this kind of thing, right?

I whispered in his ear, "Can I come on your leg?"

His eyebrows shot up.

"Huh?" I said and felt his dick. He was hard. "Can I rub up against your leg and come on it?"

He cleared his throat, then said, "No."

That was *not* the answer I was looking for. What an asshole. Didn't he know how many guys would love for me to do this very thing?

I moved away from him. But I didn't stop rubbing. I liked having control of him. I liked knowing I could do whatever I wanted and he couldn't do a damn thing about it.

"Why not?" I whispered. "Why not let me come on your leg?"

"Because I say so."

Tough shit. I began to grind against him, not letting him move until I could feel the orgasm come at me. I held onto the back of the couch and didn't stop. I rode his leg for all it was worth and it was worth quite a bit. I came then, shivering, and fell against his chest. I stayed there for a moment, wondering why the hell I'd just done that. I mean, I pretended to do it with other guys, but I'd never actually *done* it.

He wasn't pleased. I could just tell. Like I said, most guys would beg me to do that. But not him. He was some type of pervert, I could just tell. There was something wrong with him.

He pushed me off him. I glared up at him and watched as he took out his wallet from his breast pocket, took out some money and threw it on the couch. Then he turned on his heel and left the room without a word.

My face burned. The bastard. I hated him. Which is the exact reason why I began to love him.

Drunk and happy.

He'd come into the club almost nightly after that. He'd sit at the bar with another man, a bigger man, who I presumed to be his bodyguard. He was either his bodyguard or the guy just couldn't relax. He kept glancing around the room as if he were casing it. It was almost funny.

They'd watch, but he didn't request any more private shows. Or even a table dance. Fuck him anyway. The way he had acted pissed me off so much that I wanted to tell Tom to kick him and his bodyguard out. I couldn't, of course. Tom wouldn't kick him out unless he *did* something. Of course, he didn't *do* anything. He didn't cause a commotion. He was polite, a good customer. He drank the expensive but watered down drinks and smoked an occasional cigarette. He watched from the sidelines but never participated.

I knew why he came around. I knew he was there for me. And that he'd eventually want to talk to me. Maybe do more. I wasn't interested. I pretended to be uninterested. I was dying to have him talk to me. But he'd have to make the first move.

He didn't for the longest time. But then he did.

One night, I left work early. I had a really bad allergy headache and I couldn't take it anymore. Tom told me to go home. I slipped out the back and thought about getting a taxi though our apartment was only a few blocks from the club. I decided against it. I didn't like to waste money on stuff like that. Besides, the walk might help my headache.

I got on Bourbon and cut across, walking quickly. The street, as usual, was alive. People were drunk on every corner. Drunk and happy. I ignored them and quickened my pace, wanting an aspirin and bed so bad I could feel it.

I felt a touch on the back of my arm, then at my elbow. Someone was grabbing me, halting me. I automatically jerked my arm because guys always think they can pull this kind of stuff in the Quarter. They'll come right up to you and stagger around, grabbing at you like you're a piece of meat. Usually they're drunk off their asses and will mutter stupidly, *"How's about letting me buy you a drink?"*

How's about you fuck off?

"Excuse me?"

I turned around and saw his bodyguard. I was surprised, at first, but then my head throbbed again. It was aching. I groaned and held it and asked, "What do you want?"

He jerked his head to the side. I looked over at a big, sleek black Mercedes. It was a limo. *His* limo. Why do guys like that always have limos? One day, I'd love to see one of them running around in a Pinto. Or a Bug.

I looked at him. "*And?*"

"He'd like a word. Please?"

"Sorry, I've got to get home," I said and started off.

"Miss?" he called. "Please just do it. For me?"

I stared at him. He seemed almost in a panic. The bastard would probably fire him if he didn't get what he wanted. I nodded and cursed under my breath as I followed him to the car. He held the back door open and I got in.

"Nice to see you," he said before my ass landed on the seat.

"Okay," I said and winced, holding my head. "So what's up?"

"What's wrong?"

"I have a headache," I muttered.

"Would you like an aspirin?"

"No," I said. "What do you want?"

He didn't reply. He was studying me with one raised eyebrow. I gave him his look back, raising an eyebrow myself. He chuckled and looked away.

"What do you want?" I asked again.

"Would you like a ride home?"

I stared around the interior of the car, breathing in the nice scent of leather from the seats. I couldn't think of a reason *not* to let him give me a ride. Other than the fact that I never let strangers give me rides. But he wasn't really a stranger. Not really.

"Sure," I said and leaned back.

He nodded at the bodyguard, who, apparently, was also his chauffeur. The car rolled forward.

"I live at—"

"I know where you live," he said.

I stared at him, mouth agape. "Really?"

He nodded.

"Is there a reason for that?"

"No," he said.

I rolled my eyes, but didn't pursue it. I didn't care enough about him to pursue it. All I could tell about him was that he was weird. That's the only impression I had. I didn't want to know anything else. I didn't need to.

"By the way," he said, leaning over and extending his hand. "I'm Frank."

Frank. Frank. Franklin. Franklin D. Roosevelt. Frank Sinatra. Frank furters. *Frankly, Mr. Shankly*. FRANK-EN-STEIN.

I eyed his hand. His hands were soft and smooth, his nails clean and trim. He had nice hands. Big. A touch of dark hair on the side. A gold ring on his right pinky, a Rolex peeking out from beneath the cuff of his jacket.

Damn. Rich guys like him rarely gave me the time of day. I got the Timex and gold wedding band guys, but not guys like him. Not much anyway. And when I did come across them, they'd turn my stomach. They'd want a dance, maybe want to give me their number or tell me how I could "earn" some extra money, but none of them ever approached me in this kind of manner. None of them let me ride in their fancy cars or offered me aspirin. I guess that was because they all just wanted to use me.

I suddenly felt very uncomfortable.

He hand was still extended. He shook it a little, offering it again. I was almost afraid to take it, but what choice did I have?

I shook his hand and muttered, "Kristy."

"Yeah, I know you name, Kristine."

"Oh," I said off-handedly. "So what do you want?"

He leaned back and seemed to relax. He shot me a quick glance and tried to smile. He failed miserably. He said, "Nothing. Just thought you'd like a ride home."

He spoke with only a slight Southern accent. I wondered if he'd been brought up in New Orleans. Where did a guy like him come from?

I looked out the window, wishing I'd never gotten in the car. I really wasn't in the mood to play mind games. Well, I was never in the mood for mind games. Who was? I didn't like being fucked with. And I could tell he was one of those guys who would fuck with you. He'd get a big kick out of driving you crazy, and once you were too far gone, he'd get a big kick out of leaving you flat on your ass.

I decided to mess with him.

"You want to fuck me, don't you?" I asked. "That's what this is all about, isn't it?"

Again, the raised eyebrow, the slight smile combined with a little embarrassment. I kept staring at him, not letting him back down.

"No," he finally replied. "I don't suppose that's what I'd call it."

"Then what would you call it?" I asked and leaned over towards him. "Making love?"

He shook his head.

"Screwing?"

He glanced at me. "You've got a mouth on you, don't you?"

"I sure do."

"Were you raised in a trailer park?"

"No," I said. "Were you?"

"Uh, no."

He sighed, as if this was not quite going as he'd planned. He liked control. I could tell that. But so did I.

"Why are you a stripper?" he asked.

"Pays the bills."

He shook his head.

"What?" I asked.

"That's not why you're a stripper."

"It's not?"

He leaned over so our noses were almost touching. I breathed in and smelled him, his cologne, his pheromones. Him. Ahh… Yeah… *No.*

"So why is it?" I breathed.

"You're a stripper because you like to manipulate men."

I pulled back. "That's not true."

He nodded. "The first night we met, you wanted to manipulate me."

"I don't do that with everyone," I said and moved away from him.

He grabbed my arm and pulled me back. "No, you don't. You don't do it with everyone because you don't have to. You can get most of these assholes with a bat of your eyes."

"What the hell are you talking about?" I hissed. "And let go of my arm!"

He didn't let go. "You love having men in the palm of your hand, don't you?"

I took a breath and calmed myself down, thinking I could somehow take control of the situation. I placed my hand on his, eased his fingers back gently and freed my arm. He let go of it with only slight reluctance.

"Listen," I said. "I don't know you. You don't know me."

"So?" he asked softly.

"So, you don't have any right to ask me those kinds of questions."

He nodded slightly and took my arm again, pulling me closer. I didn't fight him; I slid over and liked the way our legs touched. I got an electric charge from it, just from that touch.

He muttered, "But you know what I'm talking about. You know exactly what I'm talking about. You get off knowing these men are creaming their pants over you and that they can't touch you and that they'll never have you. You flaunt your sexuality like a badge."

Well, that's one way to put it. I rolled my eyes.

"Am I right?" he asked.

Was he right? Was he? Yeah. He was right. So what? What was the harm in it?

He released me but didn't shove me away. We sat like that, that close, for a long moment, neither one of us wanting to move. I looked out the window. We were on my street. I was almost disappointed that the ride was nearly over.

"You don't like me, do you?" he asked.

I shook my head. "No, I don't really."

He chuckled. "Why?"

Why? *Why didn't I like him?* That was a good question. Maybe it was because he scared me. He scared the hell out of me. It wasn't that I was afraid of him; it was that I was afraid of myself, of what I'd do if he got me under his thumb. I'd never felt like that before. I didn't like the feeling, either.

The car stopped. Just as I reached for the door handle, he leaned over and grabbed me, pulling me back in.

"You feel it, though, don't you?" he whispered.

"Feel what?" I asked and stared into his eyes.

"That energy," he said softly. "It's undeniable."

"What are you talking about?" I whispered.

"Sex," he said. "If we had sex, we'd explode."

I looked into his eyes. He was crazier than hell. That's all. He was one crazy motherfucker. But he was right. We would explode. We disliked one another just enough to know that. To know we had it. You don't get it with everyone, that energy, that pure sexual energy. You're lucky if you get it at all.

"You're sick," I told him and meant it.

He nodded. "And you're just like me."

He was probably right. I hated that. Even so, I replied dryly, "Whatever."

He nodded at me. I opened the door and got out just as he said, "I'd like you to come to my house for dinner."

I tried to shut the door on him to put an end to this, this impending relationship or fuck fest or whatever it was we were about to embark on. I wanted to run, to try to forget about him and all this sexual energy and his craziness, and push him out of my life by simply closing the door on him. But he held it open.

"I don't think so," I said, knowing that was the best answer, but feeling disappointed by it.

"Tomorrow night," he said.

"I work tomorrow."

"I've already spoken with Tom," he said. "He's giving you the night off."

I leaned down close to him, so close that we were eye to eye. "Let me tell you one thing, I can't be bought. Not by your money, by your looks, your limo, nothing. I'm not that easily impressed. Got it?"

"I'll have Tony pick you up at eight," he said. "And wear something nice."

He eyed my jeans and tanktop. I felt a little uneasy by his look.

"I don't think so," I said and shut the door.

The car immediately pulled away, leaving me smelling its exhaust fumes. I noticed that my headache was gone.

The fuck-me dress.

Of course I went. How was I, of all people, supposed to turn down an offer like that? I was also very curious. Curious as to what kind of house he lived in and his lifestyle. And what he'd do once we were alone.

I told myself that I really didn't have a choice. Well, I did have a choice and I knew it, but I pretended I didn't. Besides, I wanted to mess with him. I wanted that upper hand. I wanted *him* down on his hands and knees, begging for me.

I should have known better.

A beautiful designer dress arrived at my apartment the next day. It was long, black and made entirely of silk, that heavy-weight kind. Jackie gasped when I tried it on. I looked like a forties movie star in it. It was that kind of dress.

"That is the most beautiful thing I've ever seen," she said and touched it.

I stared at myself in the mirror. It was beautiful. And it accentuated my curves just right, maybe too right because it made me look like sex, like walking sex, sex on wheels, on heels. It was a fuck-me dress. It was perfect. It was so not me. I never wore anything like this, even when I was working. I stuck to the simpler things, like tube-tops and Daisy Dukes. I had the Southern girl thing going, that was my act at the club—the hair in braids, the fresh-faced girl with those oh, so cute freckles. I was the innocent girl who would fuck your brains out on a haystack in the barn. All the men loved it, they ate it up, then they'd come back for more.

Frank must not like the Southern girl thing. Why else would he have sent me this dress? I wouldn't change; he'd have to know that. I was just me, that's all I was, all I'd ever be. Me. I wasn't about to change just because someone sent me a very expensive dress and assumed I'd be overjoyed to wear it. I mean, fuck him. I knew what this was all about.

I tore it off and threw it on the floor. Jackie's eyes almost popped out of her head. She bent over and retrieved the dress from the floor, then held it close to her chest as if she were protecting it.

"Why did you do that?" she snapped.

"It's not my style."

She held the dress up and shook her head. "I think it's beautiful."

That wasn't the point.

"Yeah," I said. "But it's so not me."

She shrugged. "So what?"

"So, it's not me," I said. "I'd never buy anything like that."

"You couldn't afford anything like this."

"Fuck you."

"You know what I mean," she said.

"Well, I'm not wearing it."

"Why not?"

"Because," I said and sighed. "Because he probably thinks he can dress me up and I won't be the person I am at the club."

She stared at me like I was crazy. Maybe I was.

"It's just a dress, Kristy," she said.

"I know! It's just, why would he send that? Like I wouldn't have the sense to know not to come dressed in jeans."

"You are putting way too much into this."

Was I? Maybe I was. It's just the thought of spending an evening with him—in that dress—was really beginning to bug me. I wouldn't be comfortable in it. No. It wasn't the dress. It was the idea of him, of being alone with *him*. I had enough confidence to put that dress on and parade down the street in it. But I didn't have the confidence to parade around in front of him in it. 'Cause once he saw me in it, I'd know exactly what he'd be thinking. And I'd be thinking the exact same thing. And I didn't want to go there with him. For some reason, I just didn't. He scared me. Sure, there was excitement there too, but there was also something else, something I couldn't put my finger on. Or face up to.

And I knew all I was to him was a conquest. Some guys were like that. They have to have you and once they get you, all you are is a number. Number one, or twelve or twelve-hundred. Doesn't matter which number as long as they can add you to the list. And they fuck you like you're a conquest; it's all about them fucking you. You're just along for the ride. They don't really care if you enjoy it or not, it's all about them, *their* fantasy of you but not you and most certainly not your pleasure.

I didn't want to be a conquest for him. It was that simple. I didn't tell myself I wanted to be more. All I knew was that I just didn't want to be that.

Jackie glanced at me. "I can tell he likes you."

I nodded.

"And he's really cute."

I sighed.

"I think you should go," she said.

"Why?"

"I dunno," she said with a sigh, then sat down next to me.

I smiled at her. She was little, so tiny, with a cute pixie haircut that drove men wild. Though she was my age, she looked twenty. Or younger. All the old men in the club loved her.

"It's just…" she began. "It's just an adventure. It's not everyday you get asked out by a guy like that."

"What kind of guy do you think he is?"

She shrugged. "I dunno."

"Do you think he might be a pervert?"

She burst out laughing. "No! What makes you think that?"

I thought about the first night I met him, me coming on his leg, him getting pissed off. I didn't say anything. Maybe I was the pervert.

"Nothing," I said and stared out the window.

"Look, he seems nice. He's probably just reserved or shy or something. Go have some fun and see what happens."

I nodded.

"And wear the dress."

"Why?"

"Because no man could resist you in that dress."

She had a point.

"But—" I began.

"Stop it," she said and threw the dress in my lap. "Wear it tonight and give him some major blue balls."

I grinned at her. "Okay."

"And the next time you see him, he'll be begging at your feet."

I stared at her. What a wonderful idea.

Absolutely beautiful.

Five minutes before eight, his limo pulled up. Jackie gave me a wink and a smile just before I threw open the door and ran down the stairs. Actually, I didn't run. You don't run in five-inch heels. You walk. Slowly.

Tony, the chauffeur/bodyguard, had just opened the foyer door when I got to it. We stared at each other until I burst out laughing.

"I was just coming for you," he muttered.

I nodded. "I know. I guess I just got ahead of myself."

He nodded and held the door open so I could pass in front of him. Then he raced to the car and opened the back door in a hurry. I smiled at him and got in. He shut the door and we were on our way.

Frank's house was located in the Garden District. Yeah, I had a feeling he lived there. He lived in a three story, Georgian-style mansion that was called the Chandler House. It was that old, old enough to have it's own name and big enough to dwarf the other mansions that sat beside it.

It was magnificent. I hated to admit it, but I was in awe. I never expected to be invited to one of these houses. And my poor, pitiful apartment that I had painstakingly cleaned and decorated with used furniture and flea market finds just looked like a rathole next to it. Before I saw his house, I'd actually thought I had a nice place.

I pretended to be unimpressed. I closed my slack jaw and told myself it wasn't *that* big. I'd seen bigger. And better.

The driver opened the door and I proceeded up the walk, up the steps, and to the door. I had just held out my finger to ring the bell when the butler suddenly opened the door. I jerked back.

"Good evening, mademoiselle," he said with a French accent. "Monsieur awaits you."

So formal. I tried not to roll my eyes because he seemed like a nice old guy. I gave him a friendly smile and followed him into the study. I also tried not to gasp at the size of the front hall or at all the expensive artwork or antiques or at the size of the double grand staircase.

It was just all so *gigantic*.

I affected an air of detachment and followed the butler. Frank was in a massive wing chair in front of a huge stone fireplace, the kind you can walk into. He jumped up when we came in. The butler bowed and exited the room backwards, shutting the door softly on his way out.

I could tell he was at once pleased at my appearance and with the dress. I knew I looked good. He knew it, too. I was glad to see *he* had noticed. If he hadn't, well, let's just say, *I* wouldn't have been pleased.

"Good to see you," he said, eyeing me, my ass in particular.

I gave him a grin. "Good to see you, too."

"I see you got the dress."

I turned around, then back. "Yeah. Thanks."

He nodded. "Oh, no problem. You look absolutely beautiful."

Absolutely beautiful. I almost blushed. Yeah. He'd just said that. Absolutely beautiful. It was the best compliment I'd ever received.

"Thank you," I said and smiled a little.

"Would you like a drink?"

"Sure," I said and sat down in the chair opposite his. "Whatever you're having."

He smiled slightly then went over to the bar, where he poured me a glass of champagne—Dom Perignon. I took it, sipped and smiled.

"Did you ever hear that story of Dom Perignon?" he asked and sat down in the other chair.

I shook my head. "No, what story?"

"He was a blind monk who was also a cellar master," he said. "One of the problems that French winemakers had back then was keeping their wine from going fizzy. Dom Perignon instead found a way to keep the bubbles intact."

I nodded.

"It was something to do with the cork and bottle," he said. "Anyway, after he tasted the champagne for the first time he called, 'Brothers, come quickly! I am drinking the stars!'"

"Huh," I muttered and sipped the champagne. "That's really interesting."

"Would you like another?" he asked. "You're almost finished."

I shook my head, feeling somewhat uncomfortable.

"Sure?" he asked.

"Yes, I'm sure," I replied and suddenly felt awkward. God, I was so intimidated, I was rendered shy. I'd never been shy in all of my life. We didn't try to make any more conversation. We couldn't have conversed if our lives depended on it. My heart was beating so fast. Was his doing the same? He gave me an uncomfortable smile, then leaned over and lit my cigarette when I pulled one out of my tiny evening purse.

"Thanks," I muttered.

He smiled. I attempted to smile back. The room shook with silence. The only noise I could hear was the occasional jingle of the trolley outside coming from the open French doors. And that was far off.

The butler knocked on the door, opened it and announced, "Dinner is served."

Frank stood, walked over to me and held out his elbow. I almost cracked up. I didn't. I put my cigarette out, grabbed my purse and took his arm. I liked the way it felt, too, his arm. Strong. It felt strong. Stern. He had strong, stern arms.

We followed the butler into the massive dining room/hall/big fucking room. The table was about twenty feet long, lined with elegant chairs, some of which looked like they needed recovering.

I sat down to his right, instead of at the end of the long table, which I would have preferred. We didn't speak as we were served some kind of cold soup, which I did not like, then some kind of duck, which I picked at, then some fluffy, chocolate thing, which I devoured.

Once the plates were removed, Frank leaned back and pulled a cigar out of his jacket. He offered it to me. I shook my head and pulled my cigarettes out. He leaned over and lit my cigarette, then his cigar, which he twirled in his fingers until it was red on the end and smoked like a chimney.

We smoked but still didn't talk. I couldn't take it anymore. I looked around the room, racking my brain trying to come up with something to say then I stared at the chairs.

"Why don't you recover these chairs?" I asked. "They'd look really good recovered."

He had been sucking on the cigar when I said this. His eyebrows shot up. I could tell he got a kick out of my question and he tried to hide his laughter, like I amused him. Like what I had said was such a sweet, silly little thing.

"What's so funny?" I asked, somewhat stupefied.

He shook his head and explained, not really in a condescending way, "When you purchase antiques, you don't reupholster them. You leave them the way they are."

I glared at him. How was I supposed to know that?

"I was wondering if you would ask me that," he said in a manner that made me think he wanted to lean over and pinch my cheeks.

I blushed. I felt insulted, though I don't think he meant it as an insult. Suddenly, I wanted out of there so bad I could have jumped up and ran to the door. I couldn't take the tension anymore. It was eating me alive.

He took the cigar out of his mouth, then wiped the tip of his tongue with his fingers and flicked a piece of tobacco from them, like some actor. I rolled my eyes at his behavior. Why was he putting on a show? Was he putting on a show? And what did he want? Was it just sex? Or a game, something to divert his attention from his lush, but apparently boring life. What was his deal?

And what was mine? I was impressed. I had no problem admitting that. But I knew he'd never give me anything. Nothing. I'd go with what I came, maybe without so much of my pride. Maybe I'd lose part of my heart, too. But I couldn't imagine loving this guy. No matter how good looking or rich he was. No matter. It didn't matter to me. I could take it or leave it.

So why was I still sitting here?

"It's getting late," I said, sighed and began to stand. "I should really be going."

He touched my arm, making me stop. I shivered at his touch. My heart picked up its pace, from steady to skipping, then thumping, pounding, until it swam in my head. I couldn't think straight. For a moment, all I could think about was his hand on my arm. And how it felt being there.

I moved away from him. Quickly.

"Why don't we sit in front of the fire? In the study? I had Pierre make a fire."

"That sounds very nice," I said. "But I'd rather not."

His eyes narrowed at me. I'd pissed him off. I didn't really care, though. I was tired. This evening had really turned out to be nothing more than a dud with him being the main dud. I didn't like the fancy food or the fancy cigar or the fancy house. I liked comfort, hamburgers, and soft chairs. I'd never, ever be able to get comfortable here, in this house. And I knew it.

Like I said, I was intimidated. I was out of my element. Maybe that was his whole reason in bringing me there. I didn't have the energy to speculate, though. I just didn't care. I told myself I didn't care.

"Please," he said. "Just for a moment or two?"

I really didn't want to. But his look implored me. It made me change my mind. After all, he had been nice tonight. Not really overly friendly or anything, but he had been nice. Which was more than I had expected.

"I guess," I muttered.

He rose from his chair and extended his arm. I didn't want to take it. I didn't want to touch him again. But it wouldn't be polite if I refused. I took it and we went into the study, where there was now a huge fire crackling and steaming in the fireplace. It did give the room a sort of rosy glow and made it less imposing. Not much, but some.

We sat side by side on the big leather Chesterfield sofa and stared vacantly at the fire. At least I did. I knew he was studying me, like he had studied me at the club and in his car.

I turned to him. "What are you doing?"

"Nothing," he said and rested his hand on the side of his face. "I'm just looking at you."

"No, that's not what I meant," I said. "Why did you invite me here?"

"I like your company."

"Bull," I said. "You haven't said two words to me all evening."

"I think I've said at least two," he said, his eyes twinkling. "Maybe even three."

I tried not to be charmed. "I know what it's about, Frank."

"What?"

"This. I know why you wanted me to come here."

"You do?" he asked and seemed more than a little curious.

I nodded. "It's about sex, isn't it?"

His eyebrows rose. "Uh, no, I don't—"

I scooted closer to him. "Listen, I know you want me. It's okay, a lot of guys do. But I don't need pretension."

"I'm not pretentious. This is just the way I am."

I thought about the Dom Perignon story. Wasn't that a little pretentious? I stared at him, realizing he wasn't pretentious. He was just trying to impress me. It didn't make me feel any more comfortable, but it did make me see him a little differently. It gave him a sense of humility, of humanity. Knowing this about him gave me courage to ask something. Even though it embarrassed me to death, I was going to ask. So, I did, "Why do you want to sleep with me so bad?"

He eyes darted up, then down. "Who says I do?"

"Oh come on," I said, moving even closer to him, so close I could feel the warmth from his body. "You've had a hard-on for me since the minute you laid eyes on me."

"I don't have a hard-on right now."

"Really?" I said and eyed his crotch. He was right. There was no tent in his pants. "Just tell me why."

"You're very independent, aren't you, Kristine?"

"What?"

He moved closer to me. "You like being a stripper because you think it makes you superior to men. Am I right?"

I thought about it. I did take his assumption into consideration. But he was full of shit. I liked being a stripper because I liked the money. Being superior to men was just an added bonus.

"No, you're not right," I said and moved away from him. "Besides, we've already had this discussion once before."

"I know that."

"So give it up."

"Like I said before, you love having guys want you."

I didn't answer him.

He took my arm. I tried to jerk away, but he held tight and wouldn't let it go. "You like having all the power don't you, Kristine?"

"Don't call me that," I said. "No one calls me that."

"They should," he said. "It's a lovely name."

"Let me go."

I elbowed him. I suddenly wanted out of there more than before. If I didn't get out, there would be no going back. I knew that. I struggled against him, pushing him away, but he wouldn't let me go. I began to feel a slight panic sweep over me. This was going somewhere and it made me very, very nervous. All the same, I couldn't stop it.

He pulled me back down and we began to wrestle for a moment until I grabbed his crotch.

"Like that?" I hissed. "You're right. I love having guys by the balls."

I gave him a slight squeeze, just enough to get his attention so he'd know I could do more. He didn't flinch, only reached over and grabbed me by the hair of the head and pulled me back. I winced in pain. It hurt so bad tears sprang into my eyes.

"Ow!" I yelled. "Let me go!"

"That's what you like, isn't it?" he whispered hotly in my ear. I could feel his saliva.

I pushed him away and wiped my ear.

He pulled me back. "The only man that you're interested in is one that treats you like shit, isn't it? The one who can dominate you?"

I didn't know. I'd never really had a man try to dominate me before. They, all five of my ex-boyfriends and the one ex-husband included, had been like putty in my hands. I could manipulate them in any way I chose. And they had bored me to tears. That's why I was single. Why I hadn't just settled down with one of them and lived my life like a normal person. They had been too easy. Too easy to get, to have, to contain. I'd tempt them sometimes, yell at them, scream, do anything just so they would flare up. Just to test them. Every once in a while, I'd get what I wanted. Once I got a black eye. But he had cried like a baby after he gave it to me and told me he would have rather have cut off his hands than hurt me, even offered to do it. I had run away from him, using the black eye as an excuse for escape.

From what I hear, he still has his hands.

Frank stared me dead in the eye. I stared back and waited for him to do something. We stayed like that for what seemed like a long time. Our chests pressed close, our hearts beating wildly in sync. We waited until one of us made a move. We waited on each other to make the first move. I decided to go ahead and do it, since I didn't want to be there all night.

This time, I twisted his balls. He let out a wail and released me.

"You bitch," he hissed and pushed me away from him hard.

I fell to the floor. I stared up at him just as my emotions began to run wild. I went from embarrassment to shock to anger to loathing.

"Fuck you," I said, getting up from the floor. I felt a lump rise in my throat. I was almost in tears. I was also very angry, mostly because I realized that he did have me all figured out. To a certain extent.

He eyed me dispassionately. I hated that look on his face. I hated that I didn't have him figured out as he had me.

"Fuck you," I spat and felt the tears puddle in my eyes and fall on my face. "Fuck you! Fuck you! *FUCK YOU!*"

His look changed. He almost grinned at me. He loved my anger, my seething passion. He knew I was just a touch or two away from ignition.

"Yeah, come on, then, fuck me," he said and eyed me. "Come on."

"Right!" I scoffed. "Don't you ever touch me again, motherfucker!"

He looked up at me. "Your pussy tells on you, Kristine. It's all wet, wanting this motherfucker in there fucking you."

He reached out for me. Before I knew what he was doing, his hand was up my dress. I didn't have any panties on. You don't wear panties with a dress like this. I wish I had. I wish I had because his hand was between my legs and there was nothing there to stop him. He was fingering me and he was right. I told on myself. I was wet for him. For him. In this moment. Here. I was wet and I wanted him more than anything.

He knew it. I knew it. It didn't stop me from hating myself for an instant, then reverting back to hating him.

He didn't say a word as he stroked me. As he fingered my clit, the lips of my pussy, which swelled and yearned for him to do more. But he didn't. He sat a foot away from me with his hand up my dress and finger-fucked me. Finger-fucked me until I was dissolving into a mass of quivering nerves. Until I moaned and pushed myself against his hand. His hand rested. It became still. I moved against it, feeling my own hands on my breasts, wanting his lips there more than anything. Wanting him. I fucked his hand which waited patiently for me to do as I wanted. And just as I was about to come, he pulled it away.

I gasped and opened my eyes. "You bastard."

He grinned at me. A real shit eating grin. I hated him.

"So tell me I was right," he said.

Before I could change my mind, I slapped him. I slapped him right across the face. He didn't move. He did raise one eyebrow. But that's all he did.

I shoved him away and headed to the door. I was so mad I could have spit. I did spit. Right on his Persian rug. I was almost ashamed after I did it, but I couldn't help myself.

He was suddenly on me, on my back, shoving me to the floor. He was on top of me, pulling at my dress, trying to get it off. I rolled over and kicked him right in the head. He fell back with a thump and a groan. I scrambled up and hobbled in my five-inch heels to the front door. I'd never wear these things out again! But before I could turn the knob, he was at me, pulling me down, holding me tight and not letting me move.

"Off!" I screamed as he turned me around.

"Tell me," he whispered.

"Tell you what!"

"Tell me how much you want me."

"Get off me!" I screamed and pushed at him.

"Come on, baby," he whispered, his hot breath on my ear. "Tell me how much you want me."

I stared at him.

"Come on. Tell me."

Tell me, tell me now. Tell me how low I can go. Beat me there. Hold me down. Fight with me. Kiss me. Kiss me now. Bite me. Scratch me. Make me want you. Take me away. Don't ever leave. Do what you want to me. With me. Fuck me. Fuck me now. *Make me feel alive.*

He was waiting. I tried to turn away from him. I tried to turn it all off, all the emotions I had were running riot inside me then. I wanted him. I knew it. He knew it. There was no going back.

I was still breathing hard. He was still waiting. I breathed, "I want you."

"How much?"

"I don't know," I breathed. "I just want you so bad."

"You want me to fuck you?"

I nodded.

"Beg me."

I almost regained my senses. But I realized this was his game. This is what he wanted, what he got off on. I also realized I liked it, too. And I was willing to play along.

"Please fuck me," I begged.

"Really beg me."

"Please fuck me!"

"More."

"Please, please, please! Please, fuck me. Fuck me—"

I didn't have time to finish. He covered my lips with his. He was sucking the life right out of me, thrusting his hateful tongue deep into my mouth and down my throat. I pushed at him and struggled. I could barely breathe. But he kept kissing. He kept kissing, sucking, groaning, moaning. He was right. I was wet. I did want his cock in me. I didn't melt. I exploded. I panted with lust for him, grabbing his face and holding him tight so he couldn't get away.

I suddenly wondered where the butler was. I didn't wonder long. I was too into it to wonder about anything but having him on me, in me, fucking my brains out.

He was coming out of his clothes. I was coming out of mine. I don't even know how we got them off. But there they were, strewn all over the floor and he was kissing all of my naked body, which arched under his rough and desperate touch. He pawed at me like an animal, biting at my skin until I was covered with tiny red marks. His head went between my legs and he sucked my pussy, sucked the juices right out of it and into his mouth. I gasped and rode his head, fucked his head until I screamed with orgasm. Until I screamed with liberation.

Then he was in me, fucking me. His cock went right up into me like it had always been there and he was simply returning it. I gasped with satisfaction. I gasped for him. For the moment. For the fucking. And he was fucking me then. Fucking me like no other man had ever fucked me. He was fucking another orgasm right out of my body. I held on tight and rode him as he rode me, taking it for everything it was worth and refusing to let it go until I was so spent I couldn't move.

He came then, shuddered, fell on top of me and didn't move for a long moment. He held onto me tight, like he was never going to move, never going to let me go. I found my arms holding him too, holding him like I loved him and never wanted to let him go. And I knew, I *knew*, I wasn't just a conquest fuck for him. There was something else there. I didn't know what it was, but that hadn't been a conquest fuck. It had been about us, me and him, fucking. He wasn't looking to add me to his list. And that made me just a tad apprehensive. What did he want with me?

He said, "I want you to move in."

The scary part.

I'll use him. That was my first thought.

The choice was easy after that. I made my decision that night and moved in the next day. Jackie raised one eyebrow.

"Why are you moving in with this guy?" she asked. "You just met him a few weeks ago."

I told her truthfully, "I'm going to use him."

She studied me. "Do you love him?"

Did I? No! Of course I didn't love him. I didn't even really know him that well. But what did that matter? I knew *about* him. I knew I liked fucking him. That was good enough. For now.

I told her, "I'm just going to use him. He knows that."

"You just met him, Kristy."

"You said that once already," I mumbled.

"Kristy?"

"I know," I said, shifting my feet. I mean, I knew it was all of a sudden and Frank was almost a stranger. I knew it wasn't really rational of me to just move in with him, but something told me to. Something was pushing me towards him and I was helpless to do anything other than hold on for the ride.

She narrowed her eyes at me. "Well, if that's what you want."

I nodded. It was.

She sighed. "Well, shit. Who the hell can I get to move in?"

I stared at her.

"I can't pay this rent by myself, you know?" she said.

"I'll help you until you find someone."

She eyed me. "Yeah. Right. But can you find someone to take your place?"

"I'll help you," I said and smiled at her. "I promise."

She eyed me. "Let me tell you one thing, though, okay?"

I nodded.

"If he ever hurts you, I know people."

"What do you mean?"

"I mean, I know people who can put him back in his place."

I nodded, getting her meaning.

"He's not like that," I said.

"You never know," she said.

That was true. You never know.

I moved in because I felt it was the right thing to do. I told myself I'd use him, his mansion and his money. And that's exactly what I did. He gave me everything I wanted. I'd call my girlfriends up and we'd go shopping. He never set a limit on my spending, but he did set a limit on my friendships. Quickly, I was told when to be home and that I was to quit my job at the club.

I laughed in his face. "I have to earn a living."

"You're living here."

"But for how long? How long before you get tired of our fucking and kick me out?"

"I won't get tired of it."

I eyed him. "Then set me up a bank account. I want money."

He eyed me. "You sound like a whore."

Maybe it did sound that way, but I had the stripper mentality. Men were there to be used and most times, they liked being used. As long as they were getting something out of it, everyone was happy. And he was getting a little more than something. He was getting me. And I wasn't cheap.

"I don't care what I sound like," I told him. "I won't quit my job without a little security. Why should I?"

"You've got a point," he said.

He set it up the next day, depositing a lot of money into an account, which I immediately transferred into another account, so he couldn't take it back if he changed his mind. But he didn't care about the money. He only wanted me under his control, under his thumb. Besides, I knew if he wanted that money back, he'd get it. And I really didn't care about it. I just told him to do it to see if he would. When he did, I almost fell over in shock.

What else could I get him to do if I asked?

The sex got better. Unbelievably, it got better. I didn't know if I was in love with him or in love with his dick. Maybe it was his hands that I loved. They were large, like his dick. They pawed at me, forced me to be still, quiet, then to move again. I'd never had a man fuck me like he fucked me. I worried that he might cut me off. That he might tire of me too soon. And then what would I do? What would I do with this addiction to his body?

I didn't know. And that was the scary part.

Run of the house.

I soon began to notice that my friends were slipping away. Bit by bit, I was losing contact with them even though I constantly invited them over to the house. They came, admired it then left. I got the feeling that they thought I was feeling my importance and acting snobbish. That was just stupid. I knew this wasn't going to last and I was only making the best of it. But most of my friends were strippers and most of them had little education, which made them feel intimidated, which made them act like bitches. Which, in turn, left me feeling a little indignant. It also made me not want anything to do with them.

Jackie did keep in contact. I called her everyday. We'd have pleasant conversation and we'd sometimes go shopping or to lunch, but she couldn't be with me everyday. She did have a life of her own and couldn't entertain me all the time.

I became lonely, living mostly by myself because Frank was always gone somewhere on business. And when he was home, he was never in the mood to talk. But neither was I.

I took control of the house. I had the run of it, so I figured I'd make it more comfortable for me. I had the cook make all the fattening good food I loved: Hot dogs, burgers, pizzas. I'd eat whatever I wanted for lunch, then I'd eat with Frank at dinner, picking at my food because it was always some strange concoction that looked and smelled as unappealing as it tasted.

I picked a room on the main floor and turned it into my own personal office. It was smaller than the other rooms, but that didn't make it puny, by anyone's standards. It had two camel-backed sofas sitting opposite one another before a huge stone fireplace. It had a bear rug on the polished wood floor, floor to ceiling bookshelves, and a huge executive desk in the corner. I loved it because it was painted a dark red and had lush blue velvet curtains on the windows.

I not only picked that room because I liked the way it looked, I picked it because Frank never went into it.

I had a huge TV and a DVD player delivered. For some reason, he didn't have cable so I had that installed. I also got a laptop and would surf the internet for hours to kill time between fuckings.

I got to know the cook pretty well. She was a native of New Orleans and liked working for Frank, though at first she had a hard time with the menus he wanted. She was a very nice lady, who talked a mile a minute and cracked up all the time. She told funny stories about her six grandkids. Her name was Ellen and she arrived at the house at five in the morning to cook his breakfast, stayed during the day to cook my lunch, and left just after she finished supper.

She was off on weekends.

Pierre, the butler, kept his distance. But he was always lurking around to see what I was up to, like he was waiting for me to do something so he could tell Frank on me. He got on my nerves so bad. He didn't do shit, either. He was just there to announce dinner, say hello and goodbye and to open the fucking door. I never got used to it. Every single time I came home, I'd reach for the door but he'd already have it open, thusly scaring the bejesus out of me. *Every single time.*

The chauffeur, Tony, was always with Frank. I'd only see him if we went out to dinner. He was very polite, but kept his distance. He was a young guy, around my age and every so often, I'd see him staring at my legs or ass. Occasionally, when I had a short skirt on, I'd hike it up a little so he could get a peek if he looked hard enough. Needless to say, he was a little friendlier on the days I wore a short skirt.

The only other person in the house was the maid. She came once a day to make the beds, clean the bathrooms and to do a little dusting here and there. She didn't have time to talk and when I asked her what her name was, she snapped, "Gloria! Now get out of my way! I'm trying to vacuum!"

I got out of her way.

A team of maids came once a week to do the harder cleaning and they didn't want anything to do with me, either.

So, mostly, I was all by myself. I filled my time reading trashy novels, surfing the internet, taking baths, shopping, and fantasizing about sex with Frank.

I don't know what Frank did during the day. I don't know how he got that house or all that money. He never divulged any information and I never pressed. I pretended that he was involved with the Mob, or ran a meth lab in the projects. I'd come up with all kinds of underhanded stuff he could be doing to be so rich. I also suspected that he inherited a great deal of what he had, which was realistic, but boring. When Jackie asked one day, I said, "Well, I think he's distributes cocaine. He's always flying to Colombia, so you never know…"

Actually, I never knew where he was or where he went or how he got there. After a while, I stopped asking questions. I mean, what was the use? He wasn't going to tell me, so I gave up.

I'd also visit my old haunts, run into friends, then run back and wait for his return.

Like I said, I was bored out of my skull.

This went on for a little while. It was fun at first to have no responsibilities, to be kept, to sleep till whenever I wanted, then do whatever I wanted. The fun didn't last. Soon, I was bored out of my skull. I'd run out of the house, jump into my '75 Camaro and hit the road, sometimes bypassing the city limits and always being tempted to stay on that road all the way home. One day, I got as far as Alabama. But I turned around.

P-A-R-T-Y

Jackie said, "You know what you should do?"

"No. What?"

"You should throw a huge party."

I shrugged and picked a piece of pepperoni off my pizza. "I dunno. I don't think Frank would like that."

"Well, he's going to be gone all week, isn't he?"

I nodded sadly. Yeah, all week. I'd begged him not to go, to stay or to at least take me with him. "But you'd just be bored," he had said. "And I wouldn't get any work done."

That was true.

"So why not have a kickass party?" she asked. "We could invite everyone we know and get some good tunes, some good food and have a really good time."

Sounded like a good idea to me.

"I mean, what's the use in having this great house at your disposal if you're not going to throw a party every once in a while?"

"That's true," I said.

"See? I told you it was a good idea."

"Yeah, it is," I said, really liking the idea of a party now. "Who could we invite?"

"Well, everyone at the club, for sure, except for Jeanie 'cause she is *such* a bitch."

"You got that right."

"And, of course, Chad."

I smiled. Chad, my former neighbor. He was a really nice guy who had a crush on me, though he never asked me out. I always wondered why he hadn't.

"How is Chad?" I asked.

"He's heartbroken since you moved out."

I grinned. "Really?"

"Really," she said but didn't venture. "And, let's see, some other people I know from around the neighborhood. I don't see inviting more than say…thirty people."

"That's not so bad."

"No," she said. "And we'll have it all cleaned up before he comes home and he'll never know."

"You're right," I said. "That would be fun! I need to mingle with someone other than Pierre."

"He's the butler, right?"

I nodded. "Yeah."

She rolled her eyes. I rolled mine.

"So are we on?" she asked.

"Yeah! Let's do it!"

"Cool!" she squealed.

"When?"

"How about Friday night?" she said.

"Friday night it is!"

She considered something then said, "Shit. I'm supposed to work Friday night."

I stared at her.

"Oh, fuck it. I'll call in sick."

"That's my girl."

I hired a caterer, got a few kegs, which looked ridiculous in the elegant house, and put a bunch of hard rock CDs in the stereo. Jackie and I moved a long sofa table in the foyer and lined it with liquor, glasses and ice. Then we hung streamers from the ceiling, set out a bunch of extra ashtrays, and filled the dining room table with all the good food the caterer supplied.

We got party favors, which included: Silly little hats, fake Rolex watches, dancing hula girls and bags of oregano which were supposed to look like pot. For a joke. (They were all gone first thing, then I found them discarded all over the house.)

It was the most fun I'd had since I'd moved in. The guests began to arrive around seven that Friday night.

Pierre and Tony stood around, shaking their heads, telling me that Frank would not be happy about this. *At all.* I shrugged happily and said, "It's not my idea, sorry." Besides, I wanted to have fun and I wanted everyone that came to have fun. I wanted them to eat too much, drink too much and then vomit off the porch.

In a matter of hours, the house was full of people—way more than thirty. Apparently, everyone who had been invited had invited everyone they knew. But I figured that made it more fun. I was so happy to see everyone, even people I'd never met. I'd been sequestered for too long. I needed this. I got drunk on rum punch and mingled happily with everyone, who seemed to be having just a good time as I was. We were loud and obnoxious. We had AC/DC playing on the stereo. Someone cranked up *Back in Black* so loud that one of the speakers blew out and actually smoked.

When I saw it happen, I thought it was the funniest thing I'd ever seen. I doubled over with laughter. I had been standing by the speaker singing/screaming along with the song when it happened. I was momentarily shocked. Then I just cracked up. Just looking at the demolished speaker made me laugh. I laughed and laughed and all these people stared at me, then they joined in and we laughed together until tears streamed down our faces.

Rum punch will do that kind of thing to you.

I can't remember much after that. But I do remember that Frank came home around two that morning. He had canceled part of his trip so he could be home with me. And not with a few hundred of my nearest and dearest, most of whom I had never met.

The party was still roaring. I was so drunk I was on the verge of throwing up over the stairs. I had been trying to mount the stairs and get to bed for the last half-hour, but I kept getting stopped by people who told me, *This is the best party they'd been to in years!* *("Glad you like it!")* And, *Did I want a little coke? ("Uh, no thanks.")* And, *Where is the bathroom? ("Up the stairs, to the left.")*

I finally gave up and sat down on a step, ready to hurl. My head was spinning a little, too. No, it wasn't spinning anymore. It had taken off and was now lost in space, orbiting Earth.

I don't know where Jackie went. She was probably off in one of the bedrooms getting laid. Good for her. I was just about to force myself up off the step, retire to my bedroom and leave the party to wind down on its own. I mean, there as no way I was going to break up a party that good. No way. That would be, like, sacrilege.

Then Frank came in. The look on his face was murderous.

I was about halfway up the stairs and had just glanced down at the door when I saw him. My heart leaped a little. I was actually happy to see him and was about to rush down the stairs and throw my arms around him when I realized that Pierre and Tony had been right. He was not happy about the party. Or about what the guests were doing.

Then he did an odd thing. He turned on his heel and left the house. I was bewildered by his behavior but then I suddenly retched, throwing up on the stairs, all over the carpet that covered them. Oh, no. He wouldn't be happy about that either.

What should I do? Run? Yeah, I should. But right now, I should sit down and hold my buzzing head in my hands. Maybe then I could walk and, then, possibly, run.

I don't know how long I sat there, but suddenly, the entire house was in chaos. A team of cops burst into the front door and announced that the party was *OV-ER!* And that everyone there was trespassing and to *get the fuck out!*

I briefly wondered if I should follow suit. But after I got over my initial shock, I got pissed off.

That bastard! He had called the cops! Like we were squatters or something. My drunken mind didn't rationalize. I just thought, *He can't do this! He has no right, even if it is his house!*

I looked for him but he was nowhere in sight. And everyone was emptying the house at an alarmingly quick pace. Where was Jackie? Oh, there she was, trying to pull her shirt over her head as she flew out the front door. She stopped, spotted me and gave a little wave. I lamely waved back.

I watched in dismay as everyone else followed suit. Out they went, pushing at each other as if they couldn't leave quick enough, as if the house were on fire or something. Out through the front door, out the back. I saw a few hop out of the windows. On their way out, I saw a few people grab bottles of champagne and liquor, and a few even took some really expensive knickknacks, which made me smile.

I put my head back in my hands and closed my eyes. Next thing I knew, someone was tugging at my elbow. I opened my eyes to see Tony, who smiled gently at me, almost with a sense of pity.

"Come on," he said softly. "You need to get to bed."

I allowed him to pull me up the stairs, then into the bedroom, where he pushed me on the bed gently, took off my high heels, then propped a pillow under my head.

"Thank you, Tony," I muttered and closed my eyes.

He muttered something.

"What?"

"Nothing," he said. "Just try to get some rest."

I fell asleep almost immediately.

Bad girl.

Upon Frank's return, I was given a beating.

I really didn't even suspect he would ever do anything like that. I mean, we sometimes had rough sex but it never got out of control. Sometimes he'd pull my hair and bite at my neck, and, of course, he spanked me, especially after I'd been a "bad girl," but I'd been the one to initiate that. However, I never in a million years thought he'd beat me.

But he did.

I was asleep. The house was now calm. I knew there was a big mess waiting for me to clean up, but I'd get to it the next day. Right then, the only thing on my mind was sleep, which was the only thing that would relieve the bed spins I was in the midst of.

Frank stomped into the bedroom about five that morning. He threw on all the lights and was cursing up a storm.

"Who in the motherfucking hell do you think you are, you stupid, worthless little bitch?! Do you have any idea what you've done?!"

I opened one eye but was still too drunk to be disturbed by his behavior. Like I've said, he was weird to begin with so nothing he did ever really worried me. That was just the way he was.

"You've been given too much control in our relationship," he said and stopped beside the bed, hands on hips. "I have to take it back."

I stared at him then moaned, "Can we talk in the morning? I don't feel so good."

He snatched the bed covers off me. "Get up!"

I groaned but didn't move. Actually, I *couldn't* move.

"Get up!" he roared.

I grabbed the blanket and tried to cover myself. He pulled it off the bed and threw it on the floor.

"Get up now, Kristine," he said, more calmly. "You're only making this worse."

"What the hell are you talking about?" I mumbled, wishing he'd go away. No, wishing he'd get in bed with me and hold me. I'd carried an ache around with me since the day he'd left—the previous Tuesday. I'd missed him so much that all I wanted was for him to kiss my cheek, hold me tight and mutter, "Good night." We could have sex later, when I felt better. But all I wanted now was his arms around me.

Besides, I was still partially asleep. And I kinda thought he was playing a game with me. I didn't really think he was *that* mad. Sure, I could see why he would be pissed off, but I didn't think he was seeing red or anything. I also didn't think the house was that trashed. (Later, I would fully realize the extent of the damage to the house and feel really bad about it.)

When he didn't respond, I began to fall back asleep, smiling slightly at how good it felt and noticing how warm and cozy the bed was.

He wasn't having that.

He leaned over and shook me awake. Shook me so hard, my head rolled. I screamed and swatted at him, like a bear not wanting to come out of hibernation and getting good and pissed off that someone would try to make me.

"Are you awake?" he hissed in my face, spitting on me.

"You bastard!" I yelled and wiped my face with the back of my hand. "I'm up! What do you want?"

"Take your clothes off," he said.

I eyed him. He had to be joking.

"Do you want sex?" I asked, feeling disgusted with him if he did. I know I looked like hell. And I smelled like a wino.

He shot me a look of pure disdain.

"What then?" I asked.

He turned away form me and pulled off his belt. "Take your clothes off."

"Excuse me?"

"Take your clothes off."

He had to be out of his mind. What was he doing? Undressing? No, he just had his belt off and was slapping it slightly against his thigh. I stared at the belt, then at him, trying to figure this thing out. What *was* his intention? Was he...? No. He didn't intend on beating me, did he?

He did.

He stared back at me, unblinking. I looked away and felt a sudden rush of pure dread come over my body. *What have I done? What was I doing here? Could I get out of it? What was he going to do with that belt?*

"What's the belt for?" I asked, eying it, especially the thick silver buckle.

"You know."

"Tell me."

He didn't respond. I decided to try something. I pouted and made my bottom lip quiver like I was about to cry. This usually really got to him. He stared at me and rolled his eyes.

"That's not going to work tonight."

"Come on," I pouted. "I know I've been bad, but I can make it up to you."

"Like I said, that is not going to work."

"Frank—"

"Kristine, take your fucking clothes off!"

I slid off the bed and walked over to him. "Why? What are you going to do if I do?"

"You're going to find out."

His voice was so icy it sent shivers up my spine.

"Now, be a *good* girl and take your clothes off."

It finally dawned on me. He was serious. He was actually going to beat me.

"You are not doing this," I muttered and backed away from him. "Why are you doing this?"

"Kristine, take your clothes off."

"Frank, you don't want to do this to me."

"I have to. You know that."

"But *why*?" I asked, almost crying, and this time I wasn't faking it. "Are you going to hit me?"

He nodded. "Yes, I am going to hit you."

"But why do you want to hit me?" I cried, shaking my head, trying to figure out if this was really happening or if he was playing some sort of sick joke.

"Because you deserve it."

If I hadn't been terrified, I would have laughed. Right in his face. But I was petrified. I glanced at the door. I glanced at him, formulated my escape route and his response to the escape route. But then I thought I'd give him one last chance to redeem himself. I walked over to the bed and lay down and stared at him seductively.

"If you want them off," I said softly. "You'll have to do it yourself."

"You're making this worse."

"Are you out of your mind?" I asked.

"No, Kristine, I'm not," he said and sighed. "Now you either get up off that bed and undress or I will drag you off it."

That did it. I shot up and ran to the door. I ran with all my might, with everything I could, that fight or flight instinct carrying me and carrying me with haste. I reached the door, grabbed the knob and turned. It was locked.

I whirled around and stared at him in terror. He stared back, his face devoid of emotion. I swallowed hard and wanted to crumble to the floor. I wanted to beg. Plead my case. Divert his attention. Make him stop. But something wouldn't let me. It could have been that look in his eye, on his face. It was probably pride.

"Fuck you," I said.

He took one step towards me. I tensed and looked wildly around. The bathroom! I raced towards it, but he grabbed my middle and threw me to the floor. I screamed and swatted at him like a wild animal, but he was stronger than I was. And a lot more determined.

He grabbed my shirt and ripped it—and I mean literally ripped it—off my back. He did the same to my short skirt. He grabbed for my panties but I squirmed away. He didn't let that stop him. I was still almost naked, squirming beneath him crying and begging him to stop. The lesson had been learned! I knew then I would never be able to pull anything over on him. I had pushed him too far and I knew it. I was sorry I had tried.

"Please," I moaned. "Just please stop, Frank. I'll do whatever you want, just don't hit me!"

"Shut up. Please."

I tried to grab his face; I tried to kiss him, hoping that would soften him, that it would alter his direction, his path of destruction. It didn't. He pushed me off him and I fell backwards, the back of my head hitting the floor. My head swam then began to throb. I think I blacked out. I couldn't be sure, but the next thing I know, he had me turned over and was beating me with the belt, like some sick motherfucker. He didn't just tap me, either, he belted me, lashed me at me. My body tensed and shivered with each lash. I quivered and wanted to beg him to stop, but I couldn't. I was in shock at his actions. *How long was he going to keep this up?*

I was finally able to cry, "What are you doing?"

"I'm breaking you."

I stopped moving, the terror of what he'd just said sank in and it sank in so hard I felt it land in my belly with a reverberating wallop. *Breaking me? Of what? From what? What was I? Some wild horse? Some wild animal? What the hell did that mean?*

I finally came back to my senses and was able to scream, "You're evil!"

He ignored me and gave me another lash. This time I felt sick, nauseous. I held my hand over my mouth to keep it in, but it didn't work. I threw up, gagging and coughing all over the floor.

He stopped.

I stared up at him, half-ashamed of what I'd just done, though it wasn't really my fault. I no longer felt the sting from the lashes, I felt the sting of embarrassment.

He eyed me for a moment, sighed and then went into the bathroom, returning with a towel. He threw it at me.

"Clean it up."

I sniffled and sat up. But then I felt it again. I put my hand over my mouth and made it to the bathroom just in time. After I was done, I actually felt better. I got up and rinsed my mouth out with water, then with some mouthwash.

I heard a noise. I looked up. He was standing in the doorway. He jerked his head towards the bedroom.

I glared at him and went back out and wiped lamely at the vomit. He cursed behind me, left for the bathroom again, came back with a few washcloths, then got on his hands and knees and started to help me.

"You know what your problem is?" he said. "You don't know what's good for you."

My mouth fell open. But I ignored him and finished up the job, then took the towels into the bathroom and washed my hands, dreading going back into the bedroom. When I went back out, he was standing by the bed.

"Happy now?" I hissed.

He nodded. "But it's true, you know?"

"What's true?" I snapped.

"That you don't know what's good for you," he continued. "You test people. You like to see how far you can push. But let me tell you one thing, I won't be pushed."

"Well, let me tell *you* one thing," I said and stepped up to him. "That may be true but at least I didn't do what you did."

"I had no other recourse."

I was astounded at his words and before I could stop myself, I said. "I hate you."

He didn't bat an eye. But I could tell it bothered him.

I repeated, my words getting more and more intense as I spat them at him, "I hate you. I hate you! *I hate you*!"

He grabbed me by the back of my head and pulled me up to him until our noses were touching. I wanted to slap him so badly then. Just one slap, right across his face.

"No you don't hate me. You hate yourself. You don't know what's good for you, Kristine. I am going to show you."

I shook my fists in the air and screamed at the top of my lungs, "I HATE YOU! I HATE YOU! I HATE YOU!"

He grabbed me again and this time he kissed me—a hard, lewd kiss. Slobbering. I fought against him, shoving at his hard body as best I could to get him away from me, but he kept at me, sticking his hot tongue in my mouth. I bit down hard on it. He pulled back, wiped his mouth with the back of his sleeve, stared at the blood on it then smiled. It was almost as if he liked it.

Then he suddenly changed. Just like that. It was so strange. One moment he was irate, the next, he was apologetic. I don't know. I couldn't decipher it.

He was studying me then, looking almost remorseful. But it was like something had sparked his interest. I stared back, wondering what he was thinking. I couldn't bring myself to ask, though I was dying to know. But his attention was diverted. Having it diverted gave me time to turn on my heel and run to the door. He leaned back on his heels and watched me try to unlock it. I finally got it open and turned to him.

"Where are you going?" he asked softly.

"I'm leaving you!" I yelled and threw open the door.

"You don't have any clothes on," he said and nearly smiled.

I walked over to him and slapped him. He didn't flinch. He grabbed my arm and pulled me to him. I struggled but his grip was tight and I couldn't squirm away from him.

"Where are you going to go, Kristine?" he asked, softly, staring into my eyes.

"As far away from you as possible."

He shook his head, telling me that, no, that wasn't going to happen. It infuriated me to have him do that to me.

"Let me go," I said, snarling. "Let me go."

He let me go. I was almost surprised, almost a little disappointed. I didn't spend much time thinking about it, though. I looked around frantically trying to locate my clothes. I saw them in a pile near the bed. I ran over and bent to pick them up. I shook my head at my shirt. I pulled it on. Only one button was intact. It would do. I buttoned it and turned to him.

"You shouldn't have done that to me, Frank."

He sighed like he knew this already. "Listen, Kristine—"

"I don't want to listen," I said, feeling tears slide down my face.

"Come on," he said. "Let's talk about this."

"Fuck you!" I screamed as the tears streamed down my face. "You're sick!"

He held one hand out towards me, palm up. It was a gesture of peace, his white flag, but for some reason, it almost terrified me.

"You better leave me alone," I said and pulled on my skirt.

"Kristine, come on," he said. "Let's talk about this."

"I don't want to talk!" I screamed.

"I'm sorry I lost my temper, but you—"

I pointed at him, "I didn't deserve that!"

He hung his head and nodded in agreement.

I wiped the tears off my face with the back of my hand and muttered, "You're mean."

"I'm sorry," he said, glancing at me. "Tell me what I can do to remedy this."

"You can leave me alone," I said and stepped into my heels. "For good."

"You don't mean that."

"I do," I said, sobbing. "I really do."

My clothes on, I turned on my heel and ran from the room. He followed me, but he didn't run. I knew he wasn't about to let me go but I had to get out of there. Everything in my body told me to run, run, *run!*

I raced down the hall and was about to sprint down the stairs when he called out to me, "We need to talk about this!"

I turned to see him coming at me. In a panic, I took one step down, backwards. My ankle twisted as my heel caught on the first step. I cried out, then he rushed over to me, which made me panic, which made me lose my balance, which made me stumble and fall. Backwards.

"*Kristine!*"

Before I fell, I saw his face and then his hand, reaching out to save me. I grabbed for it desperately but it was too late and I fell backwards, my body doing a somersault along the stairs before I reached the bottom, where my head was the first thing to hit and it hit hard.

I didn't black out at first. My mind tried in vain to stay active and search out something to help me. I knew I was in trouble, I knew I was in a bad way, but I couldn't do anything about it. By the time he got to me, my head was spinning. No, my whole body was spinning, out of control. It was the worse feeling I'd ever had. Not only that, I was having trouble breathing. I coughed. I tried to cough. I couldn't cough! I couldn't breathe! I couldn't do anything but lay there and allow my body to convulse, to tremble, to shudder, to shake with panic.

My eyes closed. I blacked out. I don't know how long I laid there trembling, but all of a sudden I heard something. I couldn't tell what it was. I listened closely and then recognized the sound as his voice, calling to me from what seemed like under a thick and heavy blanket. Maybe he was in another room? I stopped concentrating on it and blacked out again, then it happened once more and it lured me out of my sleep, teased me, tickled me. I wanted to reach out to it, to hold it. To have it.

Far off, I heard his voice, coming at me as softly as a June wind, "Kristine?"

I tried to say something but I couldn't.

"Kristine?"

Uhhh…uh. No. I couldn't do it. I couldn't respond, though I wanted to, so badly. I wanted to reach out and touch him, but I couldn't move. It suddenly dawned on me that I couldn't move. I could not for the life of me move. Was this shock? Panic set in momentarily. What was happening to my body? To me?

I felt something warm and wet on my face. He was washing my face, caressing it with a soft washcloth. It felt good against my face, warm, almost melodious, inviting. I could smell the fabric softener the maid used. It smelled like a baby; it was such a sweet smell. I blinked and opened my eyes.

"Kristine?" he said gently, with remorse.

I blinked and blinked, then was finally able to focus on him.

"Kristine?" he pleaded.

I managed to mutter, "Uhh…uh…"

He wiped my face tenderly, very much caressing it with the back of his hand. I tried to push it away. He wouldn't let me. He kept it there, then he turned me over, onto my stomach and I felt something red-hot on my back. I screamed and convulsed.

"Shh," he mumbled. "Shh. It's just alcohol. To clean the marks."

The marks? The marks. Oh, God. It all came back to me then, like a bad dream comes back at you once you're awake. I was suddenly frightened. I began to shake. I started to cry.

"Shh," he murmured and pressed his face against mine. "It's okay, baby."

"What are you doing?" I finally managed to say.

"I'm just cleaning your back," he said.

He was tending my wounds? Why was he doing this?

"The doctor said you were lucky," he said and I heard him dip the washcloth into a bowl, squeeze out the excess water, then bring it to my face again. "You had a bad fall, but no broken bones. I thought for a minute that you were a goner."

I heard him sniffle, like he was trying to hold back tears. I listened, hanging on his every word.

"Your ankle's twisted, though, sprained," he said. "It's swollen, but it'll be okay soon."

My ankle? Then it all came back to me. All of it. The beating, then the fall. The panic.

I finally opened my eyes wide enough to look at him. His face was plastered with grief, an unbelievable look of grief. Some shame. He gently, oh so gently, wiped my back clean, then I felt momentary relief as he put some ointment on it, which felt cool. Then he rubbed it in and turned me back over.

I looked to the side. I was now in bed. I was lying on top of the silk comforter, bleeding onto it. I was naked. I stared at the window and was amazed to see daylight. How long had I been out?

"You'll be fine," he said softly and then the bastard began to brush my hair. My hair was wet! He'd given me a bath. I tried my best to glare at him, but my face hurt so badly. And I had to pee.

I tried to speak. He bent over and pressed his ear next to my mouth. I whispered, "Bathroom."

"Oh!" he exclaimed and got up off the bed. "Can you walk?"

Could I walk? I finally managed to glare at him. *Why don't you tell me if I can walk?*

He stared back, then, without a word, bent over and scooped me up in his arms and carried me towards the bathroom. I couldn't do anything but try to hang on. Every step made my body ache like it had never ached before. I cried out several times and he shushed me gently.

He carried me all the way into the bathroom and deposited me gently on the commode. When he let go, I almost fell over. He grabbed me just in time and held me up.

Then I urinated. I was almost embarrassed, but then I thought, *What does it matter?* Besides, I had been about to burst. I urinated for what seemed like years, then finally managed to open my eyes all the way, squinting at the bright light. I finally stopped and sighed with relief as I looked around the marble bathroom, at the huge tub. I stared at the marble floor then across at the vanity where I usually put on my make-up. Then at the mirror above the vanity. Terror caught in my throat and I almost screamed.

There—right there!—was some strange woman staring in the mirror at me. And she looked like hell. But, then...

No. Oh, no. NO NO *NO!*

It was no strange woman. It was me. Me! That was me! That woman, that person with the swollen eyes, so swollen they were almost shut, that woman was me! That fragile, beaten to death woman was me! I couldn't get over it. I'd be disfigured. How many times had he hit me in the face? I couldn't remember. I couldn't remember anything.

I got up and tried to approach the mirror to get a better look. I almost fell to the floor.

"Easy there," he said softly and held me up.

I ignored him but he held me tight. I pointed and he walked me over to the mirror. When I saw what I looked like, I screamed at the top of my lungs. I screamed and I screamed and I screamed until I couldn't scream anymore, until I became hoarse. Then I screamed more and more until he covered my mouth with his hand and silenced me. Then I stared into the mirror, fully realizing how bad it was.

I was covered not only in bruises, but also in welts. All over my legs, my arms, my back, my stomach. Oh, dear Lord! I looked like I had been run over by a truck, then they'd came back and run over me again, just to make sure they got me.

I wanted to kill him then. To beat him as he had beaten me. I tried to swat at him, but I was too weak.

"I'm going to kill you!" I cried.

"Shh," he said and held me tight.

"How many times did you hit me in the face?" I asked and turned back to the mirror.

"I didn't hit you in the face," he said and shook his head. "That's from the fall."

The fall did this? I vaguely remember feeling the rough, wool carpet on my face. I stared at the welts. They were only a few of them, mostly on my back. All the rest was carpet burns. Rough, ugly, red scratchy scrapes all over my body.

But my face… Oh, dear God. My face was in shambles. It was swollen and looked so bad it made me want to cry.

"When you fell…" he began then cleared his throat. "You landed on your face."

I did? I stared back at myself in the mirror. Would it ever heal? Ever? I started sobbing and wanted to hit him so bad then. I turned and punched at him, but he ignored my sobs and my futile punches and lifted me back into his arms. He carried me into the bedroom, laid me down gently and kissed my forehead with his cool lips.

"You'll feel better soon," he said.

No, I felt like saying, *I won't.* Instead, I said, "This is all your fault."

He nodded. "I know."

I despise him, I hate him, I love him.

Days passed. Not that I could do a damn thing about it. All I could do was lie there in that bed in a pain induced haze and stare dumbly up at the ceiling. I formulated a defense and plotted Frank's murder. Then I tried to reason for him, to understand why he did what he did. I couldn't think of any good reason, other than the fact that he was nuts. And he had to be nuts. Right?

He had said, "I'm breaking you."

What kind of sick bastard says something like that? Breaking me of what? From what? And why?

Unfortunately, he stayed by my side the majority of the time. He cleaned my wounds, spoon fed me, gave me painkillers and wouldn't let anyone in to see me. He did all of this gently as a mother. He even seemed to like doing it.

In about a week's time, I felt better. Not that I could run a marathon or anything, but I did feel better. My face was healing, too, which made me breathe a sigh of relief. It didn't look like I was going to need any reconstructive surgery.

Frank moved a TV into the bedroom and flipped channels for me, stopping when I would point at something I wanted to watch. And I made him sit through chick movies, soap operas and music videos.

He didn't say a word. He didn't say how sorry he was. He would just lean over and plant a kiss on my cheek ever so often. I just rolled my eyes and counted the minutes until I could smash something heavy over his head. Maybe a lamp? A small sculpture? A broom? What would be good?

Then he'd plant another kiss on my cheek and I'd start the reasoning for him all over again. Trying to justify his actions so that I could understand what drove him to do something like this.

But he hadn't pushed me down the stairs… No. But I *had* been running away from him and that's why I fell. Because of him. It was his fault. The bastard.

One day he leaned over and planted a kiss on my cheek and before he pulled away, he said, "I love you."

I glared at him. He smiled back.

"I do," he said, almost happily. "I love you."

"*You love me?*"

He nodded and gave me another kiss. "Yes, I do."

I moved away from him, fuming. But I couldn't help myself, I had to ask, "So, if you love me, how could you beat me like that?"

He dropped his head. "Kristine, I'm sorry. I can't ever make what I did right, but I am sorry."

"But why did you do it?"

"I was extremely pissed off at you, that's why," he said. "I beat you because you did something you shouldn't have done. In my state of mind at the time, you deserved it."

"How do you justify it, though? How *can* you justify it?"

"I can't."

"That's what I thought."

"Listen," he said. "Most of your wounds are from the fall—"

"I fell because I thought you were going to kill me!"

"If I wanted to kill you, you'd be dead."

"That's really reassuring."

He nodded as if I'd given him a compliment. He had to be nuts. But what did that make me? I was the nut who put up with it. Why wasn't I gone from here? What was I waiting on? I had plenty of opportunity to leave. I could leave anytime I wanted to. Besides, I wasn't a prisoner, not that I knew of. I did have some free will. Some.

"So, you see," he said. "It's all for the best. Now I know where we stand."

"And where do we stand?" I asked, eying him.

"You know where," he said. "You know now not to pull that kind of shit you pulled."

"Whatever."

"You're not a teenager, you know."

"So?" I snapped. "And light me a cigarette."

He lit my cigarette and handed it to me, then said, "I'm just saying you're a little old to throw those kinds of parties."

I could have slapped him. Since when was thirty-two *old?* That was old? Well, if I was old, he was ancient. He was thirty-five.

"Please!" I said and took a drag. "What kind of parties should I throw? Ones where all the people come dressed in dinner gowns and tuxes?"

"Or at the very least, the people should be dressed."

We stared at each other for a moment then we couldn't help it. We cracked up.

He grinned. "I saw some of those women and I thought I was in a stripclub."

"You met me in a stripclub."

"I know."

"Why did you, of all people, come into my stripclub?"

"I met someone there. A business associate who likes those kinds of clubs."

"And you don't like them?"

"Oh, I didn't say that, Kristine," he said and leaned back on the bed, hands behind his head. "I like stripclubs but I don't have a lot of time to go to them."

I eyed him.

"I don't look down on those people as much as you think I do. In fact, I think strippers are very enterprising."

"Whatever," I said and took a drag. "Why did you keep coming back?"

"Because of you, obviously."

I hid my smile. I knew that, but it was good to hear.

"I mean, you floored me," he said.

Yeah, I knew it.

He smiled and kissed my cheek. "I had to have you."

"You could have been nicer, though."

"Oh, right," he said. "And have you walk all over me?"

I sat up and pointed at him with my cigarette. "That's what this is all about, isn't it? Me walking all over you and you can't stand it!"

He looked away towards the window.

"Frank?"

"What?" he said, still staring out the window.

"Is that why you did it? Are you afraid I'll walk all over you?"

He nodded. "Yes. Let's not talk about this."

"Why? Does it make you uncomfortable?"

"Yes," he muttered. "It does. Please let it drop."

I let it drop and smoked my cigarette, dropping the ash into the ashtray he held for me.

"I just wanted you to know, that's all," he muttered.

"Know what?"

"Know that I love you."

"Well, I hate you."

"No, you don't."

"Yes, I do."

"Kristine," he said, moving closer to me. "Right now you feel humbled. You feel frightened. You feel—"

"Stop telling me how I feel, you asshole! I feel hatred towards you right now because you beat me! I feel anxious that you'll do it again."

"I won't do it again, Kristine," he said, staring into my eyes. "Not unless you give me reason."

"Oh, and that was reason enough to beat someone? By throwing a party?"

"You did so without my knowledge, without my permission. You didn't even invite me."

"Invite you! Why would I invite you? You weren't even in town!"

"That hurt, too," he said.

"That's not enough reason to beat me," I said. "Besides, I only invited thirty people, but more came. It wasn't my fault they all showed up."

He sighed. "Oh."

"So really you had no right to do that to me. It wasn't my fault."

"Still, though, a lot of antiques were damaged and—"

"Who cares if one of your stupid chairs gets a scratch? It's just stuff."

"That's not the point."

"What is the point?"

He sighed. "The point is you didn't even consider me when you planned all this. You were only thinking of yourself."

That wasn't entirely true. I rolled my eyes and said, "You keep me locked away here. I had to have some contact with the outside world."

"Then why not throw a party in a bar?" he asked.

I looked away.

"And why stay, Kristine?" he asked softly, touching my arm. "If you hate me, why not leave?"

"Why should I leave?" I asked. "Why don't you leave? Why don't you break up with me so I *can* leave?"

"I don't want you to, that's why, and you know it."

"You didn't have to call the cops," I said.

"I didn't. The neighbors did."

I stared at him. He wasn't lying, I could tell that. Well, it made sense. I vaguely remembered a policeman at the front door telling me to wind it down soon, me promising and then inviting him in for a drink. Him coming in and getting lost in the crowd.

Well, I'll be damned.

I stared at the TV, which was turned off. He gave me a little kiss on my cheek. Then he turned my head towards his and grazed his lips against mine. Softly. Softly enough to send shivers up and down my spine. Softly enough for me to want more where that came from.

He kissed me then, kissed me gently, passionately. Wide open kissed me, all of me, my being. I couldn't stop. I wanted to stop. I couldn't have stopped if my life depended on it. I turned to him and took his face between my hands and pulled him to me, pulled his body on top of mine, helped him undress, helped him to take me. And he made love to me. We'd never made love before. We'd only fucked. Now we were making love. He caressed my body; he didn't devour it as he did before. He kissed me, stroked me. He brought me to one intense orgasm and then another. An orgasm that was tender and sweet and belonged in my body. Belonged to him. Just like I did.

After it was over, he told me again that he loved me. And he waited. He waited a long time. But he was right. I didn't hate him. Even after all that, I couldn't. My body, my soul and my heart craved him too much for hatred to dominate my feelings.

"I love you, too," I said, realizing it was easy to say, that I wanted to say it, that I felt it. That it scared me to open myself up like that. That I wanted to hide it, to take it back, but knowing I couldn't.

"See?" he said, satisfied. "You don't hate me. I knew you didn't."

He was right. And with that, I inched a little closer to being completely and utterly under his control, to losing myself in him. To losing everything that I had become and would become to him, to this man. To his love. To his prison.

But I wasn't about to let him break me. I still had too much pride for that.

Sprained ankle.

I was up in about a week. My face was healing and it didn't look like it was going to scar. My body was still sore from the fall, but the painkillers made it all easier to deal with.

I knew I looked like hell. I refused to go out anywhere and asked Frank to give all the house staff a week or so off. I didn't want anyone to see me like this.

My sprained ankle hurt like hell. It took me forever to learn how to walk on the crutches. First you have to put them under your arms, hold the hurt foot up—or out, whichever you prefer—and balance. That's the easy part. Then you have to maneuver the crutches by lifting them up at the same time to propel your body forward. By the time I learned to get around on them, I could walk without their assistance.

But before that happened, something strange happened.

One day I thought I was home alone and was walking around on the crutches and by this time I was getting around on them pretty good. I was downstairs in the living room and decided to go into the kitchen and get some tea. I got up and made my way in there. But then I thought I'd also like a sandwich. I was reading a really good book and wanted to read while I ate. So, I turned around and went back into the living room, grabbed the book, shoved it under my arm, then went back out into the hall.

As I hobbled, the book fell out from under my arm.

"Damn," I muttered and bent over to pick it up. But I lost my balance and fell flat on my ass and my foot went behind me and twisted. Again. The crutches fell noisily beside me.

I cried out in pain and started to cuss.

"Motherfucking shit!" I cried as tears began to stream down my face. It hurt like absolute hell. It was a sharp pain, way down deep in the bone. I felt it in my nerves, too. It was a taunting, deep pain and nauseating. I started to take the bandage off, but then just sat back and sighed. And then I really started to cry, like a baby. And that's what I felt like, a baby who needed its rest and food and sleep. I needed someone to help me then, to help me up, to give me a painkiller. I just needed someone because I couldn't move.

I suddenly got the feeling that I wasn't alone.

I looked up and my eyes were met directly with Frank's. He was staring at me, mesmerized. I stared back and wondered what he was doing. He didn't move. He was transfixed by something. I wanted to say something, to call out to him, but I was almost afraid to break the spell.

I didn't have to say anything. In a second flat, he sprinted over towards me. He bent to my eye level and stared into my eyes.

"Does it hurt much?" he asked softly, but with an intensity that was a little peculiar.

I shrugged and wiped my face off with the back of my hand. "Not always, but now it does. I twisted it again."

He stared at me. "I'm sorry, baby."

"I know, Frank, you tell me everyday."

"No, I mean I'm sorry it hurts."

I stared at him. What was he getting at? "Me, too," I said a little uneasily.

"Would you like me to rub it?" he asked. "Would that make it feel better?"

"Maybe," I said.

He sat down and motioned for me to give him my foot. I stretched my leg out, laid it in his lap and he took my foot between his hands and began to rub it, ever so gently.

"It's all swollen," he said.

I nodded. "Yup."

He continued to rub it, holding it in both hands. He rubbed it like a nurse would, carefully. But then he rubbed a little too hard.

I gasped and said, "Ow! Watch it!"

He stopped and stared at me. "I'm sorry. I didn't mean to do that."

I sighed and sat back. "It's okay. Just be careful."

He nodded quietly and began to rub then he stopped and stared at me. "Can I take your bandage off?"

"Why?"

"I dunno. I just want to see your ankle."

God, he's so weird, I thought, but nodded anyway. "Sure, go ahead, but be careful."

He grinned and took off the clasps, set them to the side, then began to unravel the bandage.

"You have to put it back on, though," I said as he unraveled the last of it.

"I will."

"I know you will."

He held my foot in his hands and stared at it. I stared, too. It was swollen and black and blue. It looked awful.

He bent and kissed it. I smiled. Then he pressed his face against it.

"What are you doing?" I asked.

He shrugged and smiled at me. "Nothing."

I chuckled. "You are doing something, Frank. Tell me."

"No," he said and began to lick my ankle, all over the sore spot. I sighed. Ahh, that felt so good.

"Like that?" he asked.

I bit my lip and nodded. "Yeah."

He began to caress it again. I began to feel it. I began to feel warm and want him. Just by his touch, which was so gentle and caring, I wanted him.

That was his indicator. He stopped rubbing and set my foot on the floor gently, parted my legs and bent over me. I arched and met his lips. He began to kiss me then, kiss me differently. It was a slow, amorous kiss. His mouth was open wide, then he'd shut it, like he was eating my mouth. I matched his kiss and did the same, which elicited a deep moan from him.

He pushed me back on the floor and tugged my shirt up, then dove between my legs, eating at my crotch through my shorts. I moaned and grabbed his head, tugging at him, letting him know he could take the rest of my clothes off. His hand unzipped my shorts and he pulled them down my legs, threw them over his shoulder and came back up the inside of my leg using his tongue.

By this time I was so wet, I slid around on the floor.

I grabbed at his zipper and pulled it down. He helped, pulled his dick out and put it in. Then he fucked me. I sighed with relief. For a while now, we'd been making love, which was great, but fucking was what I liked best. I liked the way his dick filled me then thrust into me.

"Ahh, yeah," I said and bit at his ear. "Fuck me, baby."

He did so and gave a thrust that made me pant. He took my leg and held it up, so he got in deeper. I liked that. I told him so. He grinned at me and kissed me again, then bent and bit at my nipple, which made me rise off the floor and meet him thrust for thrust.

"I'm gonna come," he moaned and buried his face in my neck, which he ate at like a vampire.

I held his head and grunted, "So am I."

And I was. I was coming fast and hard, being so turned on I couldn't contain myself. And it was a deep, intense one. So intense I grabbed out for him and scratched his chest.

"Ahh!" he yelled, obviously in pain.

"I'm sorry," I breathed but didn't stop.

He didn't stop, either. We couldn't have stopped no matter what. We were like two wild animals on the floor fucking like we were supposed to fuck and when we came, we both cried out in pain.

It was that powerful.

He fell away from me, panting. I laid there panting. We didn't move for a while. I noticed we were both sweating profusely. I leaned over and wiped his brow. Just as I was about to take my hand away, he grabbed it and put it around his dick. I complied and moved my hand up and down it, then bent and put it in my mouth. Even though it was rapidly deflating, it was still hard. And as I sucked, he came again, came right into my mouth, his sperm. Not a lot of it, but some.

He grabbed the back of my head and held onto it, held me there and he let out a loud cry as if it were the best thing he'd ever felt, but it hurt a little too.

I stared at him. He stared back. We couldn't believe he'd just done that. Neither one of us. He grinned sheepishly and opened his arms. I lay down on his chest and he kissed the top of my head.

"Do you just come again?" I asked.

He nodded and cleared his throat. "I guess maybe I didn't get it all out the first time."

"I've never seen anything like that."

"I've never done anything like that."

"Wow," I said and sighed. "You were horny, weren't you?"

"Yes, I was."

"Why were you so horny? We just had sex this morning."

"Why do you always ask these stupid questions? I'm always horny for you, you know that."

I grinned. I did know it, but it felt good to hear, too. "Thanks for rubbing my ankle," I said, then laughed. "Why did you do that?"

He shrugged.

I sat up on my elbow and stared him down. "Tell me."

He said, "I don't know what came over me, but when I saw you like that, all weak and helpless, it just drove me crazy."

"Really?"

He nodded.

"Did it turn you on?"

"Yes, it did. Tremendously."

"Wow," was all I could think of to say. "What else turns you on?"

He smiled, but didn't reply. I was about to find out.

Honey.

After the sprained ankle incident, things began to change in our relationship. All relationships are about sex to a certain degree, but ours became about games. And that's what started the games. That's where the door cracked, then swung wide open.

It all started innocently enough. I guess it was just a natural progression in our relationship. They were fun games, silly even. They made us laugh. The day after a game was played, I'd sit and think about it and just crack up. They were that fun.

Just after I was done with the crutches, the phone rang about ten in the morning. It was a Wednesday.

"Hello?"

"Kristine," Frank said, calling from work, or whatever he called it.

"*Franklin.*"

"Kristine," he said. "I've given Pierre and cook the day off."

"Ohhh...kay."

"What are you going to do?"

"Going to do?" I asked and glanced around the living room. "Just watch some TV or—"

"No," he said, silencing me. "What are you going to do for supper?"

"Oh!" I exclaimed and thought about it. "I could order in or maybe we could—"

"No," he said, again silencing me. "You will not. You will cook supper for us tonight."

I wasn't so convinced. Cook? For him? There was no way. I made a mean spaghetti and meatballs, but he wasn't the spaghetti and meatballs kinda guy. He ate veal that had little green things sprinkled all over it. He ate things I couldn't pronounce. He ate things I didn't like to eat because I didn't like fancy food. I was too meat and potatoes for escargot or any of that other fancy stuff.

Besides, I wasn't going to eat snails even if they did give them a fancy crème sauce and a fancy name to go along with them. Nuh uh. No.

He cut into my thoughts, "I have prepared a menu."

"Tonight?" I asked hesitantly. "You want me to cook tonight?"

"Yes, Kristine," he said, losing patience. "You will cook for us tonight."

"I will?"

"Yes!"

I still wasn't convinced.

"Kristine," he said in that warning voice. "Listen to me. I have prepared a menu, which I will fax to the house."

"If you say so," I said and stifled a yawn.

"You will receive it shortly," he said and hung up.

I stared at the receiver then set the phone down. Not a minute later, the fax machine on the desk was spitting out a menu. I grabbed it. Menu: Pot roast, mashed potatoes, green beans, rolls, lime jello.

Lime jello?

Well, that was certainly an all-American meal. I smiled. I could do this in no time. He must have guessed I couldn't cook anything fancy.

I rushed to the grocery store, bought up the items, rushed back and found a crock-pot in the cabinet. I prepared the pot roast, stuck it in there and started peeling the potatoes. I worked my ass off until about two that afternoon, only stopping once to light a cigarette, which dangled from my lips as I chopped vegetables, like a short-order cook in a greasy spoon diner.

He called around four. "I will be home at six. I expect supper to be on the table."

Then I suddenly got it. He was playing a game. He was acting like a man—a man with a woman at home, who stayed home, who cooked for him, who took care of him. And that woman was me.

He continued, "I have purchased you a dress, which will arrive at the house shortly. Please put it on, with the stockings and the heels."

"Yes, sir," I teased.

He growled, "Don't 'yes, sir', me."

"Uh, sorry. Sir."

"Kristine," he said. "I am your husband. You don't have to call me sir."

My husband? Well, well, well. When did *that* happen?

"Can I call you master then?" I teased, twirling the phone cord around my fingers. "Please, master."

"No," he said. "You can only refer to me tonight as 'honey'."

"'Honey'?"

"Yes. 'Honey'."

"Okay, honey."

The doorbell rang.

"Go get that," he ordered. "That will be your dress."

"Bye!" I squealed and hung up before he could respond. I ran to the door, threw it open and a tall, elegantly dressed woman jerked back.

"Oh, sorry," she drawled. "Are you Kristine?"

"Yes, that's me."

"I'm Liddy," she said and patted a thin dress box. "This is for you."

I reached out for it. She held it back.

"No, sweetie," she said, smiling as if she were embarrassed for me. "I have to make sure it fits."

"Oh," I said. "Okay."

I led her into the living room. She sat on the sofa and placed the box in her lap, like she was protecting it. She smiled. I smiled back and waited for her to let me have it.

"You'll need to try it on, of course," she said and laid the box on the couch, then opened it delicately.

I stood back and watched her, thinking she must have some prize in there. I was astounded when she pulled out a rather plain, but pretty, black dress. Kind of like the ones Mrs. Cleaver would have worn on *Leave it to Beaver*.

She held it up and smiled at me. "Please be careful. This is on loan."

I had to ask, "What is so great about this dress?"

She gasped. "It's vintage Chanel, sweetie!"

"Oh."

She nodded. "Your husband wanted it, but I couldn't part with it, so we worked something out so you could wear it tonight."

I didn't bother telling her Frank was not my husband. Or that that this was all a game. I nodded at her and held my hand out for the dress.

She shooed my hand away and stood. "Just undress and we'll make sure it fits."

Being a former stripper, I didn't mind this. The only thing that bothered me was a prominent bite mark on my ass that my "husband" had given me the previous night. But I had panties on, so I doubted she saw it.

After I was undressed, she held the dress out and I stepped into it. It fit like a glove, which meant I could barely breathe in it. It also smelled musty and the old material was rough, like a thick sewn silk or something. But once I turned and looked in the mirror, I grinned. I looked like a hot fifties housewife. It *was* a beautiful dress.

She bent this way and that, tugging at the dress, then she sighed, "Well, you don't need any alterations. It fits perfectly."

I nodded and twirled around. "I love it!"

She smiled and touched my arm. "Please, be careful. This is a one of a kind and I have it displayed in my shop."

"Which shop?" I asked.

"Tree Jordan's," she said. "On Magazine."

I didn't know it, but I nodded like I did.

She reached back into the box and pulled out vintage heels, an apron and a set of pearls, then silk stockings, a garter belt and a girdle. I'd never worn a girdle in my entire life.

"Now," she said. "With a little make-up and hair, you'll be the perfect housewife."

I stared at myself. "Yeah, I guess you're right."

"Well, that about does it," she said and tried to smile. I could tell she was having a hard time letting this dress go.

"I'll be extra careful with it," I promised.

"Please do," she mumbled, then let herself out.

"Poor thing," I muttered after I heard the front door close. I glanced at the clock. It was five. I barely had enough time to finish up the meal and to get some make-up on.

I rushed around and was seated in the "parlor" with a cigarette—in cigarette holder—when I heard Frank come in. I tensed with anticipation.

He walked in, ignored me, threw his briefcase down, and plopped in the chair opposite me.

"Hey," he muttered.

"Hey yourself," I said, unsure of where this was leading.

"Where's my drink?" he asked.

"Oh!" I said and jumped up. I smiled at him before racing over to the bar where I fixed him his favorite martini—vodka with an olive. I slowly walked back towards him, swinging my hips. I bent down, delivered the martini and stood back up.

"Thanks," he muttered. "What's for dinner? I'm starving."

"Pot roast," I said and sat down in his lap. "With mashed potatoes and—"

"Good," he said and pushed me out of his lap. "Let's eat."

I watched in befuddlement as he left the room and headed for the dining room. Well, alright then. I followed him. He was already seated when I walked in the dining room.

"Smells good," he mumbled then opened a newspaper and flicked it so the pages would smooth out.

I stared at him. He stared back, over the newspaper.

"Well?" he asked.

"Aren't you even going to say anything?"

"About what?"

"About anything!" I half-yelled, really getting into my role as the over-looked wife. "Look at this meal! At me!"

He eyed me, the meal. He nodded. "Good job, honey."

I stared at him. Well, he had told me I'd done a good job. I decided to go with it. "Thanks. Honey."

"Am I going to have to beg for it?" he asked.

I sighed loudly as if I were *this* close to telling him to fuck off then fixed him a plate, plopping the food down onto it. I shoved it under his newspaper, then sat down, crossed my arms and glared at him.

He didn't take notice. I almost smiled. He was really playing it up. He started to eat while reading the paper, just like I wasn't even in the room.

He glanced over at me. "Aren't you going to eat?"

"Oh! Yeah, I almost forgot," I said and prepared myself a plate.

He shrugged and gobbled down everything on his plate. Then he looked around. "Where's my beer?"

"Your *beer*?"

He nodded. "Yeah. You know I like a beer with pot roast."

"Oh, sorry," I said. "I've had so much on my mind lately. I'll get it."

I hopped up and raced into the kitchen, where I located a six pack in the fridge. I grabbed one, then a glass and raced to the door. I stopped at the door, pushed it open with my hip, and sauntered in, really swinging my hips as I walked over to him. He didn't notice, so I stopped about half-way there and walked like I usually do.

He glanced up at me and winked.

I smiled and put the swing back into my hips and made my way over, stopping at the table. I bent over and poured the beer while he stared at me from the corner of his eye.

"There you go, honey," I said sweetly.

He nodded, sipped the beer, then he held out his plate to me.

"Yes?" I asked.

"May I have some more pot roast? Please?"

I grabbed the plate and loaded food onto it. I plopped it back down in front of him then picked up my fork and moved my food around a little, staring at him from the corner of my eye.

He folded the newspaper, grabbed the plate, hunched over it and ate it like a truck driver. Or a coal miner. He didn't even pause to wipe his mouth. I watched him, mouth agape. Then he leaned back and gave a big burp. I cringed.

"Would you like some more?" I asked.

"No, thanks," he said, eying my plate. "Aren't you hungry?"

"No, I had a big lunch."

"What about the lime jello?"

"Oh, I forgot," I said and retrieved it from the refrigerator. I put some on a desert plate and slid it over to him. He ate it in exactly the same manner as the pot roast, then pushed the plate towards me.

"You can clear the dishes now," he said.

"Of course."

"And bring me another beer."

"Sure, honey." I said began to clear the dishes.

"Be sure to wear latex gloves when you wash the dishes," he called as I carried them into the kitchen. "You don't want to ruin your manicure."

I stared down at my nails. He was right.

I smiled at him, kicked the door open with my foot, walked over to the sink and threw the dishes down. One of the plates broke in half. Oops! Oh, well. What did it matter? I grabbed another beer, went back in, handed it to him then gathered the remaining dishes and smiled at him. He didn't smile back. He now had his feet propped up on the table and was leaned back, smoking a cigarette and sipping his beer. I bent over in front of him to grab his plate and his hand came down and slapped me right across the ass. It stung like hell.

I jumped up and whirled around. "What the hell was that for?"

"An ass like that," he said, grinning. "Deserves a good slapping." He slapped it again, this time squeezing it with his hand.

"Watch it," I said, going back into the kitchen. "Honey."

I washed the dishes in about ten minutes. Then I went back into the dining room. He was still in the same position, only his cigarette was extinguished. He eyed me.

"Honey," he said. "I want you to get up on the table now."

"Excuse me?"

"Get up on the table."

"For what?"

"I want to see what's under that dress."

I began to tense and tingle with anticipation. I did as I was told. I slid up on to the table and crossed my legs.

"No," he said. "On all fours."

I got up on all fours.

He grabbed my legs and pulled them apart and peered between them. I almost cracked up. What was he doing? Giving me an exam?

He sighed and I felt his warm breath on my legs. I felt myself getting warm, growing moist. He did that to me. He could just look at me and I'd be ready.

He laughed. "What the hell is that thing you're wearing?"

I stared back at him from over my shoulder. "It's a girdle. It completes the authentic look."

He shook his head, still eying the girdle. Then he reached between my legs and began to tug it off. I wriggled so he could get it down. He threw it over his shoulder.

"That's the ugliest thing I've ever seen," he muttered.

I laughed. It was ugly as hell.

His hand went up between my ass cheeks sideways, then down. He stopped to finger me. I was now dripping.

He slapped my ass again like I was a piece of meat. I wiggled and stared back at him. He didn't return my gaze. He just kept looking at my ass like it was the first time he'd seen it. Then he ran his hand up my leg, holding it, squeezing it.

"I like your stockings," he said. "And I see you have a garter belt on."

"Yes, honey."

"The dress is nice, too," he said. "Did you get it on sale?"

I smiled, playing along. "No. It was full price. Is that okay, honey? That I paid full price? We can afford it, can't we?"

He shrugged. "This time, but you're going to have to stop your damn spending."

I hid my smile and said very seriously, "I'll do better next time. I promise."

He was now fingering my clit, stroking it, bringing it and me under his control. I moaned and spread my legs wider.

"Honey," I moaned. "Climb up here and fuck me.

He only response was another hard slap to my ass, then a grunt, like he liked doing that, slapping my ass. I know I liked it. He squeezed it again.

"You're fucking the neighbor, aren't you?" he asked suddenly.

I tensed. "No."

"Don't lie to me," he growled. "I saw you."

"No, no," I said, playing along, pretending to be in a panic. "You didn't see me. I only fuck you."

"Don't lie to me, bitch," he said and I heard him pull his zipper down. "Is his cock as big as mine?"

He pushed it between my ass cheeks, running it up and down. It slid along happily, getting lost in my juice. I moaned.

"No," I murmured. "Your cock is much, much bigger."

"Then why are you fucking him?" he growled and pulled my head back. He began to lick and kiss my neck, suckle it.

"I just did," I moaned. "I don't know why!"

"Yes, you do," he said. "You did it because you're a little slut. Isn't that right?"

He gave another jerk to my head. I moaned with ecstasy.

"No!" I cried. "I did it 'cause you work all the time! You don't pay any attention to me! You don't love me!"

"Love you?" he hissed and let my head fall. "How could I love a woman who sticks another man's cock in her mouth?"

"I didn't do that with him," I moaned. "I only let him fuck me."

He leaned over and whispered, "Where did you let him fuck you?"

"Just up the ass," I whispered. "I told him my cunt belonged to you."

He laughed harshly. I knew he'd like that one.

"Come on, baby," I said. "Stick it in my pussy, your pussy, it belongs to you. I'd never let another man touch it."

He did as he was told. He stuck it in, filling me up with every single inch of his hard cock. He took me like a bitch. Fucked me like a bitch. I couldn't get enough. I wanted it all, then some more. More, more, more.

"Besides," I moaned. "You're fucking your secretary."

"So what?" he said. "She doesn't give me shit and she works cheap."

"She's a whore!" I screamed. "She sucks your cock every day before you come home! There's nothing left for me!"

"I got plenty for the both of you," he said and leaned over and kissed my neck, then bit at my ear. "Then some."

"But I want it all," I said and moaned. "It's mine. Your cock belongs to me."

"No, it doesn't," he said. "I can fuck any bitch I want with it."

He accented the last syllable with a hard thrust. I gasped. Then he grabbed the front of my dress, yanked it, and, consequently, tore it apart. It fell off me in pieces. I stared down at it. Oh fucking shit!

"Oh shit!" I yelled. "She'll kill me!"

He was fucking me, not missing a beat as he asked, "Who?"

"Liddy! The dress woman! She said this was on loan!"

Oh, God I'd never be able to fix it! I almost stopped him, but of course, I didn't. Forget the dress for now. There wasn't anything I could do. I'd worry about it after we were done.

"Fuck Liddy," he muttered.

Yeah, fuck her.

"Oh, honey," I moaned. "Fuck *me* harder. You like giving it to me, don't you?"

"Uh huh," he said and complied, driving his cock deep inside me. I pushed back against him, which pressed it in deeper and deeper.

He grabbed me by the hair of the head and pulled my face to his. He hissed, "I don't like it when you fuck around on me."

"I won't do it again," I said and begged, "Please, fuck me harder."

He gave another push. "You should pay for what you did."

"I won't do it again! I promise!"

"I think you need a spanking," he said.

"Noooo!" I wailed as he pulled out. "Don't!"

But he had me turned over and pulled off the table, and I was bent across his lap, my bare ass sticking in the air.

"I'm going to spank you now," he said and reared back. His hand landed on my bare ass with a resounding *whack!*

I screamed, "No!"

"I'll show you to fuck around on me," he said and gave me another whack, then another, and another until I was writhing in his lap, until I was squirming, coming, coming so hard I nearly fell to the floor. I wanted my hand—or his hand—on my pussy so bad then. I put mine there, but he pulled it back, held my arm tight and wouldn't let me touch myself.

"Please," I begged. "Please let me touch it!"

"No," he said and gave me another good whack, so hard this time I nearly jumped out of my skin and ran away.

"Please," I begged and tried to get my arm back. "Let me rub it a little."

"No."

Another whack.

"Oh, God!" I screamed. "Please fuck me now!"

He grabbed me by the hair again and hissed, "Promise me you won't fuck him again."

"I won't fuck him again! I promise!"

He seemed pleased with my answer. I almost smiled gratefully at him.

He gave me one last whack, then bent and kissed my now red ass, picked me up, sat me on the table, then spread my legs and dove in, sucking and eating at my pussy, getting lost in there like I was lost in him. I grabbed his hair and held him still as I wrapped my legs around his head and humped his face. Humped him until I came. I screamed as I came, screamed his name with all my might.

"Now fuck me," I said.

He got up, stuck it in and fucked me, pushing me back on the table, pushing me down and overcoming me with his cock. I grabbed onto his ass and pushed him deep inside and I didn't let go until I came again. Until he came. Until it was over. And when it was over, we fell away from each other gasping for air.

He glanced at me and said, "You're a good fuck, Kristine, but you can't cook for shit."

I didn't reply. He was right.

Maid for a day.

The next time:

"I will be home in one hour," he said.

I smiled and stared at the clock. One hour away was six o'clock.

"The maid is off this week."

"Yes?" I said and smiled.

"You will need to scrub the kitchen floor," he said. "When I come home, you will be down on your hands and knees scrubbing the floor. You will wear the maid's uniform that I put in your closet yesterday."

"When did you do that?"

"Kristine," he sighed. "Just put it on. Oh, no panties. Got it?"

I nodded. "Yes, got it."

"Also, do not clean the floor with ammonia. It will strip the wax. Use oil soap."

"Okay."

He hung up.

I raced upstairs and found the maid's uniform stuck in the very back of the closet in a garment back. I grinned. It was a French maid's uniform—a little black uniform that consisted of a short little skirt with ruffles and a plunging neckline.

I put it on, then a garter, stockings and, lastly, a pair of black pumps. No panties, of course. I put my hair up, pulled strands down in my face and went all out on my make-up.

Damn. I looked hot.

I found a bucket, a sponge and the oil soap. I checked the clock. He'd be home in ten minutes. I filled the bucket with water and got down on all fours, pointing my ass at the door. And I waited.

In ten minutes he was home, slamming the front door. He came directly into the kitchen. I scrubbed the floor and ignored him. He stood in the doorway and watched me. I moved my ass a little as I scrubbed and hummed like I was alone. He didn't move from the doorway for a long time. I could tell he was devouring me with his eyes. He liked to watch.

I sighed and sat up, then dipped the sponge in the water. I squeezed it out all over my white shirt, until it was drenched and my nipples were visible and poking through.

I got back to work, moving backwards towards the door. Towards him.

He still didn't move.

I kept cleaning and moving backwards, until I felt his foot. He lifted my skirt with it and looked in. Then he bent down and cupped my ass, running his hands up and down my bare skin, sending goosebumps all over my body.

I shivered and continued to clean. He continued to paw at me.

"How long have you been a maid?" he asked.

"All my life," I said, not looking at him.

"Do you enjoy your work?" he asked, pushing a finger into my pussy.

I stiffened. "Sir, please. I don't know you."

"Yes, you do," he said and bent down. His tongue flicked out and grazed the lips of my pussy, spreading them open. "You've been my maid for a long time."

"Sir, please," I begged. "Please don't make me."

"But your pussy is so sweet," he said and began to really kiss it. "You've always wanted me. I can see it in your eyes. I can see it when you stare at me from across the room. I've always known it."

"But what about your wife?" I asked.

"She's not here. Don't worry about her."

He put two fingers in me. It felt so good I nearly jumped from the floor. Then he moved them around.

"You're so wet," he muttered. "You're so wet for me."

"Yes."

"We'll do this," he muttered. "Then we'll pretend it never happened."

"Oh, sir, no, please, I can't!"

I pretended to try to get away, but he held me tight, grabbing me by the waist. He turned me over, tore open my shirt and devoured my breasts, squeezing one with one hand while the other one was in my pussy. I moaned and raised my hips off the floor. He pulled his hand out and stuck his finger in his mouth, tasting me. He held the finger to my mouth and I took it, tasting myself.

"You've wanted this for a long time, haven't you?" he asked and unzipped his pants.

I nodded shyly.

"You've wanted me to fuck you," he said. "Now I'm going to. How does that make you feel?"

"It makes me feel good."

"Good?"

I nodded.

He sighed as if this were the answer he wanted all along but was somehow disappointed by it. He took his cock out and forced my mouth to it. I gobbled it up, sucking at him so hard he had to hold me back.

He pushed it in then and fucked me, grabbing my legs and putting them on his shoulders. This allowed him to go deeper inside me, deeper and deeper and deeper, making me gasp and grunt like an animal. He hammered into me until I screamed with pleasure. I pulled his face to mine and sucked on his tongue, sucked and moaned and began come and come and come. He was coming too. Just before he did, he pushed me back and stuck his cock in my mouth, spewing his hot cum. I took it and sucked it dry, then I grabbed him and kissed him, pushing his cum back into his mouth and we shared it. We kissed and kissed until our mouths were sore and we didn't have anything else to give. When we pulled away from each other, we were still hot with the lust we'd shared. And I wanted more. I started to reach for him but he held me back.

"Kristine?" he said, not looking at me.

"Sir?"

"You're fired."

"Damn," I said and bit at his nipple. "And I really needed this gig, too."

He eyed me from the corner of his eye and cracked up. I laughed with him and we laughed until tears formed in our eyes. Then I began to tickle him and he tickled me back until I screamed for him to stop, getting so mad at him that I beat his back with my fist.

"Stop it! You're killing me!"

He finally stopped and said, "Come on, let's order a pizza. I'm starving."

The other woman.

It was inevitable. Something was bound to happen. I was snapped out of my sick, happy world one day while I was taking a walk around the Quarter. I'd just stopped at a shop near Jackson Square and was proceeding on to the casino where I was going to meet Jackie to play some slots, then we were going to have a late lunch, then I was going to go home.

Then I saw him.

Frank was walking along happily with her, some woman. He assisted her all the way to his car, placing a hand on the small of her back almost as if to make sure she didn't tip over. To anchor her.

Her. Her. Who was she? His secretary? His lover? His sister? He didn't have a sister. *Who was she?* And what was she doing with him? Obviously they'd been out to lunch; it was about two in the afternoon.

I watched as he smiled at her as she whispered something in his ear before getting into the car. He nodded and glanced in my direction. I didn't move. I wanted him to see me. He didn't. I was only a face in the crowd to him, someone anonymous. Unknown.

What struck me as odd was the way he handled himself around her. Gently, reserved. It was puzzling. That's the way he was acting right then. Ambiguous. Not like himself. He rarely smiled. He did smile. Some. When he was pleased.

But with her, he acted well-behaved. He used his manners. He held onto the small of her back, pushing her gently into the car, smiling nicely as she swung her legs in. Smiling as he got in after her.

I was so jealous I couldn't see straight.

The car pulled away almost immediately. I raced towards it on foot and followed it until it disappeared into the traffic. As soon as it was out of sight, my first instinct was to leave. Again. I wanted out. When things got tough, I fled. It was my nature to avoid conflict. But why should I leave? And, more importantly, why should I let him get away with it?

It wasn't jealousy I felt. No. That's a lie. It was jealousy. That petty little insecurity that feeds on anger. I was suddenly flushed with anger. As soon as the car disappeared, I was angry. Mad, fighting mad. My ears roared with it. How could he? How dare he? And how dare *she*? Those were my smiles she was stealing. They belonged to me!

I hung my head, on the verge of tears. Betrayal set in. I had been betrayed. I kept repeating, *How could he?* over and over and over. I began to walk and I walked a long time, ignoring everyone on the streets, ignoring the Mississippi River to my right. I ignored my date with Jackie, pushed it from my mind and walked for about an hour, then two. I walked until I had blisters on my feet and I walked until I found myself in front of the house, staring at it, my decadent prison. My home. His home. Where we belonged to one another and to no one else.

Should I go in or keep walking? What should I do? Everything in my bones told me to go in, proceed with what was to come. Something else told me to leave, to pack it in, to run away. But I'd been running a long time. Running from one relationship to another, never finding anything worth sticking around for. Was this worth sticking it out? And, if so, why was it so worthy? It was the worst relationship I'd ever been in, yet the best. I played games, I submitted, I relented, I shook with passion inside this relationship. No one had ever given me this. No one ever would, I knew.

I hung my head and walked in.

He called around five that afternoon. He called and set up our latest game. He said he wanted me to pack a picnic lunch, grab a blanket and go to the park.

"Then undress," he said. "Recline backwards. I'll be there at six."

He hung up. I hung up and sat down, put my head in my hands and cried. We'd already played this game. I'd done as he said, found a secluded area and did exactly as he told me. He fed me the food from the basket and kissed me all over. It was one of the better games. Easy enough to do.

I hated it. I hated that game. It was boring to me. Not much of a challenge. I wasn't going.

I stood and went upstairs, where I crawled into the bed, covered myself and fell asleep. He woke me up a few hours later. He was angry.

"Where were you?" he demanded to know.

I ignored him and stared at a picture on the wall, concentrating on that picture, tracing the lines of it with my eyes, then back again.

He touched my shoulder. "Where were you?"

"I don't like that game," I said quietly, not taking my eyes from the picture.

"It doesn't matter if you like it or not," he said.

"We all have our limitations."

He pulled me back and forced me to look him in the eye by holding my head still. "Why didn't you go?"

"I told you," I said. "I don't like that game."

"That's no excuse."

I didn't respond.

"Are you sick?" he asked.

"Yes," I said. "I am very sick."

"What's the matter?" he said, turning on the concern.

"Nothing."

He sighed heavily and shook his head. "Then why are you acting like this?"

"Acting like what?"

"Like something is wrong. You know what I'm talking about."

I glared at him. If he only knew what I knew about him. If he only knew, he'd be sorry then. I would tell him. I said, "I saw you today."

"Oh?" he asked and his eyebrows shot up.

"Oh, yeah," I said. "I saw you with her."

"Her?"

"The woman who was getting in your car."

He studied me then turned around. "So?"

"Who is she?"

"She's a client."

"Oh really?"

"Yes."

The sad fact was I wanted her to be his lover. I wanted something on him. I wanted it so much, I made myself believe it. So I could start to hate him and get out, out, out! I don't know why I wanted out. I'd never been so happy and content in all of my life living with him. But it scared me. He had so much control over me and I wanted some of it back. I wanted to be in control. I knew I'd never be, though. And that I might as well give up. But there was that little something in me that refused to let me relinquish it all to him.

But she wouldn't do. The woman. That woman. Who, really, wasn't anything to him. I knew that. Even if he had fucked her, she didn't mean anything to him. Not like I did. And that scared me even worse, knowing he felt the same way about me as I did about him. It scared me because I was afraid we would both spiral out of control and explode.

"And what type of client is she?" I asked, giving it up, sending the argument to bed.

"You know," he said. "I don't like to discuss business at home."

My face burned along with my ears, neck and shoulders. My entire body just lit up like a Christmas tree. I was shaking now, shaking with fury. *How dare he?*

I sat up, leaned over and slapped the side of his smug head. He didn't even flinch. He acted as though he expected me to do that, to slap him. I tensed. I thought he was going to do the same. When you're in a volatile relationship, you tend to expect these things. I tensed and waited.

He didn't slap me. He stood, went to the door, opened it, walked through, and then closed it gently.

I was stunned but of course, I followed him. I let an hour pass then I ran down the stairs, calling for him. He didn't answer. I ran through all the rooms searching for him. He was nowhere to be found.

He stayed gone overnight. I fell asleep in his chair in the study. I'd fallen asleep crying, wondering if he was ever going to come back. Wondering what I had done that was so bad. I knew I shouldn't have slapped him, but he *spanked* me and we fought all the time. So what was a little slap?

But of course, when he spanked me, we were usually in the throes of a game.

When he came home, he didn't wake me. He came in and sat in the other chair and watched me until I woke up. He sat there staring at me like I was an object of some kin, like he was trying to figure out what the hell to do with me.

When I opened my eyes, I didn't smile. He didn't either.

He said quietly, "She's a client of mine. That's all. We were on a business lunch. Take it or leave it."

I took it. And the games began again.

The stranger.

"We're going to meet at a party. Walk in like you don't know anyone. I'll be there around eight. Pretend you don't know me."

"Okay."

"And Kristine?"

"Yes?"

"Wear that little plaid mini-skirt. It really shows off your legs."

I smiled. He loved my legs, their shape, the muscles in my claves. He told me I had "diamond" calves that people would kill for. Before him, I didn't think my legs were anything special. And I'd never heard of diamond calves.

"Got it."

"Oh, and one more thing," he said, lowering his voice. "Don't talk to anyone you don't know."

"Frank, I don't know any of those people."

"Exactly."

I rolled my eyes and we hung up.

I arrived at the party around eight. It was just down the street from the house, so I walked by myself. I nervously rang the door and a butler let me in. The host and hostess greeted me, smiling. The host stared at my legs then caught my eye. I smiled at him. I knew what he was up to.

"I'm Kristine," I told them and held out my hand. "I'm a friend of Frank's."

"Oh!" they exclaimed and shook my hand warmly.

"So you're a friend of Frank's?" the host asked.

I nodded but didn't say another word. The hostess gave me a little smile. Luckily, a couple walked in behind me so their attention was diverted and I was able to walk away quickly, going into the living room. I noticed all the people in there were very elegantly dressed. I looked around for Frank, but didn't see him. A few people smiled at me and a few nodded, but other than that, I didn't really communicate with anyone. No one seemed to know who I was and that made me feel very vulnerable. I was almost afraid I'd get kicked out.

Nine o'clock came and went and Frank still didn't show. I was trying to have a conversation with a man who had this awful looking toupee on his head. I couldn't concentrate on him and all his words come out in a jumble: Egg salad…business associate…the color green…olives…

I smiled at him and forced my eyes away from his toupee. He didn't force his eyes away from my tits or ass. I allowed him to look; I didn't mind it at all.

I felt a hand on my shoulder. I turned to see Frank. I smiled at him.

"Yes?" I said.

"Do I know you?" he asked.

I smiled at him like I was considering. The toupee guy had asked me the very same thing.

"Uh, no," I said. "I don't think so."

He grinned and turned to lean against the couch we were standing behind. I smiled back and raised one eyebrow.

"Hey, Frank," the man said.

"Hello," he said without taking his eyes off me.

I tensed. What was he going to do?

Frank pointed a finger at me. "I know who you are. You're the debutante from Alabama."

I almost cracked up. I didn't. I concealed my laughter and said, "Oh, you found me out."

He nodded. "What's it like being a debutante?"

"Boring as hell."

He laughed softly and the other man stared at him, then back at me.

The man asked, "You're from the Williams' family, right?"

I nodded, going with it. "Yes."

"I know your father very well!"

"Really?" I asked just as Frank jerked his head. I stared at him and he held his finger upside down and rotated it. I obeyed, turned and took one step back towards him.

"Yes," the man continued. "I did business with him a while back."

"That's good to hear," I said and felt Frank's hand on the back of my shirt.

"He's a great man, your father."

"Really? That's funny because he's always been a bastard to me," I said and tensed. Frank's finger slid down my back, between my ass cheeks and was now lifting the bottom of my skirt up.

The man eyed him, but continued. "Uh, what was that?"

"Nothing," I said as I felt Frank's finger slide along the seam of my g-string.

"So, what do you do?" he asked, still eyeing Frank.

"I'm a stripper," I said, just to see if he was paying attention.

He wasn't. He was watching Frank and what he was doing to me. I could tell he was getting off on it, which was fine by me. I smiled at him, but he didn't notice.

He said, "Oh, that's an interesting field."

"Yes, it is," I said and felt his finger on my clit, arousing it. I almost stopped him, but I couldn't. His finger went up into my pussy and moved around a bit, while his other one stayed on my clit. I moved my hips just a little and felt the full force of the finger. Just as he was about to make me come, he pulled his finger out and staring at the man, stuck it in his mouth and sucked it dry. The man, having just taken a sip of scotch, nearly choked.

Frank touched my shoulder and gave me one tiny kiss on the back of my neck. I shivered with delight and anticipation.

"Well, it was nice talking to you, Miss Williams," he said and walked away.

"You, too," I called as if he we'd just had a pleasant conversation.

The man smiled and leaned in towards me. "So, how about if we go find somewhere to sit and talk?"

I turned on my heel. "Thanks anyway, but I have to get home."

I hurried out of the house, slipped my heels off and started to run, hoping to beat Frank to the house.

"Kristine!"

I turned and saw him standing by a Rolls Royce. He jerked his head towards it. I grinned and flew over to him and we got in the back. I fell down on my back and he was on top of me immediately. I wrapped my legs around his waist as he tore off my g-string and pushed his hard cock into me. I gasped and grabbed his head, kissing him passionately, grinding myself against him as he squeezed my breast with the palm of his hand. It didn't take much at all. The orgasm—for both of us—was instantaneous. We were that turned on.

We laid there gasping for a moment then I looked around the soft blue interior of the car.

"Kristine," he said.

"Yes?"

"I thought I told you not to talk to strangers."

I smiled and hugged his neck. "Frank, give it a rest."

He chuckled and nuzzled my neck. "Okay."

"Whose car is this?"

"I have no idea."

Silly games.

As I've said, they were silly games. We loved them. We loved every part of them. Each day brought a new game, a different game, a game that was better than the one before. A game that always ended in us fucking like animals.

I didn't take them seriously, but I was seriously falling in love with Frank. I couldn't help myself. I would wait all day for his call. I stopped seeing my friends. I didn't want any friends. I didn't want anyone but him.

The next game changed my mind about him. It hurt me. Somehow, I was convinced I loved him. Maybe it really wasn't love, but infatuation, obsession that had been realized and had spiraled out of control.

"There's an alley beside the Hotel Brazil," he said.

"An alley?"

"Yes, an alley," he said. "Meet me there."

"In the alley?" I asked.

"Yeah," he said and his voice took on a tone of excitement. "I thought… Never mind. Just show up. You know what to wear."

Short skirt. Tight top. High heels. My typical uniform.

"Okay," I said.

"I'll see you then."

"Okay. Oh, by the way, what am I today?" I asked and glanced at the clock.

"You're a whore."

He hung up.

I was slightly stunned. A whore? I was whore? For some reason, that didn't sit well with me. I certainly didn't think of myself as a whore. Or maybe I felt like a whore, living with him, off of him. All he ever got in return was the unlimited use of my body.

Ah, hell, it was only a game.

I convinced myself of that and rushed around getting ready, then took a cab to the hotel and found the alley, which was very narrow and, thankfully, deserted. I sniffed. God, it stank. So rank. Garbage was overflowing in the dumpster.

Did whores come here to fuck their johns? I didn't know. If I was a whore, they'd have to pay for a room. I'm sorry, but I wasn't into fucking in alleys.

I waited for a little while, swinging my purse, then laughed out loud, thinking about Frank. This must be one of his older fantasies, meeting a whore in an alley and fucking her, then... What would he do after? Would he pay me? And how much? What was someone like me worth? A grand? At least. Fuck that. Five grand, especially if they didn't pay for a room.

I stared up at the sky. It was darkening. He'd better hurry up. The afternoon lull was almost over and soon this very alley would probably be crawling with the real hookers.

I heard footsteps. They were his, I could tell. Heavy, deliberate footsteps, always walking quickly and with a purpose. I glanced up and smiled. He was walking towards me with a very determined look.

"Hey, baby," I said. "How's about a date?"

He nodded, eying me. "How much?"

"For you," I said and traced a line along the collar of his shirt. "Free."

"No," he said, shaking his head. "I can pay. I want to pay."

"How much you got?"

"Whatever it takes."

I eyed him as if I were considering. "Umm... I'll give you a discount. A couple hundred."

He nodded. "Deal."

"Cool," I said and smiled at him.

"What's your name?"

I considered. "Ummm...Gabrielle."

"I'm Ted."

"Nice to meet you, Ted. Are you ready to fuck?"

He nodded. I set my purse on the ground and before I could stand back up, he came at me and began to tug at my skirt. I pushed him off.

"Hey," I said. "Why don't we get a room?"

"I don't have the time," he said hurriedly. "I've been thinking about this all day."

"Thinking about what?"

"Fucking a whore."

Again, that unsettling feeling sank into me. I almost pushed him away and walked off, but it was only a game. Right?

"Okay," I said. "Let's do it."

I grabbed for his face to kiss him, but he pushed me away and shoved me up against the coarse brick wall. What the hell? I pushed him back, but he pushed me back again, grabbing my crotch, pulling my skirt up, and sticking his stiff cock into me without a word. He fucked me dry, not caring if I was wet or ready or even enjoying it.

I was almost in shock. What the hell was he doing? He fucked me for a good five minutes and anytime I tried to kiss him, he wouldn't let me. He only sucked on my tits and fucked me.

"Frank—"

"Shut up," he muttered.

What the hell was wrong with him?

He finished and pulled away from me, then zipped his pants, took out his wallet and threw a couple hundred dollars at me. I didn't grab for the bills and they fell to the ground. I was stunned. What the hell was this all about?

"How does it feel to be a whore?" he asked.

"What?" I asked, aghast.

"You're a whore, aren't you?"

I moved away from the wall. "Frank—"

He pushed me back and whispered in my ear, "You're a whore today and I want to know how it feels. How do you like being a whore?"

That flew all over me, I was all of a sudden angry. I hated him with every fiber of my being. It might have upset me because maybe, just maybe, that's what he really thought of me. Nothing more than a body, something to stick his cock in. A whore.

I shoved him off.

"I'll show you what kind of whore I am," I hissed and kneed his balls. He doubled over in pain and groaned. I whacked him upside the head, pulled my skirt down, grabbed my purse and ran out of the alley.

"You can't leave! Our time isn't up!"

"Oh, it is, it is certainly up, asshole!" I yelled. *Fuck him!* I ran as fast as I could before he could get to me. I was so angry, I saw red. I ran to the closest bar, stopped, caught my breath and went in.

I'd show him. If he wanted me to be a whore, I'd be whore. I'd be the best fucking whore in the world.

I surveyed the room and picked out my target. There he was—a young man, early twenties, big feet, cute, easy target. Good enough.

I sashayed over to him, sat in the seat next to his and smiled. He straightened up and grinned from ear to ear like he couldn't believe his luck.

"Hi," he said.

I didn't beat around the bush. I said, "Hundred bucks."

"Excuse me."

"I'll fuck you for a hundred bucks."

"Really?" He leaned back and checked me out, as if to see if I was serious. "Really?"

I nodded. "Give it to me."

He stared at me like he didn't believe me.

"I'm serious," I said. "Get it out."

He pulled his wallet out and fumbled with it, counting money. "I only got fifty."

I held out my hand. "Give it to me. I'll give you a discount."

He handed it to me. I shoved it in my bra, pulled him up and started out the door.

"Where are we going?" he asked.

"In the alley," I said and he followed me to the same place Frank had just fucked me.

"Here?" he asked, looking uncertain about the whole thing now.

"Shh," I said and kissed him. His lips were chapped and he had that after cigarette taste in his mouth. I tried not to think about that as I allowed him to kiss me back. He kissed like a teenager. It was all tongue. I felt his crotch. He was hard. He'd do.

I grabbed a condom out of my purse—what whore leaves home without one and authenticity always counted during our games—and then I unzipped his pants, helped him put it on, then pulled my skirt up and helped him put it in. He fucked me. I stood there and let him, not feeling any of it, just like a whore. I felt tears stream down my face. I felt so bad, so awful. I wanted him off me. But I was whore and whores don't do that. They let their customers finish. I decided to fuck him back, to give him his money's worth. He deserved it. He didn't deserve some whore who didn't like her job.

He moaned and buried his head in my neck as I held onto him. I felt him move faster and knew he was about to come. I was relieved. I was so relieved because I knew I was leaving. I was leaving. I was leaving! I made the decision as he fucked me. I would go home. I might go to Florida and start a new life. But I was leaving. I was leaving Frank. He'd never see me again. All my stuff was at his house. But I had fifty bucks. No car. My car was at his house. I could get a bus ticket to somewhere.

I cried harder, knowing it was going to be hard as hell to leave, but knowing I should. Why did he have to do that? Why? I didn't like that game. I hated being called a whore. Guys in the stripclub would call us whores when we wouldn't fuck them. "So what?" they'd say. "You take it off. What's the difference?"

Was there a difference? Was there? What fine line was there separating me from the others, from the whores? Maybe there wasn't a difference. Maybe all men classified all women as whores, like we sometimes classified all of them as jerks.

Maybe Frank classified me as a whore.

And that's what had done it. That's why I had freaked out, why I was letting this guy fuck me. Why I wanted to leave, to run away. Did he think I was a whore simply doing his bidding? Doing everything he wanted and asking for more?

Yeah. He must feel like that.

The guy was done. He pulled back and moved away from me. I looked away from him and pulled my panties up just as I heard him pull his zipper up. Then he came at me and tried to kiss me again. I pushed him away, but he wasn't budging. *Oh, God, what did I get myself into?* I was about to knee him in the crotch when, suddenly, the guy was pulled off me and thrown on the ground. I gasped and looked Frank right in the eye. I scowled. He looked at the guy, who stared up at him in disbelief.

"What is your problem, buddy?" the guy asked.

Frank pulled him up and punched him in the nose.

"Hey!" he yelled, holding his nose. "What'd you that for?"

He gave him another punch.

"She's a whore, man," he groaned.

"No, she's not, motherfucker!" he hissed and really went at him, pummeling him with his fists, beating him to a bloody pulp. I watched in horror as the guy fell to the ground. I had to go. Go. Go now.

I turned and raced out of the alley. Frank was immediately on my heels, pulling me off the crowded street and into his limo. He shoved me in, got in, slammed the door and the car took off.

"Why did you do that?" I asked.

He was breathing hard, but he was trying to stay calm. "How could *you* do that?"

"I did what you told me to do!" I screamed in his face. "I'm a whore, remember?!"

He backhanded me. I fell against the seat and groaned as my head swam. He'd never done that before, backhanded me, like a pimp backhands his whores. I held my face and stared at him in disbelief, feeling all the love I had for him drain from my body. I couldn't give it to him. I didn't want to give it to him. Not anymore.

I took it back. All the love I had for him, I took back. And I was leaving him, no matter what, I was leaving. He was no better than any other man I'd ever had.

I grabbed the door handle and tried to get out. It was locked from the driver's side. I couldn't get out. I banged on the window.

"Let me out, Tony!"

Tony ignored me.

"Fucker!" I yelled at him.

"Shut up," Frank said.

"Fuck you!" I screamed and pulled on the door. "Let me out! I'm leaving!"

"Leaving?" he said and grabbed my arm, pulling me next to him. "And go where? Back to your little shitty town? To where? You got nowhere to go but home. With me."

"I would rather die than go home with you!" I spat in his face. "Now let me out!"

He released me and turned to stare out the window. I almost panicked. But I had to stay calm. Once we got to the house, I'd jump out first, then run like hell to get away.

And I would not, I repeat, would not, look back.

The wine cellar.

Before I had a chance to put my plan into action, he opened his door, grabbed my arm and pulled me across the seat and out of the car, then into the house. I beat at him with my free arm and screamed bloody murder, which he did not heed. Neither did the neighbors.

He pulled me through the house, down to the basement and to the wine cellar. He shoved me on the floor, left the room, and locked the door behind him. I stared up at the ceiling. Only one bulb hung from it.

Oh shit. Shit. *Shhhhiiittt!*

I jumped up and ran to the door, beating it with my hands and screaming. I couldn't get out of there and I knew it. The only way out was that door and it was old, made of rough wood and at least three inches thick. It made my hands bleed as I beat it. But I didn't care. Someone had to hear me. Pierre, the cook. Maybe even Tony would take pity and rescue me.

I beat that door for ten minutes. Then I beat it for an hour, three. And no one came. I was a prisoner. I wasn't getting out.

I was all alone.

I gave up and backed away from the door, glaring at it. Then I grabbed a bottle of wine and hurled it at the door. It broke and red wine went everywhere. That felt *good.* So, just for fun, I broke a few more of the old wine bottles, laughing crazily to myself, thinking about how mad it would make Frank when he found out. Then I thought I might need them. So I decided to make a party of the whole thing and get drunk.

I looked around. No corkscrew. Huh. I grabbed a bottle and slammed the neck against the shelf. It cracked open. I took a drink and spit it out. Good—no glass slivers. It had been a clean break.

I drank the whole thing and got another bottle from a very good year. I sat down and drank the bottle clean, threw it the side and started to cry. I cried for a long time. I cried until my eyes were dry.

I begged the ceiling, "Please, God, let me out of here. Make him stop this."

I finally fell asleep. I slept for a long time on that cold, concrete floor. When I awoke, there was a tray of food by the door, if that's what you could call it. Bread and water. Pâté. Pâté? He knew I hated pâté! The bastard. All Served on a silver platter. I was definitely a prisoner.

But I was hungry. I gobbled the food and water up and threw the tray at the door.

No one came.

I wandered around in circles for a while then I sat down and cried. I schemed. When he came to let me out, I'd hit him with a wine bottle. Get him real good. Make him bleed.

When he came…

When would that be? How long had I been here? I looked up at the light. It flickered. Oh fuck. No. *Nooo!* It flickered again and went out. And I was in the dark.

I hated him then. More than ever, I hated him. I really, really did. But what could I do? I was stuck. I knew he had conscientiously thrown me in the cellar so he wouldn't be tempted to beat me, like he had the first time I'd really pissed him off.

What a great guy.

I'd never give him anything anymore. He had ruined it all, by acting like an animal, by treating me like a whore, he had ruined it.

But why should I go? Where should I go?

I decided I'd stay. I'd play his games and I'd steal from him. I'd be that whore he wanted me to be. I'd grub for money. I'd ask for it. And when I was ready to leave, I'd leave a rich woman.

He deserved no better. He couldn't love me. He didn't love me. If he loved me, he would have never, ever treated me like that. I didn't like being treated like a whore. That was my pet peeve. It got under my skin so bad it drove me crazy. I hated, and I mean hated, men who treated women like shit. Like whores.

I would be nice. I'd play his games. Hell, I'd even enjoy them, but something in me, God knows what it was, would not allow me to give him my love. Not anymore. He'd almost had me. He wasn't going to get me anymore. He could fuck me, but that would be all. He could not have me.

I would be his whore. Nothing more, nothing less.

He called softly, "Are you ready to come out?"

I sat up and rubbed my eyes. The light was back on. He'd replaced the bulb.

"Frank?"

"No," he said. "It's Tony."

I was almost disappointed. "Tony?"

"Yeah, it's me," he said softly. "Are you ready to come out?"

"Where's Frank?"

"I dunno, but I can't let you stay down here much longer."

I focused on him. He was a good man. Why couldn't I have picked a guy like him? He was big, kind. Yeah, we know what was wrong with him. He was boring. He wouldn't put me in wine cellars or fuck me in alleys.

"How long have I been here?" I asked.

"It's been a couple of days."

A couple of days? Surely not. I had slept most of those days, though. Time moves quickly when you sleep all the time. Like when you get sick and all you can do is sleep. You get sick on Monday and the next thing you know, it's Thursday.

"Kristine?"

I stared at him. "Does Frank know you're letting me out?"

He shook his head sadly. I stared at him, then away and curled back up in a ball and closed my eyes.

"You've got to leave now," he said. "He'll be back anytime."

"No, Tony," I said. "But thank you anyway."

"Kristine, you're crazy!" he muttered.

"I know, but I can't let you do this. Please go."

He sighed but didn't argue. He shut the door quietly and I fell back to sleep.

When I awoke, Frank was curled up next to me, a blanket covering us. I was relieved to see him. I tried to put my arms around him but he grabbed my hand and kissed it and put it next to his cheek. I closed my eyes and we slept. I had been in there two whole days.

We never mentioned the incident again.

Even though Frank could be a complete bastard, he took good care of me. When we woke up, he led me to the kitchen, letting me lean on him as I faked being weak. He prepared me a big breakfast of bacon, eggs and biscuits and gravy. He poured me a coke with ice, just the way I liked it. I made my hand shake as I lifted the fork to my mouth, like I was weak from being "starved." He stared at my hand and shame came over his face. Good. Good enough for him. I wanted him to feel bad for what he'd done. He deserved no better.

He took the fork out of my hand and fed me, like I was a baby. He wiped the corners of my mouth off, held the straw to my lips so I could drink the coke, and kissed my cheek.

He told me he loved me. Loved me. Loved me, loved me, loved me.

I smiled, repeated his line to him and ate.

When breakfast was over, he took me upstairs, where he drew me a bath. He put me in the tub and washed me from head to toe, again, like I was a child. He did so gently, patiently.

Then he combed my hair, towel dried my body and took me to bed, where he laid me down and began to kiss my body, every inch of it. Soft, whisper kisses. Kisses that made me moan and pull him on top of me. Again, we made love. We didn't fuck as we did before. When it was over, I fell asleep in his arms, as content as a… As a baby.

Blindfolded.

"Here," he said, slipping a white silk scarf over my eyes. "Put it on."

I smiled and tensed. It had taken him awhile to warm up to the idea of blindfolding me. But I knew it was coming. He'd hint at it every so often, and I'd smile and say, "Whatever you like. You're in control."

Whatever you like. You're in control. And not me.

"Lay back," he said.

I scooted back on the bed and tried to relax. I felt his fingertips glide along my body, stopping every so often to tease me. I reached out for him. He pushed my hand back down.

"No," he said and I heard him rise and move away from me.

"Where are you going?" I asked.

"Shh…"

I lay there quietly for a few moments, tensed and ready. I could feel him bend down in front of me. I wanted to reach out and touch him, but I couldn't see anything, which was the point of it all. I didn't really like the blindfold because of that reason. I liked to have all my senses alert and ready. Just in case.

"Are you ready for me?" he asked softly.

I sighed. He took that as a "yes."

"Relax."

I attempted to relax then I felt a light, tickling sensation.

"Can you feel that?"

"Oh, yes."

The sensation had started on my knee and was slowly moving up my body, cruising by my inner thigh, trailing along the outer lips of my pussy, skirting up my belly, between my breasts, then stopping to caress each nipple, then it lingered on my face.

"Ahh…" I moaned.

He gave a slight sigh as if my response pleased him. The sensation was now in the crook of my arm. What was it? A feather?

"Ummm…" I moaned. "What is it?"

"A mink stole."

Oh. Mink. It was so soft. Light. It tickled me just to the point of pleasure and never went beyond. It slid along my body, readying it for more. And there was more on the way, I could tell.

"See if you can tell me what this is," he said.

I waited. Then I felt something cool, almost cold, slide down between my breasts, then puddle onto my stomach. It bubbled slightly.

I smiled. "Champagne."

"I am kissing the stars," he said with a chuckle and bent over and began to kiss the area around the champagne before he slurped it up into his mouth. Then he leaned over and pressed his lips against mine. I opened my mouth and he deposited the champagne. I swallowed.

"Thank you," I said and smiled.

"You're welcome," he said. "Tell me, Kristine, do you like being blindfolded?"

I considered. What's not to like? Especially since it had all been good. Maybe it'd get better?

"Yes," I said.

"Good," came his reply.

I heard the clink of ice cubes in a glass, then I felt an ice cube between my legs, then inside of me and it was slowly melting, making me numb down there. His face was down there, his tongue gently probing it in, puckering his lips until it disappeared.

Ahh, that felt good.

Two fingers were in me then, twisting, finding my spot. My hips rose off the bed. He pushed them back down.

"No."

"What?" I moaned and tried to raise my hips to meet his lips again. But he had moved. I put my hand between my legs and started to rub, but he took it off.

"No," he said. "Not yet."

"*Please!*"

"No. Not yet."

I grunted and groaned and shook, but he wouldn't let me. He wouldn't let me touch myself to bring any sort of release. And it was killing me. I was so wound up, so turned on, so hot I could have spontaneously combusted.

"You're not very good at this game," he said.

"Why?"

"You want to touch yourself too soon."

"What's wrong with that?"

"Nothing, if all you're concerned with is getting off."

I sighed, my shoulders slumping. He was right, but I had somehow thought that was the point. Of sex, I mean. To get off.

"You see," he said and I could tell he was looking over at me. "The point is arousal, so much arousal that is never fulfilled by orgasm at once. You build it up. So, when you have your orgasm, it's more intense than it could ever be before."

Had he read that in a book?

"How would you know?" I asked.

He sighed. "It builds up for both of us, Kristine."

"And how would you know?"

"It's just an idea I had," he snapped and snatched the scarf off my face. I blinked in the bright light. He glared at me. I looked away. "Do you want that, Kristine? Do you want that intensity?"

"Yes, of course I do," I said, wondering exactly what it entailed, wondering exactly what would be expected of me.

"Can you handle it?" he asked softly.

I stared him dead in the eye and responded, "Of course I could handle it."

He nodded slowly, not very pleased with my answer. "No, you couldn't handle it."

"Yes, I can!"

"Then do this," he said. "Refrain from touching yourself. All day tomorrow. And after I've gone to sleep."

"I don't do it that much."

"No, you don't have to because we fuck every day. Today we're not going to fuck. Or tomorrow. Got it?"

I sighed. Well, I could always lie to him

"Kristine?"

"Okay. I'll do it."

You will be punished. Severely.

I sat on edge all day waiting for his call. It didn't come. He didn't come home until late and when he did, he ignored me, went up the stairs and into the bedroom without a single word.

I willed myself not to succumb to any anger. I willed myself up the stairs and into the bedroom.

He was in the bathroom, brushing his teeth. I went in, sat on the commode and stared straight ahead. He ignored me.

"Frank?" I said.

He didn't respond.

"Why are you mad at me?"

"You know why."

"I do?"

He shook his head. "Yes, you do. Now leave me alone."

He was right. Damn him. I had to give it all over to him to experience this intensity he wanted us to experience. I knew that. But I wasn't ready. I didn't know if I would ever be ready for it.

"Did you masturbate today?" he asked.

I jerked at his question then stared back at the wall, almost embarrassed. Well, yeah, I had. But I didn't tell him that. I lied, "No, I didn't."

He stared back at me, his head nodding slightly. "Bring me your toys."

"What?"

"You heard me."

"No," I said, crossing my arms, thinking of my vibrator. No way was I giving that up.

He sighed and went back to looking at himself in the mirror. He ran his hand over his face once. I sighed.

He said, "You masturbated today, didn't you?"

It wasn't so much a question as an accusation.

"Yeah," he said. "You did. I know you did."

How in the hell did he know that? It's like he could just tell, even after I'd lied to him. He must be psychic or something.

"How do you know this?" I asked.

"I can see it in your eyes," he said, all knowing. "I can see that you did it when I asked you not to."

I almost cried. I wasn't going to. I had tried not to masturbate, but then I started having this fantasy of us and the next thing I knew, I was on the bed giving it to myself, coming and coming quick. After it was over, I had another and another until I was exhausted.

"How do you know?" I asked.

"I just do," he said. "I know you. You never listen to anything but what's between your legs."

I sighed. He was right. But why did that make him so mad? I decided to make it up to him. I went behind him and slid my hands up his back. He stiffened. But he didn't move.

I tiptoed and kissed the back of his neck, pushing my hands into his hair. Suddenly, he whirled around, grabbed my wrists and twisted me until I was nose to nose with him.

"I am not in the mood," he said, then moved away from me.

Tears sprang up in my eyes. I hated him then. I hated every cell in his body. I hated his blue eyes, his handsome face, his dark hair, his cologne.

I peered through the doorway and watched as he got into bed. I loved him. I loved every part of him, even this. No, no. Not loved—wanted. I *wanted* every part of him. There was a difference. It was all lust now, the love wasn't there anymore. But it didn't make me want him any less. I knew he was holding out on me. Making me wait. Making me want it. Making me want it so bad I'd explode.

I went to the bed and sat down, not looking at him.

He eyed me and sighed as he said, "It's just that I want you to give more of yourself."

I was stunned slightly. *More* of myself? More of *me*? I was giving him everything I knew how to give and more than I'd ever given anyone else. I'd taken shit from him I would have never taken from any other man. I put up with it because I'd never felt this way about anyone else. He knew it. I knew it. It was no secret. I would pretend to love him, give to him until I was ready to leave. Then I'd turn it off. That was the plan.

"What are you talking about?" I asked.

"You hold back."

"I do not!" I said, indignantly.

"Yes," he said. "Yes, you do."

"How?"

"You always want that quick orgasm, instead of holding out for more. You're like a teenage boy."

My face flushed. Maybe he was right, to a certain extent, but wasn't that what sex was all about in the first place? Getting off? I wasn't into Tantric or any of that *Kama Sutra* stuff. I liked fucking and fucking liked me and we went well together. Why mess with a good thing?

"I don't know what you're talking about," I said and crossed my arms.

He pointed at my arms. "That's what I'm talking about."

I rolled my eyes.

"Yeah, go ahead and roll your eyes. You're very good at that, aren't you?"

"Fuck off," I said and started to rise.

He pushed me back down on the bed. I struggled against him for a moment, then he kissed me and I melted. Oh, yeah. Oh, baby. I opened my mouth just as he pulled away and he pulled quickly, abruptly, as if I disgusted him. As soon as I melted, he pulled away. And refused to let me pull him back down.

"That's what I'm talking about."

"What?!" I half-yelled, getting pissed off.

"Our games, these games, are fine," he said. "For beginners. We're not beginners anymore, are we?"

I studied him. I tried to figure him out, I really did. I couldn't. I just wasn't getting it.

He leaned and whispered in my ear, "I want to show you something. Stay here."

He jumped up and went into the closet. I sat on the bed and wondered what he was doing. I could hear him rummaging around. He came back a moment later carrying something behind his back, like it was a surprise. I eyed him, wondering what his hand held. Candy? A rose? Sometimes he brought me little gifts like that. Once I got a Cartier watch. Once a pair of diamond earrings. What was it this time? When he finally pulled it out, my jaw dropped to the floor.

He had a switch. Not a rose. Not candy. And most certainly not a watch. It was a switch, the kind pulled from a tree to swat the backs of children's legs when they're being brats. The kind my mother used on me from time to time to keep me in line. A switch.

He cracked it in front of me. I almost cracked up. *Was he serious?*

"May I?" he asked.

Before I could think of an answer, the switch came down and hit me smack dab on my outer thigh. I screamed with pain as it cut right through my skin and scorched the muscle. It hurt like hell. Like a papercut. That's what it felt like. Tears sprang up in my eyes, burning into them.

He bent down in front of me and whispered, barely audible, "Did you like how that felt?"

I began to shake my head. No. That would be a negative. It hurt too badly.

"Kristine," he said. "Tell me. Tell me now. Did you like how that felt?"

No, I didn't. I couldn't. How could I like that? He was inflicting pain on me. I didn't like pain.

"Tell me. Please?"

I didn't like it. I didn't like it. I didn't like it.

"Tell me."

What kind of sick person likes something like that?

"Tell me?"

If I liked it, then that would mean… What would that mean?

"Tell me."

Would it mean I was a sick person? That I had been brought to this level by him? What *did* it mean?

"Tell me."

No. No. No, no, no, no, no and no!

"Remember the first time I beat you?"

Oh, yeah. How could I forget? I still had scars. Not from the belt, but from the fall, but scars nonetheless. Scars that reminded me of the incident, of his anger towards me. Of my fear.

"Remember how it hurt?"

Of course I remembered!

"Remember afterwards? Remember how I took care of you? Remember how it felt, especially afterwards."

I didn't like it. I didn't—

"You liked it, Kristine," he said. "I could tell you liked it. You liked having me in control of you, you being out of control, you liked it. A lot. Didn't you?"

No, I did not.

"You liked it so much you tested me," he said, his face in my hair, near my neck. I could feel his hot, sweet breath. He smelled like mint toothpaste. He smelled so good, fresh, clean. I wanted him so much.

"You've tried to get me that upset again," he murmured. "But it scared me. I was scared of it because I was afraid I'd lose control and really hurt you. But now I understand and I'm asking you. Did you like it? Did you like the way it felt to have no control? To not know how it was going to turn out? To give yourself over to that moment?"

That moment. Oh, God, that moment. That moment where nothing made sense but everything did. That moment where I was at my weakest, yet I'd never felt stronger. That moment where everything fell from the Earth and I could care less. That moment when clarity took over and suddenly I knew what it was all about, all of it. And everything was about that moment—every single thing. And I'd wanted it back so I could feel alive, so I could get that close to him again, that under his skin, that close. So close I couldn't breathe if he didn't tell me to.

I knew what he was talking about. And it scared me. I couldn't think. I couldn't think straight. I began to quiver, panic.

"The way you responded to me blew me away. And you've been testing me ever since, trying to make me do it again."

He was lying.

"You know you have. You've been testing me ever since."

He was telling the truth.

"You accused me of sleeping with another woman so I would hit you. Didn't you?"

The other woman. Oh. Uh... Oh, no. Oh, no. It wasn't about that. It was about me leaving him, finding an excuse for escape so I could take off. That's what it had been about. But even as I sat there and tried to make myself believe it—and it was true to a certain extent—I knew he was right. He knew me too well. I could never admit it, though. I could never admit wanting to give myself over like that. That would make me as bad as the men who played these games, who inflicted the pain.

"Kristy," my mother would say. "Never trust a man because as soon as you do, they'll be gone. Out the damn door. Just like your damn daddy. And you'll be on your ass. Never, I repeat, never trust one enough to let them have control."

Never, never, never. Never let anyone have any control, have anything on you. They'll use you. They'll treat you like shit. You—

He said, "You liked me taking control and you liked me taking care of you afterwards."

Did I? If he said it and thought it and believed it to be true, than did I as well? Did I believe that?

"You have to know," he whispered, so softly. "You can trust me. Trust me, Kristine. Let's see how far we can go. I would never do anything to you that you couldn't handle."

I wanted to cry, throw up. This was too much, too, too much. I wanted to run away and forget it all. But I couldn't. I was cemented to him now. We both knew we'd already crossed that line and now we were dancing along it, twirling, nearly falling, regaining control and laughing about it.

"Trust me."

Trust. Trust, trust. Trust him.

"Just this once."

This once... Now. Today. This moment. Trust him now. Do it before it's too late. If I didn't accept, it would be over. And I didn't want it to be over. Not yet. I was still having too much fun for that. And I still hadn't robbed him blind like I'd intended after he had thrown me into the wine cellar. I hadn't done it yet because... I didn't know why.

Then he did it. He gained my trust. He said the one thing he needed to say to win me over. He said, "We'll take it slow, at first."

I couldn't control myself. I wanted to jump on him, fuck him, and have him fuck me. I wanted to succumb to his every wish, to his every desire. To whatever he wanted.

I breathed, "I'll do it. Just this once."

He smiled. "Then let's do it."

I reached over and found the scarf, which was lying on the nightstand, and handed it to him as an offering. He eyed me.

"Are we going to do it right this time?"

I nodded feebly.

"I don't have much patience," he said. "If you're not committed to this, I will be very angry."

I nodded.

"You sure?"

"Yes."

He said, "Now you have to let me have control. You know that. If you do anything that pisses me off, you will be punished. Severely."

I stiffened. Did he just say that? *You will be punished. Severely.* What exactly did he mean by that? And what did "severely" entail?

I started, "Frank, what—"

"This is your first and your last warning," he said. "You either let me do it or we stop."

Let him do it. Stop. Let him do it. Stop. Surrender or stop. Stop or surrender? Which one?

"Okay," I muttered.

"You have to totally submit to me, Kristine, in order for this to work."

Totally submit. Submit. Submission. Let go. Concede. Acquiesce.

I took a deep breath and nodded, staring up at him.

"So are we set here?" he asked, in a very business-like tone.

"We're set."

"Good. I assume you're ready?"

"I'm ready."

He blindfolded me before pushing me back on the bed where he began to undress me. He took his time, loving having me under his control.

"Relax," he whispered.

I couldn't relax. I wanted to but at the same time, something kept me from it. A sense of fear. A sense of panic. My senses became alert, ready. Steady. I could hear everything that went on inside the room. His bare feet padding on the wood floor. The ticking of his alarm clock. The vent pushing warm air into the room from above. The soft bed covers. The silk of the comforter.

He rolled me over onto my stomach.

I felt the tip of the switch tracing along my skin ever so gentle. It rode along me, forcing me to tremble with anticipation. Then, all of a sudden, it came down and came down hard. Right across my back. *Ouch!* It was the papercut feeling. I hated that. I shivered.

His lips were on the mark now, kissing it, his hands caressing it, fondling it, easing the pain away. Ah, that was better.

"Would you like another?" he asked softly.

I was so excited, I could barely breathe.

"Kristine?"

"Yes."

And the switch came down. This time across the back of my thighs. It almost tickled. Then the sensation eased. I felt relief, release. Surrender.

"Can you handle another?"

"No," I said sitting up. "Not just yet."

He got up, turned me over, bent and kissed the tip of my nose. I began to quiver.

"Lie back."

I lay back.

"No touching yourself, okay?" he said. "Promise?"

"Yes," I breathed. "I promise."

His hands were all over me, the palms sliding along my body, kneading me, bringing all of my senses out. My nipples hardened and wanted his lips. I moved to the side, towards his face, but he pushed me back down.

"I'm warning you."

"About what?" I moaned, teasing him.

"I told you."

"Told me what?" I asked and almost laughed at his seriousness.

All of a sudden, I was turned, flipped onto my stomach and I heard a crack and his belt—not the switch—came down across my ass. I let out a wail that shook the chandelier.

"Why did you do that?" I cried and felt the welt on my ass.

"You know why."

I stiffened and started to take the blindfold off.

"If you take it off," he said methodically. "We won't start this game again."

My hands dropped involuntarily. I couldn't take another day without sex. Even if that meant he was going to give me a few more lashes.

He turned me back over and his hands began to play along my body once more. I moaned. It was killing me to lie there and not do anything. I wanted his hands on me, but more importantly, I wanted my hands on him. I wanted to touch him, his skin. I wanted to pull him tight and hang on forever.

He opened my legs and got between them, positioning himself there. I could tell he was staring at me. This made my juices flow even more, to have him stare at me like that. I moved a little, trying to entice his lips to move in that direction, down there.

"Do you need another lash?" he said as I moved again.

I halted myself. "No."

"Good."

I balled my fists up and waited for him to continue.

His fingers began to play with me then, one went into my pussy, moved around a bit, then the other stroked my ass. The pleasure was so intense, I nearly cried out. I bit my fist and tried to contain the cry. Something came out anyway. I think it was, "Please."

He sighed, got up, turned me over and gave me another lash with the belt. This time, it didn't hurt. Well, it did. But it was different. It was so different, like nothing I'd ever felt before. As the belt hit me, I felt a deep surge of power from it, as if it were giving me power. I shivered and began to shake. It took everything in my body to keep me from asking for another.

Then, as soon as it hit, it was gone and I felt light, almost airy.

He turned me back over.

This time, he dove in, eating at me, licking, almost chewing. I moaned. He kept at it. I was almost there, the orgasm was coming and it was coming hard and then…

He stopped. "You're doing it again."

The switch came out again and he began to tap me with it, lightly at first, then with more intensity. Tap, tap, tap. It went all over my body, every square inch of my body became alive as the switch played with me, teased me, controlled me. It wasn't painful, not really, it was more of a tickling sensation, just this side of irritating. I laid there and allowed it, allowed it until I couldn't handle it anymore and I screamed for him to stop, but he didn't. I begged and pleaded and I promised myself I wouldn't want it again, that I couldn't take it. It was too much. No orgasm was worth this. But just before I broke, he turned me around and kissed me, sending me into a totally different realm.

"Get up on all fours."

Uh, what? No. You get back down there and finish what you started.

"Now."

I got up on all fours.

He pulled my legs apart and then he began to eat me from behind this time, licking every crevice. I was so wet his face just slid along. He sucked at my clit for a moment, then pulled back and fingered it gently. I moaned and before I knew what I was doing, my hand was on it and I was trying to get off. He didn't give me a warning this time. The belt came down across my ass. I let out one scream, then my body began to shake and I rode the tide of euphoria out.

I collapsed on the bed and gasped, "I can't take it anymore. Please do it."

He grabbed me by the shoulders and kissed me, pushing his tongue into my mouth until I moaned. He pushed me back on the bed and fucked me so hard it knocked the breath right out of me.

But I took it and wanted more and I began to come then, so hard. It was like nothing I'd ever felt. The orgasm seemed suspended in the air, holding on to me tight, never letting me go. I screamed with it and screamed until it fell away from my body.

He turned me over and put one of my legs up on his shoulder then he put his hard, throbbing cock in me. He began to ride me then and I laid there wanting to move but unable to do anything but pant.

He was now pumping into me. I could tell he was about to come. He fell on top of me, taking my arms and holding them above my head. I began to move with him. We stared into each others eyes as we fucked and we reached that plateau together, nearly fainting in our lust for each other, nearly blacking out as we came together.

As soon as it was over, we didn't say one word. We didn't have to. There was nothing to say.

After that, the blindfold became a regular. This continued for a while, the sex becoming so intense, so powerful that we could do nothing afterwards but gasp for air. A few times, he incorporated a gag into our sex, so I couldn't talk. I mean, so I couldn't beg.

It continued like this until he said those magical words, "Tomorrow I'm going to tie you up."

Stop.

"What?" I asked, staring at the rope in his hands.

"A word," he said. "Any word. A safe word. We need a word. If things go too far, you say the word and I stop."

I felt a wash of relief come over me. I smiled and thought about it. And thought some more. What word? Then I had it. I stared him in the eye and said, "That's easy. Stop."

He nodded and I could tell he was pleased. I was pleased, too. He said, "Then let's do it."

So we did it. He tied me, spread eagle, to the bed. I laid there and waited.

"Remember our word," he said.

I nodded. He checked the knots on the robe to make sure I was secure. I smiled at him.

"With blindfold or without?" he asked, ever so politely.

"With."

He nodded like my answer pleased him then blindfolded me. Within two seconds, I began to panic. I couldn't move. I couldn't see. I was trapped. I was alone.

He was there. He was there beside me, his hand on my arm, caressing it, caressing me. I willed myself to be strong.

"What would you like me to do?" he asked.

"Anything," I breathed, squirming under his hot touch. It was almost as if his hands burned into me. I wondered if they had made a mark.

His hands played with my breasts for a moment, then moved down my belly and between my legs. I moaned and tried to raise my hips off the bed. I couldn't. I was tied too tight.

"Ohh," I moaned.

"Shh," he whispered in my ear.

I quieted myself.

His breath was on my neck again, his lips near my ear. He whispered, "I want to put it in your ass."

Uh. Uh?

"Can I do that, Kristine?"

We'd never done that before.

"I'm going to put it in your ass," he said.

I said, "Frank, I don't think I want you to."

And then, the switch came out, hitting me across the leg. I trembled but didn't let out a wail. That's how much self control I had.

"I'm going to put it in your ass," he said and began to untie me.

"Why are you untying me?" I asked.

"We can't do it like this," he said as he untied me.

He was right. As soon as he had me untied, I sat up and was told to lie on my stomach. I did as I was told, then he tied me to the bed. I laid there and tried not to cower.

I heard his zipper come down. I tensed as he pushed two pillows under my ass, so it was sticking in the air. He pulled my buttocks apart and his finger slid along my ass, then in it. I tensed. I liked that part. I was just unsure of the other.

I felt a cool liquid then. Lube. He was lubing me up. I tensed. Then I heard my vibrator start, its soft buzzing floating into my ears like music. I almost smiled.

"We'll start like this," he said. "To get you ready."

"Okay," I sighed.

The vibrator had nothing on the size of his dick. I could handle the vibrator. He'd even put it in there a few times. I sighed as it went in, pushing deep inside me, making me feel whole as it stretched my ass to accommodate its size.

He played with me for a little while, getting me ready and by that time, I was more than ready for his dick to go in. I felt the tip of it at first, then it disappeared, then he gently pushed the rest of it in there, all the way down until I could feel his balls bounce against my ass.

"Ahhh…" I moaned.

"Ahhh…" came his reply.

He began to fuck me then, up the ass. It was so tight, my ass with his dick in there. I tried to move. I couldn't move. I had forgotten I was tied to the bed.

Before he moved again, he took my vibrator and put it next to my clit, turning it on high, just the way I liked. I could have cried my thanks, but all my thoughts were on his dick then, so much a part of me. He began to move, which made me move as he pounded up against me, his balls slapping against my ass as he thrust.

"You are so tight," he moaned. "I've never seen such a tight ass."

My eyebrows shot up involuntarily, but I didn't pursue the thought of whose ass he might be comparing mine to. I couldn't do anything but allow my clit to reach orgasm as he reached his. It was intense, much more intense than I thought it'd be. It was the pain, the ever so slight pain, combined with the joy that made it the way it was: Intense beyond compare.

"Oh, Kristine!" he grunted. "I love fucking your ass!"

"I love you to fuck my ass!" I grunted back and the orgasm intensified. "Fuck my ass harder!"

"I'll fuck your ass harder," he grunted and did just that, but not before giving me a good, hard slap across my ass cheek, which made me shiver and made the orgasm intensify more. It just grew, that orgasm, and I thought it was never going to end. I laid there as he fucked me and it grew and grew and grew and I wailed with it, because of it, taking the corner of the pillow and biting into it to help ease the pain of it and make it last.

"I'm coming," he moaned. "Oh, God, I'm coming!"

I was already there, had been there. I was still getting jolts here and there from it. In a moment, it was gone.

He pulled out of me just as it faded away. I was gasping by that point. Then his mouth was on mine, his tongue probing it open and my tongue in his mouth, where he sucked on it until I fell away from him.

"I love you," he said and gave me little kisses all over my face before removing the blindfold. "I love you so much."

I blinked in the bright light and looked into his eyes. It was true. He did love me. And for some reason, that was scarier than any game we'd ever played. And I was at a loss for words.

He waited on me for seconds, not moving. He waited for me to respond, verify. I did love him. I loved him at that moment. I loved him during sex. And I didn't have a problem admitting it to him, only to myself.

I smiled and said, "I love you, too."

He sighed with relief.

"What's for supper?" I asked, hoping to change the subject. "I'm starving."

Slave to love.

That was the way it was.

He'd tie me up. Or not. If I begged, he'd switch me. Once he tied me to the bedpost and left me. He wanted to see how long I could handle it.

"*Frank!*" I had screamed thirty minutes into it. "Frank!"

God, was this going to be like the wine cellar but with no wine and no floor to lie down on? I stood there for a moment considering my options. Well, I could stay here. For a little while, then he'd surely be back.

I decided to do that and I hung from the bed for the longest time. I have no idea how long I was there.

I stood there and stood there and my arms grew heavy and numb. They were asleep. And one of them was itching so bad I was about to start gnawing at it.

I stood there and willed myself to be good.

I stood there and waited for him to come get me.

I stood there and fantasized about beaches and Bourbon Street and a new car.

Hanging there like that made my thoughts torturous. I kept thinking, *He doesn't love me, he doesn't love me. He wouldn't do this if he loved me. He couldn't love me and do this to me. He couldn't.*

I sobbed, realizing it was true. It had to be. He would never do this to me if he loved me the way he said he did. I should accept it. I should be on my way. But I was powerless around him. He had me in his orbit and I was spinning out of control.

I stood there and cried. And cried and sobbed and wailed. It was the crying that broke me. I began to cry and feel sorry for myself. I began to feel bad, anxious. And when the crying stopped, I began to scream. I screamed for Frank, for my mother, for God, but especially for him.

And no one answered.

Just before I broke and screamed "Stop!" I thought I couldn't stand it another minute. Not one second longer. I thought I was going crazy. Then he came rushing into the room as if he couldn't get to me quick enough. The rope was untied and he massaged my wrists and arms and kissed my cheek. When I told him how it felt—how it felt that I couldn't move or do anything about it—he chuckled and said, "You've never had any patience."

"It wasn't you hanging there," I said.

He nodded. "Maybe this isn't one of your strongest games, baby."

He was right. We never tried it again.

Happy man.

I have never been so addicted to another person's body before. I craved him. When he was away from me, I ached as though I had lost part of myself. Upon his return, I was whole again.

Everything became about him. About us. I ceased to exist other than for him. We became so close an army couldn't have torn us apart.

We began to talk. We talked so much I can't remember what it was about most of the time. He began to tell me everything about himself, telling me he had inherited everything he had, even his huge real estate business, from his father, who had died when he was very young. He had been raised by aunts.

He never spoke of his mother. I asked him about her once, but all he did was shake his head sadly. I didn't pursue it. When he was ready, he'd tell me.

I told him what I thought he should know, leaving out the boring stuff. The past ceased to matter anymore. I lived in the present, in the now. In our next tryst, knowing it would fill me to the point of exhaustion.

We only had meals I liked. No more frou-frou stuff. Meat and potatoes. Chocolate cake. Soda pop.

We rarely went out, even to eat or shop. He gave the servants more and more time off so we could be alone in the house. The world outside that doorstep ceased to matter. All that mattered was when he would be home and what we would do next.

I was obsessed with him and his body. With his hands and what they did to me.

I loved every single minute of it. I loved knowing he was in control and I didn't have to think about anything. All I had to do was lie there and let the pleasure begin and end. Then the cycle would start all over.

It was natural, a natural progression. I didn't wonder or worry about what was going on or where it was headed. I knew it would eventually end. I took it for what it was and it was our life. And that was the way we lived it—secluded and sequestered from the entire world. Alone we stood, holding onto each other as tightly as we could. We regretted to fall asleep because that would be time that we were apart. He began to come home earlier everyday. As soon as he could, he was skipping up the walk and into my arms.

And once we were together, once we were alone, nothing else mattered. Nothing else ever would.

Afterwards, he'd give me a bath, or rather, we'd bathe together, giggling as we soaped each other up. We got so lost in each other during those sessions, I sometimes wondered if it were healthy to be that enamored of another human being. He cleaned my wounds if there were any and he'd feed me off his fork, as I'd feed him off mine.

But I knew my time was almost up. My deadline was nearing. I knew I had to keep it. If I didn't, I was going to be there forever and though I was more than sure I loved him, I knew sooner or later it would be time to move on. I figured sooner was much better than later.

"Frank," I said, staring at him. "Would you do something for me?"

His head jerked up and he smiled, "You know I would do anything for you."

I smiled. Who was the real slave here? I lied, "I need some money. For my mother. Could you give me some money?"

He nodded and walked over to his desk, pulled out his checkbook and handed it to me. I fingered the thick leather and stared up at him.

"Just write the amount and I'll do the rest," he said, sitting back down. "I can even cash it for you tomorrow on my way home."

Should I? Did I dare? Why not? He tested me all the time. I'd test him. I wrote in a preposterous amount, even becoming embarrassed at it, but he didn't blink an eye and the next day, he brought the money—in fifties and hundreds—to me, delivering it in a bank bag. Delivering it to me with a big smile on his face, as if he were happy to deliver it, glad he could accommodate me.

He bent and kissed my cheek, before turning to leave the room. He called over his shoulder, "I've made dinner reservations. Please be ready in an hour."

I stared after him. It suddenly dawned on me. He was happy. He was a happy man. I'd never really noticed this about him before. Had it always been there? That happiness? He was so happy, he was nearly elated. Had I done that? Had I made him that happy? If so, why wasn't I feeling it too? I discovered the answer to my question about as soon as I asked it. I couldn't feel it because I wouldn't let myself feel it. I didn't want to give it away. I didn't want to lose control, like the way he apparently thought I had. I could fake it, sure, for a little while, but soon he'd catch on. He was too smart not to.

All I had to give him was my body. I knew it then. I knew it and it saddened me. But I couldn't do anything about it but hang on and hope it would change. But can a leopard ever really change its spots? No. And neither could I. No matter how badly I wanted to.

Birthday girl.

Frank decided to throw a big party for my birthday on December 10th. I'd never had anyone do something like that for me. He told me to invite anyone I wanted and he'd invite a few "friends." I didn't know he had any. He never took or made calls from the house. No one ever stopped by. Maybe he communicated with them via email.

I was excited as a teenager on her sweet sixteen. I picked a perfect little black dress, perfect heels and had my hair done. He took care of the rest. The house was decorated with flowers.

I invited all my stripper friends who I knew would stir up a little trouble. And I invited my old friend, Chelsea, who had been the one to bring me to New Orleans in the first place. She was very excited when I called, but couldn't come. She promised to come down later on. I was disappointed. I really missed her. I was even beginning to miss my little hometown from time to time. I'd think about the one red-light or the hardware store and I'd get all nostalgic. But I knew I belonged here. I loved New Orleans. I wasn't about to leave. At least not anytime soon.

The morning of my birthday, he woke me up with breakfast in bed. On the tray were two little blue boxes. Inside one box was a pair of platinum and diamond earrings that took my breath away. In the other box a huge diamond and platinum ring. It looked like an engagement ring.

"It's a family heirloom," he said and slipped it on my finger.

I waited for him to continue. Was he going to ask me to marry him? He didn't. He only smiled at me.

"I wanted you to have it," he said softly.

I stared at it. I didn't dare ask, but then I had to. "Isn't this an engagement ring?"

He shook his head. "No. I'd want to give you a much bigger ring than that."

I blinked. Bigger than this?

"I haven't found the right one yet."

The right one? *Yet?* I almost panicked but I pushed the thought of leaving out of my head.

"Thank you," I said. "It's beautiful."

"Not as beautiful as you are."

I smiled and laughed a little. "Come here."

He bent over me and I put my arms around his neck, pulling him down on me and I showed him my appreciation immediately. Jewelry always seems to have that effect on a girl.

I scampered around all day, singing *Happy Birthday* to myself and to anyone who would listen. I ate pizza for lunch and washed it down with a beer.

The guests began to arrive around eight. Jackie and two of the other girls I'd worked with—and had partied with at the other party I'd thrown—were the first ones to arrive. When we saw each other, we hugged and jumped up and down. They admired my new earrings and the ring and told me I was one lucky bitch.

I knew I was.

His "friends" were fashionably late. Same look as he had, same reserved manner. They came in with their highly fashionable girlfriends, who hung like starlets from their arms.

One of them told me, "Frank is such a good guy and so sexy! All the girls have wanted him for years."

I smiled smugly to myself.

"So, how'd you manage to land him?"

If she only knew... I sighed and said, "Don't you mean, how did he manage to land *me*?"

She threw her blonde head back and gave a fake, high-class laugh. I tried not to cringe.

The party was in full swing by ten. The food and drink flowed. People seemed to be having a really good time. Around midnight, I glanced up at the top of the stairs. Frank was leaning on the railing and staring down at me. I lifted my glass to him. He smiled genuinely at me as though he were more than happy he was able to please me. Then he jerked his head to the side, indicating he wanted me.

My heart began to pound.

I set my glass down and tried not to run up the stairs to him. I took one step at a time, loving the way he looked at me as I neared him. I loved the way he waited patiently until I was on the top step and I loved the way he extended his hand to help me to the landing. He encircled my waist with his arm and led me into one of the guest bedrooms.

I nibbled at his ear and whispered, "Thanks for the party."

"You are more than welcome," he said and opened the door.

I went in and he closed the door behind him. I turned and grabbed his head, pulling him into a wet, lusty kiss. He let me kiss him for a moment, then pushed me down on the big, four-poster bed.

"Get undressed."

I grinned. He was taking control, as always. I loved it. I loved it when he took control. I was lost in his control and I could let my body do what it wanted to do: Get off.

I sat up. "Please help."

He reached over and unzipped my dress, all the way down. I liked the way the zipper sounded; I liked the way the dress fell off my back. I liked the way his eyes devoured my body each new time, as if this were the first time he'd seen it. I liked that he never tired of it, of my body. Or of me. I liked that I didn't tire of him.

"You don't have any underwear on," he said.

I shook my head. "No."

"Why not?"

"I like the feeling of the dress against my skin."

He seemed pleased with my answer and told me, "Keep your heels on."

I did as I was told.

"Get up on your hands and knees."

I did as I was told.

"Spread you legs."

I did as I was told.

He didn't say anything else. He came towards me, tracing an invisible line along the outline of my curves with the tip of his finger. I shivered in delight. My breathing became sporadic as I tensed in anticipation. What would it be this time? Rough? Would he grab my head and pull me back and suck on my neck? Would he glide in gently, taking his time to fill me? Would he let me to play with myself while he fucked me?

"I want someone to watch us," he said suddenly.

I froze. *He wants someone to watch us?*

"Would you like that?"

He leaned over and touched my breast, grazing his finger along the nipple until I purred. He said, "Someone is going to watch us, Kristine. He's in the bathroom right now, watching through the door."

I jerked my head towards the bathroom door, which was indeed open a slit, the light peering through. I couldn't see anyone.

Then I heard the crack. Of the switch. My heart began to pound twice as fast. My breathing became labored. I couldn't catch my breath.

Before I could mutter a syllable, the switch came down on my ass with a *crack!* I shuddered in misery, in pain, in elation, in desire, in ecstasy. I shuddered with release.

Again, another whack, then his hand rubbing the mark gently then the switch sneaking up my cunt and the tip flirting with my clit. I shivered, shuddered, moaned, shook, shimmied.

He pulled it away, leaned over and placed his hands where the switch had been. I glanced over at the door. Whoever was inside the bathroom had now moved closer to the light and I could see his shadow. He was a big man, whoever he was. Knowing that made me even wetter. Knowing that some man, some stranger, was in the doorway, peeking at us, watching what we did, how we did it, how long we took was more than enough to make me hotter than I'd ever imagined.

He was suddenly in me, bearing down on me, fucking my brains out. The switch was discarded, tonight it had been used only a teaser, something to get me started, to let me know that there was more, lots more, where that came from.

I stared over at the door, at the shadow of the man inside. Who was he? A friend? A business acquaintance? A hustler? Someone he picked up on the street for this very purpose?

Then he stopped fucking.

I groaned and tried to put him back in me. He pushed my hands away and told me to close my eyes. I closed my eyes. The scarf was now covering my eyes. I was blindfolded. Protected from the other man's identity, from Frank's face. I was blinded to the world then, blinded from what he was going to do.

I heard scuffling feet. I jerked my head towards the noise. I heard a zipper and I knew. *I knew.* Yes, yes yes!

The fucking resumed but Frank wasn't the one doing it. He was gone now. No, he wasn't. There was something in my face—his hands, his lips on my mouth, his tongue in my mouth, then mine in his, his mouth sucking on it, sending shivers up and down the entire length of my taunt body. The other man's dick was in my pussy, fucking me. He was a little hairier than Frank. He didn't move around like Frank moved, either. He kept it in one place, fucking me from behind, holding my ass still as though he wanted to make sure it wouldn't get away.

I almost laughed. If I hadn't been so turned on, I would have.

Then I felt the smooth shaft of Frank's dick. He was rubbing it along my face. I moaned and grabbed for it with my mouth. He allowed me to have it after he teased it along my mouth for a moment. I took it and sucked it, licked it up and down, then nibbled at it, just the way he liked.

He moaned with approval. I wondered if he and the other man were staring at each other as they both took care of business with me, with one woman, whose orifices were being filled by both of them, by both of their throbbing cocks.

Then they switched.

Ah, yeah. Frank was back in me, where he belonged. Frank began to slap my ass, the way he always did when he did me doggie. He'd slap it, then grab at it, running his hand along it. Then he'd give a thrust—AH! YES! Just like that one!—and slap it again.

The other man began to run his big hands all along my body, grabbing at my breasts and squeezing them hard. He manhandled me, treated me like a piece of meat and I couldn't get enough. I was so turned on I was going into overload.

They switched again.

As the other man fucked me, Frank took the switch and began to give me little taps with it. I moaned loudly as it hit me, as the man fucked me. Then Frank's hands were all over my body, making me want to come. I writhed and wiggled and moaned and had to bite at the pillow to keep from howling, to keep the guests at the party from knowing what we were doing. And what we were doing was dirty but it was so good, it felt right.

Then the other man was gone and Frank was back inside me, pumping into me. He kept at it, hitting all my hot spots until the orgasm drained all the energy from my body. He fucked me until he came, until he was dry.

I collapsed on the bed. That was too much. Frank fell beside me and said, "Happy birthday, baby."

"Thank you," I said and smiled at him.

He took the blindfold off. I blinked and rubbed my eyes. He smiled at me. I smiled back and pulled him down on me, kissing his face and lips and him. He kissed back and we kissed for minutes, kissed until my legs parted and his cock got hard again. And then he fucked me while I wrapped my legs around him and fucked his orgasm out of his body, fucked him until I came and came and was left without breath.

He rolled off me and gasped once, then resumed his normal breathing. I moved in close to him and rested in the crook of his arm.

"So?" I asked.

"So?"

"Who was he?" I asked, really wanting to know.

"No one special," he replied.

"Oh, Frank, come on! Tell me!"

He eyed me. "No."

I sighed. "Then who?"

"Do you really want to know, Kristine?"

I stared at him and answered the answer I knew he wanted to hear. I said, "No."

"Good."

We left it at that.

End in sight.

This went on for about a year. For a year, we lived and played our games to the breaking point. He was always in control of us, of the situation, of me.

As I said, I loved it.

But obsession will wear off. None of us are immune to that. I wanted him with every fiber in my being and I wanted it to continue forever.

One night after we were finished and he was making the bed, I sat there and watched him, wondering if this was the way it was always going to be. Not that I minded if it were.

But then, I thought about him. He loved being in control so much and I loved surrendering it to him. What would it be like if I were in control of him? Just once?

I decided to test him. I stood and walked over to him, smiled, pushed him on the bed and sat in his lap. He hugged my middle and kissed my naked shoulder.

"Frank," I said. "Let's try something new."

His eyebrows shot up. He didn't like me saying that. He arranged the games. I was only the player. He was the coach.

"No, listen," I said. "Don't you ever wonder what it would be like to be me?"

"No."

"Come on," I said. "Haven't you ever even considered what it feels like for me, lying there, letting you take control? It feels wonderful. I want you to experience it."

"No."

"Frank—"

"No, Kristine," he said and pushed me out of his lap. "Let's go to bed."

When I woke the next morning, he was gone. He had left a note on his pillow, telling me he would return in a few hours and for me to stay put. It also told me he loved me.

It was Saturday.

I wadded the note up and got out of bed. It felt strange doing that. Usually, he woke me up so we could shower and get ready together. So I could have breakfast with him and kiss him at the door, wish him a happy day, then do whatever I wanted. And what I wanted was for him to come back soon.

It's funny, but it never felt strange. Until now.

I showered and got ready. I fumbled around looking for the toothpaste. Where the hell was it? I finally found it inside the medicine cabinet and brushed my teeth. I stared at myself in the mirror and suddenly got that strange feeling I get from time to time. *Who am I?*

I shook it off and suddenly started laughing. Who *was* I? What did it matter? I thought about that and it did seem strange. Not only strange, but also funny. I started to laugh and I couldn't stop laughing. I had to sit down on the floor as I convulsed with laughter. I laughed until I cried, then I got up laughing, put my clothes on and I left the house, straight out the front door. And I didn't leave a note.

My car was parked in the garage. It hadn't been driven in so long, I was almost afraid it wouldn't start, but it did and I backed it out and got on the street.

I don't know what my intention was. I just wanted to see something different. Some different faces, some different places, something different other than that house, Frank and all the same places we went to. I saw a mother pushing a stroller with a little, bitty baby in it. I smiled and drove to the stop sign at the end of the street, looked both ways, turned left and headed to the Quarter.

It was early, but there were a lot of people out. It was summer and crowded. People were all over the place, walking out in front of my car without looking. I had a sudden urge to return to the house and escape all this chaos, but I had my mind set. There was a little bistro down here where I used to eat my breakfast. They had the best biscuits and gravy. I was dying for them. Frank made them for me but he always got the gravy wrong. It either came out way too thick or way too thin. It was usually inedible.

I drove around for a few minutes until I found a parking space, pulled in, got out, put some money in the meter and walked to the bistro.

It was busy. I found a seat in the back and sat down. A waitress came by asked me what I'd like and I was stunned at myself when I rattled off, "I want two eggs, scrambled, biscuits and gravy, two slices of bacon—extra crispy—and a sweet tea."

I hadn't even hesitated. She didn't seem to notice.

She nodded. "Anything else?"

"Yeah," I said. "Do you have a newspaper?"

"Sure," she and jerked her head towards the bar. "Over there."

I spotted it and rose, grabbed the paper and hid behind it. In no time, I had my tea, then my food. I ate some of the food, but it tasted different. Maybe they had a new cook. I pushed it away and stared around the room. Strangers. All these people were strangers. Tourists. Visitors. Where were they going? Where had they come from? And when were they headed home?

Home. Home. I suddenly wanted to go home so badly, I could have run there in no time. I hadn't seen my mother in a long time. I should call her.

I threw some money on the table and left the bistro. I walked out, deciding to do some shopping or maybe just walk. I wanted to be out with people. I needed that.

I walked for a long time, getting lost in the crowd. I didn't get my palm read or my future told. I didn't go into any shops. I didn't buy anything. I just observed what everyone else was doing. It seemed strange to me, in a way. I had forgotten what it was like, doing normal stuff like this, getting excited over a good buy, or squealing with delight at the sight of the horse-drawn carriages that lined the street with the flowers on top of their heads. I always loved those horses.

Maybe I'd ask Frank to buy me a horse. That would be fun. I loved to ride. Maybe he did as well, though he'd never said one way or another.

Would he buy me a horse if I was leaving? Could I take it with me?

I stopped my thoughts. I wasn't leaving. Not yet. No. I couldn't. Could I?

I shook my head and found myself over near Jackson Square where all the palm readers set up shop. I had just about decided to go home when I heard someone calling my name. I stiffened, thinking it might be Frank, but it wasn't. It was Chad, my neighbor from my life a million years ago.

"Hey! I thought that was you!" he exclaimed and gave me a big hug.

"Hey yourself!" I said and hugged him back.

He pulled away, marveling at me. "I haven't seen you in forever! I thought you'd moved!"

I smiled at him and said, "No, I'm still here."

He nodded. "I was just about to grab a bite to eat. Want to join me?"

"No," I said. "I've already eaten."

"Already?" He glanced at his watch. "It's only eleven."

"What?!" I said and grabbed his arm. It was eleven. I'd been wandering around for three hours! How had I lost track of time?

"Come on," he said. "My treat."

I stared at him. He was so cute. Tall, lanky. Good natured. He lived in the apartment below mine and Jackie's. I was always running in and out of there and he'd always say, "In a hurry much?" which would make me smile. God, I missed him. I missed running around. I missed Jackie.

"How's Jackie?" I asked.

"Didn't you hear?" he said. "She moved to Ft. Lauderdale."

"What?"

He nodded. "Someone told her the strippers there were making twice as much as they do here and she left."

She hadn't even called me. She hadn't said goodbye. I hadn't been around for her to say goodbye. We were so close once and now she was gone, to a new life.

Oh, shit. Shit.

"So, how about it?" he said and wiggled his eyebrows.

"Sure," I said. "Why not?"

We went to a little Greek place and ordered gyros. Chad talked my ear off, asked me a million questions, which I didn't answer, then told me we should go out sometime.

"If you like," he said. "I always meant to ask you out, then you moved and I kicked myself in the ass. I told myself that if I ever saw you again, I'd ask you. So how about it?"

I smiled at him. Something in me made me almost want to accept, but I couldn't, of course. I couldn't because I wasn't a free agent anymore. I had my man and he had me.

A sudden gust of panic set it. It ate at my insides and made me slightly nauseous. I suddenly remembered my deadline. Knowing it was past made me panic. I wanted to jump up and run, get out before it was too late.

Chad was staring at me as I swam inside these thoughts. I shook myself and smiled at him. "Sorry," I said. "I'm kinda…"

I trailed off. What was I involved in? What kind of relationship was it? Was it the kind that involved a nursery? No. The kind with diamond rings? No. The kind with white wedding cake? No. Then what kind was it? I didn't know and that saddened me. For a moment. Who cares about that kind of stuff anyway? I knew life was no fairy tale and that included knowing weddings and marriages weren't either.

"Oh," he said and squeezed my hand. "When you get tired of him, give me a call."

I smiled at him. "Sure."

"Great," he said happily.

I nodded and stood. "Listen, I have to get going. I have an appointment I need to keep."

"I understand," he said. "Keep in touch, Kristy."

I stared at him. No one ever called me Kristy anymore. Always Kristine.

"Will do," I said.

He stood and gave me a peck on the cheek. I stared into his eyes, wondering if he could see through me. If he knew what was going on. He couldn't. He smiled back at me and told me to be careful.

I didn't go immediately home. I wandered around a little while in the Quarter, then I got in my car and drove around, looking at strip malls, at houses in the suburbs, at things like I was a foreigner and all of this was new to me.

And it was. In a way.

After darkness had fallen, I decided to go home. He was waiting on me. As soon as I pulled into the driveway, he was at my car, opening the door, demanding to know where I was, who I had been with and why I had left.

"I don't want to talk about it," I said and pushed him away.

He watched me disappear into the house. I went straight for the liquor cabinet and poured myself a shot of Jack. He stopped in the doorway and watched me.

"What's the matter?" he asked quietly.

"Nothing," I said and took the shot.

"Where did you go?"

"Out."

"Why?"

I poured myself another shot and said, "No reason."

"Kristine," he said. "Just tell me what's wrong."

"What's wrong?" I said and waved the bottle at him, pouring whiskey all over the floor. "What could be wrong, Frank? I have it made here. You do everything for me. You give me all I ever wanted and more."

He swallowed hard. "Just tell me."

I stared him dead in the eye and said, "I can't do this anymore."

"Can't do what?"

"Be with you like this. I can't give it to you anymore. I want to and it kills me to say this, but I can't do it anymore."

"What happened?"

I scoffed, "What do you think happened, Frank? I woke up!"

He stared at his shoes. "What do you want?"

"I don't know," I said and started to cry. "But I don't want this anymore."

"What do you want?"

"I don't know, but I don't think you can give it to me."

His head shot up and a dark cloud settled over his face. I wished I hadn't been so honest.

"What's wrong, Kristine?" he said. Now he was concerned.

"I can't do it anymore, Frank," I wailed. "I just can't!"

He stared at the switch on the floor, where he'd dropped it the night before and never retrieved it, then back at me. He looked almost defeated.

"Do you not love me anymore?" he asked quietly.

No, I didn't. I couldn't. I had shut it off. Today. This morning. Time was up. I had all the money I'd wanted from him and it was, simply, time to go. Move on. Away. Run. Run away.

"Of course I love you!" I said, shaking my head.

"Then what?"

"I don't know!"

And I didn't. It was as if the tables were suddenly turned. I didn't know what to do now, besides leave and start over. I was good at that, starting over. I liked it. I liked the newness. I didn't like what I had here anymore. It was so comfortable, it suffocated me.

"If you only knew how it felt," I said. "If I could share that with you—"

"No," he said.

"Please," I said. "Just once. Just let me tie you up once."

"No."

"Either do it," I said. "Or I leave."

And I would, my bags were packed. I had packed them before I left that morning. I had stored them in the trunk of my car. I had planned on leaving and I had driven around to prolong it and then I had come home. I had promised myself I was going to leave and now I couldn't. Not until it was finished. And I still didn't want it to be finished, over, done with. But I had to see what he'd do. I wanted to know how far I could push him. I didn't know what I'd do after he had been pushed, but I wanted to see. Pushing him would tell me something which included whether I should stay or whether I should go.

He knew I wasn't bluffing. He knew I would stand my ground on this one. He knew I wouldn't back down. Now it was in his hands—what to do. What would he do?

"Either give me control or let me leave," I said.

He started to laugh, but stopped himself. He bent down and picked up the switch and said, "Follow me."

I followed him.

We went upstairs and into the bedroom where he solemnly and ceremoniously handed me the rope and the switch. It felt funny in my hands, the rope. I'd never noticed its coarseness before now. The texture was rough, uneven. It scratched my skin.

Frank was staring at me, wondering what I would do next. What was I going to do now that I had the control?

"Please undress."

He complied, watching me out of the corner of his eye. I stared at him, then at the wall. When he was done, I told him to lie down on the bed.

He lay down.

"Spread your legs and grab hold of the post."

He did as he was told.

I walked over and tied him to the bed. He began to squirm. I hated that. It didn't feel like I thought it would feel. It felt affected, put on. Not exciting, not like when he tied me to the bed.

After he was tied, we stared at each other for the longest time. The tables had turned. I was now in control. Neither one of us liked it. But there was no going back.

I lifted the switch and brought it down on his leg. He didn't even flinch. I felt sick. I ran into the bathroom and vomited into the commode. I got up and rinsed my mouth out with water.

I went back out and stared at him, tied to the bed. Seemingly helpless. But he still had it, no matter how tightly I had tied him to the bed, he still had me under control. He had only given it to me this one time to make me stay under the false pretense of giving me what I wanted.

And I didn't want it. I didn't want it any more than he wanted me to have it.

I sat down beside him and kissed him, crying as I kissed him, knowing I would miss him so much I'd want to die. I already missed him and I hadn't left yet.

But that was my nature. I don't deny my nature. Not even with him. I pursue something until I get it and once I get it, I'm done.

And so was he. I left him lying on the bed, still tied up. I left with tears in my eyes, with his money in my pocket, with regret in my heart. I left, knowing I would never, ever find anyone like him, but knowing that that was fine. That it would have to be fine.

Run, run, run.

I wasn't running home to my mother. I wasn't running anymore. I didn't have anywhere to go. I had never felt better.

I'd never felt worse. I wandered around, driving for endless hours, endless nights, never sleeping, barely eating enough to sustain me. I stayed in cheap hotels just long enough to take a shower and rest then I ran again, running so much I eventually found myself in a circle, circling New Orleans, circling him.

Sometimes, late at night, I could hear him calling me. From far away, I could hear his sweet voice, telling me everything will be fine, good, better than it ever was before. I wanted to run and find that voice, but I didn't. I didn't need it anymore. I wanted it, but that's another matter.

I told myself to stop. To stop loving him. To turn it off. It was over. It had to be over. Nothing ever lasted and this couldn't last either. I had to leave. I had to! I couldn't go back.

Why?

I asked myself that over and over. Why? Why not return to him? Why not? Why was I running in the first place?

I knew why. I was afraid. I was afraid, not of Frank, but of his love. It was terrifying to me, his loving me. I was terrified I couldn't return it. I didn't know if I had it in me to love him as he loved me. I just figured that it couldn't last, the infatuation, the love, the passion. And if I gave it back, what if he took it away? What would I do then? I'd crumble. That's what I would do. I'd crumble. And I was too strong to crumble. No one had ever gotten the best of me and I didn't want to start that now.

But it was lasting. The love I had for him was lasting. It wasn't going away. It was tormenting me to know what I had left behind. What I had given up.

But I couldn't go back. There was too much there. Too much. It was too much.

A week passed. A lonely, long week. One week. Only one week and I couldn't take it anymore. I told myself to take it, to let it go, but I kept hearing his voice, sometimes coming at me in a dream, telling me to come home to him. That voice broke me. It carried me home to him. It was my saving grace and my prison. That voice, his voice, which was his love, which I needed, which I told myself I didn't need, that I couldn't need. That I ran from, which I was now running back to.

I ran to it, to his voice, so far away and to him. I ran all the way home, crying, hoping, praying he would be waiting. And he was. He was waiting, his arms spread open. He kissed me passionately, chaining me to him and never letting me go. And I never wanted to be let go again. I never wanted to succumb to my doubts or my resolutions. I didn't have to live my life the way everyone else lived theirs. It was my life and I chose to live it with him. I chose it, to be there. It made me happy to be with him. He was mine as much as I was his. Time had done nothing to our passion. It was as if it had stopped for us and once we met again, it resumed.

"I knew you'd come home," he said.

I had a feeling he did. And that's when I realized what it had all been about. Frank hadn't been trying to break my spirit or my back. He'd been trying to break down that wall I had around myself that never let anyone in. He wanted to break down those walls so he could see, so he could tell if I really loved him. He wanted inside that wall because he loved me. And he knew if he broke it down, I'd love him back. He'd beat me that one time because then, that's all he knew to do. He threw me in the wine cellar for the same reason. He was unsure of my love, unsure of me. And it frightened him and he took his fear out on me. He did those things because he really didn't know if I loved him or not. And that's what made him crazy. He was just as afraid of not being loved as I was. The games had been the way for us to find our love and stake our claim to it. He'd only beaten me to the finish line and he knew I'd soon follow, if he could only hang on for a little while longer. He knew me better than I knew myself.

"Don't ever go again, Kristine," he said, cupping my face in his hands, staring deep into my eyes. "If you ever leave again, I won't be able to take it."

Neither would I.

"I love you," he said, kissing me, holding me, loving me. "I love you so much."

"I love you, too," I murmured and took his kisses and gave them back.

"Stay with me forever," he said, forcing me to look in his eyes. "Tell me you'll stay forever. Promise me."

"I'll stay forever. I promise."

And I kept my promise. This time he kissed me and I felt it wash all over me and I fully understood what it was all about—the games. The games were not about succumbing to his control, they were about losing it, they were about letting myself go, letting myself run wild like the wild horses run inside of me, letting myself free, freeing myself to the feeling not of ecstasy but of love. The games were about nothing other than love. I knew that now.

And with that realization, I shuddered with release and I let everything go. Nothing mattered. With that final resolution, he broke me. He broke me. No. I broke myself. I broke myself of those chains that never did anything but hold me back in the first place. I loved him. And I allowed myself to love him the way I wanted to love him, the way I had to. The way I needed to. And I allowed myself to accept his love.

And there was no going back after that, never again would I show any ambivalence on it. I loved him. He loved me. That was all we had and that was enough.

The girl has been broken.

EAGER TO PLEASE

Here I am. Take me. Use me. Do whatever you like.

"Shh," he said and put a finger to my lips. "I'll untie you now."

"Please hurry," I begged as the pain shot through my arms again.

"I said I would do it," he said and began to untie the ropes.

I immediately felt relief, though only slightly. It took a minute before he was done and I began to whimper with pain. I don't know why it hurt so badly today, but it did. It was excruciating pain, a burning pain. It hurt so bad I couldn't stand it. It was usually more fun.

"Shh," he murmured.

Even though it's my pet peeve to be shushed, I shushed. Even though I was in so much pain I could barely concentrate, I shushed. He could shush me because he was in control.

Once the ropes were off, a feeling of relief, like a rebirth, came over me. The constriction was too much to bear. I stared up at him, almost smiling, though he was the one who had tied me up.

"Now lie down," he said. "It's my turn."

His turn. His turn to do whatever he wanted. We had played my game, the tying of me to the bed game and before that we had played my spanking game. Now it was his turn. His game was fucking. He did the fucking and I hung on for the ride. It was the best part of the night. The other games were merely a precursor. They got us both ready for the intensity of what was really important.

"Don't move," he said.

I stared up at him, knowing exactly what he was going to do. My heart began to beat wildly in my chest. He set the fire in my soul. He made me come alive. He knew what was going through my mind and that was, *Here I am, take me, use me. Do whatever you like.* And he would. Submission was the name of the game and dominance was inevitable. It was our favorite game, the one we played over and over but never tired of.

As instructed, I didn't move. I just lay there and let him look at me. I was naked, completely and utterly naked and not just in the sense that my clothes were off. He saw me then; he saw every single part of me from the tips of my toes to the curve of my earlobe. He saw my soul, my heart. He liked what he saw. I could tell as his eyes glided over me and settled on my mouth, which longed for a kiss.

Another pain shot through my arms as the feeling began to return from being bound. A cry came out of my mouth before I could stop it and I began to shake my arms to get them awake. It was a terrible ache I felt. I had to get them better.

"I told you to be still," he said, his English accent coming out strong.

But I couldn't stop moving. The pain I had felt earlier was still there, though it was numbing. "I can't," I said and held out my arms. "They hurt."

He eyed me, sighed and sat down on the bed. He took my arms and began to massage them until the life came back. I moaned. That felt so good.

"Is that better?" he asked.

"Yes," I said. "Thank you."

He stared into my eyes, not blinking. "Then be still."

I was still.

He got up and went to the foot of the bed and continued to stare me. He loved to stare at me, take all of my body in. Although it was natural to feel self-conscious when someone looks at you like that, when he did it, it gave me power. I wanted to show him what I had, from the top of my head to the bottom of my feet. I wanted him to *see* me. I couldn't stand it when he looked away.

He looked away.

"What did I do wrong?" I asked.

"Nothing," he said.

But there was something wrong, something amiss. I could feel it, I had felt it earlier. That's why it wasn't as fun as it had been. I had to asked, "What is it?" though I dreaded the answer.

He stared back at me and said, "Tomorrow you're going home."

My mouth dropped and before I knew it, tears were spilling out of my eyes. I began to cry so hard I could barely breathe. *No!* I didn't want to go home! I wanted to stay here, in this dilapidated, abandoned house forever. I wanted to stay with him.

"Shh," he said again.

I couldn't stop crying, not even for him. The thought of being away from him, even for a minute, was killing me. And I wouldn't see him after tomorrow. I didn't know much, but I knew that. He'd be gone forever.

"I said to *shh*," he told me.

I stared at him and bit my bottom lip. He stared back and shook his head slightly, as if he felt sorry for me.

"Please," I said. "I don't want to go home."

"But you have to," he said and climbed into bed.

I stared at him, at his big arms that held me tight, at his hands that made me squirm. I stared at his handsome face, at the laugh lines around his deep blue eyes that crinkled when I said something to amuse him. I stared at the whiskers on his chin that tickled my legs when he kissed his way up. I stared at him and felt a connection so strong it made my heart sick.

He bent over me and said, "You knew this day would come."

"I won't go," I said.

"You have to, Kara."

I stopped crying. "No. I won't."

He smiled. He liked my defiance; it amused him to no end. He almost laughed but then he didn't. His mind was on other things.

"Don't think about it right now," he said and leaned down for a kiss. I rose up on my elbows and met his lips, but then he pulled away, teasing me. I couldn't help but smile, even though I felt terrible inside. He leaned back down and pulled away again, teasing me, making me come to him. He did this until I grabbed his face and pulled his lips to mine. We began to kiss, kiss like we always kissed. A little forceful at first and then we would begin to eat at each other's mouths.

I moaned, "Oh, Nate, you taste so good."

He climbed on top of me, pushing my legs apart with his knee. I pressed against his leg, feeling the coarse outline of his jeans. His jeans felt cool and unyielding. I began to move against his leg, allowing myself to scrape along it. He began to grind into me. His cock was so hard I could feel it even though it was still inside his jeans. It pressed up against them and made a big outline. I wanted it. I rubbed it and kissed his neck, sucked it. He moaned and moved so I could kiss his chest, then down to his dick, which awaited my mouth. He was squirming for it. He wanted to take as much as I wanted to give.

He rolled off me and I climbed on top of him, straddled him began to move down towards his cock. But he grabbed my hips and pulled me back to him. I bent over him and he started by kissing my breasts, grabbing them with both hands and squeezing them. *Mmmm*...I wanted more. He nibbled at my nipple then sucked on it before he pushed me up until I was standing over him. He grabbed my hips and pulled my pussy down on his face and began to lick and suck it, finger it until I was humping his face and wanting his cock even more.

"Ahh," I moaned. "Oh, yeah, oh, baby... Let me do you."

I pulled his hard cock out of his jeans and went down on him. He gasped a little. *Ahh, yes.* I kissed the shaft then slid my tongue down along it until I came back up and deepthroated him. He moaned. I stopped for a minute and smiled up at him, loving the look on his face as I controlled of him. I went back to his dick and sucked it with everything I had.

I didn't have time to do any more. He suddenly moved me off him, turned me over and put me up on all fours. Then he was on my back, licking it, kissing it, reaching around to squeeze my breasts.

I couldn't take it anymore and demanded, "Put it in. Now."

He didn't need to be told twice. I moaned as he began to fuck me, fuck me hard. I pushed back against him, loving the way his dick filled me up and made me whole.

Then I felt the first slap of his hand on my ass. *Oh, God, yes!* I shivered and wanted another. He gave it to me then resumed his fevered pace. I couldn't keep up. I grabbed the bed for leverage. He was going for it. He was taking me, consuming me, using me. It was dirty and slightly vicious and was what sex was really all about when you got right down to it. It was about getting and taking what you wanted. And what you needed.

Just then he slowed and bent over my back, kissing it. I moaned and began to wriggle. I trembled with delight as he pawed at me before he went right back at it. He slowed again and his hand came around and rested on my clit. Without hesitation, I began to move against it, moved until I felt the orgasm. It began to tickle me so I paused and moved against his hand and then back against his cock.

I shuddered. This was going to be an enormous orgasm. Before I could enjoy the moment before the release, I felt it. I felt it then, all of it, it was almost painful, but so deliciously painful it made me want it more. That's when I took it and began to come and come hard, so hard I was wailing. A strange sound came out of my throat and that was his cue to take over again.

I don't know how long it lasted. All I know was that we were going at it so hard the bed threatened to fall apart. But that didn't stop us, even if the pictures on the wall were shaking and the windowsills were rattling. Nothing mattered as we fucked. Nothing ever would.

He came just then, just after my orgasm began to fade and he grabbed onto my ass and pumped into me so hard I thought I would break in two. He pumped into me and moaned and...then... He was finished. We collapsed on the bed, with him on top and tried to catch our breath. We lay like that for a long moment, barely breathing. The intensity always winded us.

When we were finally back from euphoria, I rolled out from under him, draped a leg across his chest and kissed his cheek. He grabbed my hand, kissed it, and then kissed me.

"I love you, you know that, right?" he muttered.

I nodded. "I love you, too."

He eyed me. I stared back. Say it, say it, say it *say it!* Tell me we can make it work, that we can figure this thing out. Make it work; give me some hope that it can.

He turned away.

I almost started crying again but I didn't. I couldn't. I would figure this thing out. I would make it work. I don't know how, but I already had a plan working and nothing was going to keep me from him. He was mine and no one was going to take him away.

"Let's go to sleep," he said.

"Uh, Nate—"

"Shh," he said and nuzzled my neck. "Let's sleep, love. We can talk in the morning."

"But—"

"Shh," he murmured and closed his eyes.

I thought about my plan. I knew what I was going to do. I turned over and we spooned. He fell asleep but I stayed awake for a while. As I listened to his breathing, I figured and formulated. I stayed up half the night and didn't move an inch from his arms. I wouldn't have moved for anything. I lay there and felt so sheltered and so secure and so wanted. I loved that feeling, of being wanted by someone who wanted me as much as I wanted him. It was a good feeling.

I tried not to fall asleep but before I knew it, I had. When I awoke he was gone. At first I thought he might have just gone downstairs for breakfast. Sometimes he did that and would carry a tray back up for me. He was considerate and wouldn't disturb me when I slept. He would let me sleep then he would bring the tray up, set it on the nightstand quietly and lie beside me. He would hold me until I woke and turned over to him. A smile would flicker in his eyes before it crossed his lips. He would always say, "How late can you sleep? It's nearly noon."

I stared at the clock on the wall. It wasn't even nine. And that's when I knew he was gone. I felt sick, so sick I could have thrown up. He was gone. He was really gone. And he had taken my heart with him. There was no way to get it back.

I jumped up off the bed and looked around. I don't know why I looked because I knew deep down that he wasn't there and that he'd been gone for some time. There was no "goodbye" note on my pillow. His side of the bed was cold. There was nothing left of us. I began to cry. I was crying so hard I couldn't breathe. I fell down on the bed and buried my face in his pillow, which still smelled of him. I breathed the smell in and knew that in a matter of hours it would be totally gone from the room and from my memory.

"Good God, Kara."

I froze.

"Put your clothes on."

A dress came flying at me and landed on my back. I turned and looked up. It was Grant, my husband. He was standing in the door dressed, as usual, in a business suit. He never wore jeans and he never got his hands dirty. He never did anything he didn't want to. I had never wanted to see him again. I didn't usually get what I wanted.

"We're going home," he said. "Now get ready."

And with that, he turned and left the room. It was true. Nate was gone for good. And I was all alone—again.

The beard.

"Grant, why did you marry me?" I asked once.

He stared at me for an instant before replying, "I knew my parents wouldn't like you."

He had that right.

It was strange how we met. I had been working for a catering service and had met his best friend, Todd, at one of the events. Todd was good looking, charming and such a snake. He charmed me right into bed. He would drop by my apartment just to have sex. I was so enamored of him that I didn't mind when he'd leave just as soon as he came. I didn't mind because I was in love.

I was such an idiot. Today, I could see right through a guy like Todd. I could see that I was just a piece of meat to him—something to devour and throw away once all the fun wore off. Back then, I couldn't see it for the life of me. Maybe because I was a romantic at heart and believed in love and happiness and all that other crap storybooks and movies feed you.

Todd was a good lover, though. Well, I guess he was. I was practically a virgin and not very experienced when I met him. I wouldn't let many guys close to me because my mother had always warned me about men. "Men will use you," she would say over and over to me and my two sisters. "Don't let them near you."

She was right. At least about Todd, she was. He was a user and he used me. I think he did like me but saw me as some sort of trailer trash, and therefore, beneath him. But I wasn't trailer trash. My parents worked and did the best they could and though we never had much money, I never wanted for anything. And if I did, I would get some little odd job here or there to pay for it.

I had been seeing Todd for about six months when I was asked to work at a birthday party at a mansion just outside Nashville. I remember being in awe of the house as I pulled up in my junky little car. It was huge—sprawling. It was made of stone and looked imposing. It had halls and wings, that's how big it was. The owner was a manufacturer of various goods and very wealthy. The party was for his only child, a son named Grant.

I didn't even know that Grant and Todd were friends. Todd never told me anything about his life and I didn't press him for information. I was also a doormat and doormats don't pressure others into talking about things. The sad part was I just wanted him to like me.

So, I went to work at the party, serving the plates of delicious food on the back lawn, which was covered with tables dressed in white linen and fresh flowers. The pool was huge and flowers floated in it. A champagne fountain gurgled in the center of it all and next to it stood a huge table where a gigantic birthday cake sat, waiting to be eaten. It was definitely the most expensive party I'd ever worked.

I hustled and bustled and out of nowhere, I heard Todd's voice. I turned around and there he was, his arm draped around a gorgeous woman's shoulders. They were conversing intimately and I knew—*just knew*—they were lovers. It hurt mostly because a woman, particularly a young woman, in love despises all other men, especially those who love her. And I'd turned down a lot of guys to be with Todd. Now I felt like a fool. I particularly felt hate for the other woman, whoever she was. She was someone special to him and that meant I wasn't.

I was so hurt that tears sprang into my eyes. I was even more hurt when he glanced over and saw me. When he saw me his face took on a look of annoyance, like he hadn't expected me to be there and it pissed him off that I was.

I held back the tears long enough to deliver the rest of the drinks on my tray and long enough to excuse myself to the ladies room. Of course I couldn't find it. I ran through the house looking for some place private where I could break down.

I went back out and finally found a secluded spot in the garden. I sat down on a stone bench and sobbed, oblivious to the beauty that surrounded me. The European style garden looked like a picture. There were sculptures and topiary but it was just lost on me. My heart was breaking.

I was also very angry at myself. It was easy for me to see what I had been to Todd after he had given me that look. And all I had been was a secretive lover, someone he could fuck and then forget about. Nothing more.

I felt so stupid and foolish and just hopeless. I was insecure, too. I had such insecurity issues, I was bordering on self-hate. I didn't consider myself to be beautiful. Other people did. But I didn't come from that kind of background. We didn't tell each other that we were attractive. We told each other how "stupid," "dumb" and "ugly" we were. I was in my late twenties before I realized that I might not be the ugliest person on earth after all. I didn't think that my blue eyes or pert nose or my high cheekbones were nice. I didn't think that my little body, firm and curvy, was what men lusted after. I didn't think my long, dark hair was anything special. I thought I was ugly. I only saw the flaws when I looked into the mirror. My nose was slightly crooked because my sister had hit me with a basketball when I was thirteen. I thought the freckles on my face were ugly and I longed to get rid of them. I thought the plumpness of my lips were an atrocity. Who could possibly find *me* attractive?

Not that it ever did me any good, being good looking. People always say that good looking people have it easier than the not so good looking people. That's a lie. It only helps to attract assholes like Todd into your life who will screw you and leave you. They like the way you look, they just don't like anything else about you.

The sobs were coming harder as I thought about him. I almost wanted to die, but mostly I wanted to find him and kick him in the balls. *Hard.* I wanted him to double over in pain and then I wanted to punch his face and—

"Are you okay?"

I jumped and saw this extremely handsome guy standing in the shadows. He was dressed in an expensive suit and his blond hair was short and perfectly styled. He looked like a lighter James Bond.

"I'm sorry," I said and regained my composure. "I know I'm probably not supposed to be here. I'll just—"

"It's okay," he said and walked towards me.

I stared up at him and nodded. He sat down beside me and we didn't say anything for a few seconds.

"What's wrong?" he asked.

"Oh, nothing," I said and wiped my eyes.

"Here," he said and took out a handkerchief and handed it to me.

"Thanks," I said and blew my nose.

"You're welcome," he said and smiled. "You know, it's supposed to be a happy time."

"Excuse me?"

"A party," he said.

"Try working it," I said dryly.

His smile disappeared. "I didn't mean—"

"No, no," I said. "I'm sorry. I know you didn't mean anything by it."

"Why are you crying?" he asked.

I stared him dead in the eye and blurted, "I just found out that the guy I thought—for some strange reason—was my boyfriend really isn't. Does that make sense?"

He nodded.

"I mean…" I trailed off. Why was I telling this guy all this?

"Does he go by the name of Todd?"

My eyes widened.

He sighed and pulled a pack of cigarettes out of his jacket and handed me one. I took it and he lit it, then lit himself one, and then he said, "He's like that."

"Do you know him?"

"He's my best friend," he said.

I gulped. "Oh, shit."

"Don't worry about it," he told me. "He does that to a lot of girls."

Yeah, but I thought I was different. I was so stupid.

"Just don't take it personally," he said. "The guy's a dog. One day he's gonna get his ass kicked for it, too."

"I hope," I muttered and took a hit off the cigarette.

He cracked up and held out his hand. "I'm Grant."

★ ★ ★ ★ ★

I had always been eager to please. For what it's worth, I was a good girl. And I wanted to please Grant. I wanted him to love me.

He'd only married me to get his trust fund. He didn't want a wife in the first place, mainly because he was gay. And, yes, I was his beard. I was the one he picked to properly fool everyone into believing he liked girls. I was a little hick-ish and a little starry-eyed at the whole concept of someone having *all* this money because I came from none. I was naïve and he seized upon the opportunity to marry "down." Or, rather, to piss his parents off.

Of course his parents didn't like me. They pretended to, though not very well. It's hard to hide disdain. The only problem was that Grant represented everything they were. He was tall, very blond and very handsome. He looked successful though he'd never worked a day in his life. He didn't have to work. He had the manners and the sophistication that came with his fortunate birth. He had the right connections and had attended all the right schools. Yet, he hated where he came from and he hated who he was, mainly because he was living a lie. That fact made him despise himself.

I'd always believed that he was a very insecure person. His family was not very touchy-feely. The thought of his very stiff mother and father actually having sex to procreate was unthinkable. They didn't even move their hips when they walked. And I never saw either of them dance. How they made Grant was a mystery to me.

Once they found out he was gay, the shit hit the fan. But they wouldn't accept the fact that he was gay and pretended that he was just going through a "phase." They had a very tight hold on him, always talking about "loyalty" and all that other bullshit which just means, "You're stuck here so get used to it."

I kinda felt sorry for him.

Oh, he wasn't a bad guy. He was just living this big lie and it made him miserable. So, he thought that everyone else should be miserable as well, to keep him company. It was almost funny, in a way. He should have known that his parents would have had to give him his trust fund no matter what girl he picked. He once told me he picked me because I made him laugh. And I did. In the beginning, we made each other laugh. It was all a big joke to us.

The plan was to marry, then to "live" together and then to divorce a year later. *That* had been the plan. In the process, he'd get his trust fund and I'd get a part of it for just pretending to be his wife. Didn't fool his parents a bit, though I don't think he was really trying to. He was only trying to pacify them. That didn't work either. They were a little smarter than he gave them credit for.

Right before the wedding, I got cold feet. I begged him to let me out of it but for some reason, he wouldn't. I was the woman elected to make him look straight. He had picked me to do the job and there wasn't much I could say that would convince him otherwise. Once he had his mind made up about something, it was made up. It didn't matter how I felt about it, either.

Deep in my heart, I knew it was a mistake and called the wedding off several times. It just didn't feel right. I was only marrying him for the money anyway and I told him that. Also, I had a feeling that if you married for money, then you'd end up getting screwed. I'd never known one single person that married for money whose marriages worked out.

In our case, it couldn't work out because it wasn't meant to be. People don't change and I should have known that.

But Grant convinced me by saying any girl he married would only marry him for his money so it might as well be me. He said I could do whatever I wanted once we tied the knot and then after he got his trust fund, I could leave if I wanted.

It sounded like a plan to me. When you're only twenty-two, things like that always make sense and you readily, foolishly, let other people talk you into doing things that you don't want to. Now for the life of me, I don't know how I was talked into it. I'm not a greedy person. I think I just wanted to please him because he was so unhappy. He told me constantly that we were doing the right thing and that everything would turn out fine.

And I believed him. I believed him because I wanted it to be true.

We had a big wedding and everyone was properly fooled into thinking we were this great, good looking couple who had the world on a string. During the reception, we'd glance at each other and crack up. We posed for the pictures and kissed and held hands. I began to wish we really could be in love. I *wanted* to be in love with him. He was perfect. The only problem was that he didn't like girls.

We did have sex during the honeymoon in Paris. We both picked up two really attractive guys. He went into one room and I went into another and we both had wild, monkey sex. In the morning, we laughed about it.

He wasn't so bad in the beginning. We did have fun. We traveled around the world first class. We were treated like royalty or rock stars. We went on shopping sprees and slept till noon every day. He bought me a few horses, a few diamonds and all kinds of designer clothes. During that first year, I lived a life of luxury. I know now he was giving it all to me so it would be harder to leave later.

It was only after the year was up that he began to change. He got really possessive of me. Personally, I think he was looking for a sweet, loving mother figure. I tried to be that for him because I honestly did care about him. When he was sad I would hold him in my arms but he wouldn't cry; he'd just be very still. I don't think his mother ever held him like that. I would tell him how special he was and about how proud I was to be married to him. I wanted him to be happy. I really did.

At one point, I even thought I could turn him straight. As I've said, I was very young and naïve. Somewhat delusional, too. I did everything within my womanly powers to turn him on to me. I tried lingerie, herbal supplements, even aromatherapy. But he just couldn't get it up for me, not for any woman. We'd try to make out. He'd try to feel me up, but then it would become this very awkward situation that made both of us cringe. He'd apologize and tell me it wasn't me. But it felt like me. It felt like there was something wrong with me. I would end up feeling perverse, so lowly. There had to be something wrong with me if I couldn't make this work. But the fact of the matter was that no matter how hard either of us tried, it wasn't going to work. I had married a gay man and a gay man he would stay.

I was jealous of the men he would see, too. At first, anyway. What did they have that I didn't? Well, they had dicks. That pretty much summed it up. But being so young, I just thought he was rejecting me because there was something wrong with me. A young woman never takes no for an answer and she takes defeat to heart. The rejection I got from him was heart wrenching. I would cry my eyes out. But one day, I stopped crying. I stopped crying because it finally sunk in. There was nothing I could do about it.

A year into our "marriage" I wanted out, not that it did me any good. Grant wouldn't get a divorce because his father was grooming him to take over his empire. And he needed a wife to help him with the little things like throwing parties and looking straight. Besides that, *any* woman would do and, as I said, I was the woman elected to do the job. If they could pretend everything was okay, then it was.

I cried and told him I wanted a normal life, that money really didn't matter that much to me anyway. And it didn't. I mean, like everyone else, I liked money and I liked buying things and going on nice vacations, but I didn't need it. And he didn't either. He was smart and he could have done something else with his life. He would have made a good doctor or a lawyer or whatever. But he was always searching for approval from his parents and he was stuck doing what they wanted him to do. They wanted him to carry on the tradition. And they wanted him to be heterosexual.

So, he was. At least in their eyes.

But deep inside he was a miserable bastard and nothing I could do was going to change that. After a while, I stopped trying. And I wanted out. But he wasn't about to let me go. Whatever he was getting from me, he needed. He was a control freak and, even if he wasn't in love with me, he wanted to control me.

I wasn't about to let that happen, so I started having affairs. Of course, he caught me. I was in a hotel room with this guy I had met at one of the parties his parents threw and forced me to attend. I hated those parties. Everyone pretended to have a good time but no one really did. Well, the guy wasn't having that great a time, either, so we struck up a conversation and the next thing I know, we're down at the pool house doing what came naturally. We started seeing each other pretty regularly and I was very discreet. I don't know how Grant even found out, but he stormed into the hotel room just as we were getting dressed and proceeded to beat the shit out of the guy.

I ran away. I only had ten bucks in my purse but I ran away. He found me and begged me to come home. I could have anything I wanted, he said. But all I wanted was my freedom. That he wouldn't give. Nor would he give me understanding.

"But why do you have to do it?" he asked. "Why do you feel the need to have sex with other men?"

I was astounded at his reasoning. He really didn't want me to have sex with other men though he was incapable of giving it to me. I knew he had the occasional affair, too, but he thought *I* shouldn't do it. It was pure possession. He thought of me as a possession, someone to keep up the charade with, someone to be there when and if he needed. If I was dividing my attention with other men, that meant he wasn't getting the best of me, which he fully deserved as he was my "husband." It made me sick to my stomach to be thought of like that.

"This just doesn't make any sense! You don't give it to me!" I screamed. "For God's sake, Grant, can't you see that? We're living a lie here. You're not happy and I'm not happy."

"But I am happy," he told me.

And that's all that ever mattered—his happiness. Mine didn't matter. It couldn't have mattered much because I never left him. I guess I could have, but I fell into a pattern. I still had the occasional affair here and there but nothing satisfied me. All the money at my disposal meant nothing. I didn't have any real friends and I was totally alone. I wanted love, love that could be reciprocated. But when you can't form any lasting bonds with anyone, you can't have love.

So I didn't.

After we married, much to my chagrin, we moved into his parent's house where we had our own wing. Grant had a set of rooms and I had a set. It was like a luxurious apartment. I even had my own kitchen so I wouldn't have to go all the way to the main kitchen if I wanted a midnight snack or a soda. I had my own butler who made sure I was taken care of and always picked up after me, though he did sometimes chastise me for being such a slob.

In the first few years, I rarely saw his parents except when we had the obligatory dinner here and there and of course, all holidays. My family didn't matter after I married him. I was supposed to spend all holidays with his family so we could look "normal," though they didn't give a rat's ass if I was there or not. It just wouldn't look "right" if I was off somewhere else. Someone might suspect *some*thing.

Yeah, like your son's gay?

It pissed me off at first and I would rant and roar to Grant who never did shit about anything and then I would concede and stay home with them. I would send my family their gifts and call and apologize for not being home for any holidays. My mother was upset at first, but then she began to accept it. Just like I did.

His parents retired to a few years ago to Palm Beach and we got the whole place to ourselves. Lucky us. I wished it would burn to the ground. Of course, it had an elaborate sprinkler system, so if I got any crazy ideas, it wouldn't have done me a damn bit of good. Not that it kept me from fantasizing about it from time to time.

Have a drink on me.

I always wanted a birthday party when I was a kid. I never got one. I usually got a chocolate birthday cake with a few candles and a five-dollar bill in a card. Nothing fancy.

Grant made sure to give me one every year not to make up for my "disadvantaged" childhood but because it gave him the opportunity to mingle with other people in the business and make contacts and all that other bullshit. It pissed me off that he used my birthday to do that. But every year, I had to get up early and start telling people where to put stuff and where things were. And I hated it. I just wanted to sleep in, eat some pizza and drink some beer.

He would go all out on my birthdays. The parties were so grotesquely expensive we should have been beaten for having them. I always felt a twinge of guilt because there *are* starving people in the world.

But that's not the way rich people think. They have these lavish parties because they can. And every year, I got one. Because my birthday's in December, Grant had the whole back lawn converted into a gigantic tent with little fireplaces so everyone will be good and warm. There was always a string quartette playing the "classics"—no rock and roll allowed. There was always a champagne fountain. There was always caviar, which I didn't like and wouldn't eat. There were always lots of people I didn't know.

I wished he wouldn't bother. When I was kid, I would have loved a party like this. But I wasn't a kid anymore and the parties grew tiresome. Bedsides, the parties weren't for me. They were for Grant.

This year was no different.

I stood alone on the veranda watching everyone have fun. I was dressed in a floor-length light gray ballgown made of silk and chiffon. It was entirely hand-sewn, down to the tiniest sequin on the bodice and had cost a fortune. The earrings I wore had been passed down in his family for several generations and were worth a fortune as was the thick diamond bracelet that slid down my wrist. I looked like a million bucks standing there. I would catch people staring at me. I smiled not because they stared but because they didn't know how uncomfortable I always felt dressed like this.

I watched as the crowd moved across the lawn. I was thirty-three now and I was getting older. It scared me in a way. But then again, I was very happy to have another birthday, so I didn't bitch about turning a year older. Turning a year older was a good thing. I was sad because Grant had told me he wanted a baby.

"By the time you're thirty-five," he had told me the other night. "We have to have a baby."

I just stared at him.

"We need to have one," he said and nodded like his mind was made up.

"What's all this 'we' shit?" I asked. "Besides, do you know how babies are made? I mean, do you have any idea what's involved?"

His face reddened. "Don't be a bitch."

"I'm not being a bitch," I said.

"Kara," he said and gave a loud sigh. "Two more years, okay? Then you need to... *We* need to have a baby."

"It's your parents, isn't it?" I said. "I knew it! I just wonder why it took them so long to get around to this."

"It has nothing to do with them," he hissed. "I want a child."

"*You* want a child?" I asked and shook my head.

"Yeah," he said. "I think it's a good idea."

"Yeah, it is a good idea," I said. "We can hire a nanny to watch it because we're much too busy ourselves. When it turns five, we can ship it off to school and after it's done there, it can return home stiff and unhappy and be just like its daddy. Is that what you want, honey?"

He glared at me and stormed out of the room.

"If you want a baby!" I yelled after him. "Bring me a turkey baster!"

"Fuck you!" he yelled back.

But I meant it. How else was I supposed to get a baby? That was the only feasible way. I wouldn't mind having a baby but I most certainly didn't want to have one with *him*. I thought if I kept putting him off, the bastard would divorce me and get him another beard. *She* could have his baby.

I sighed and sipped my champagne. I wondered if I could get away with sneaking off. But, no. Here he came, my husband. And, oh, he looked at me like he loved me, smiling slightly and with pride. *Look, everyone there is my beautiful wife. Let's celebrate the day of her birth.* He was so good with that shit it was scary.

I wanted to kick him in the balls. I wanted to scream, *It's all a sham! He's gay and I'm a bitch and we don't love each other! We only pretend to so all of you can come here and get drunk and tell everyone what wonderful parties the Claiborne's throw.*

I played my role well. I smiled back and when he offered his hand, I took it and kissed it. Everyone went, *Ahhhh...* I tried not to throw up and allowed him to kiss my cheek and lead me down the stairs and over to my birthday cake where I was forced to blow out the candles. I smiled and clapped my hands together playfully when I managed to blow them all out at once. I feigned happiness and answered all those annoying questions they had to ask, most of which had to do with my age. Every year the same people asked me the same question, "And how old are you?" Couldn't they count? They'd started coming to my birthday parties around the same time I had.

And every year, I tell them the same thing, in a teasing voice, "I just turned twenty-one."

Grant said, "She turned twenty-one last year, too."

Everyone collapsed in laughter. It was such a bad joke but it was *our* joke. *Lovely.*

Grant gave me his gift. Oh, what could it be? Why, it was a stunning emerald necklace. He put it around my neck and everyone admired it. He got me one that looked exactly like it last year. I think he just went out one day and bought a bunch of them and put them in a safe. That way, he never had to shop for my birthday.

I didn't even like emeralds. I mean, I wasn't in my sixties. I liked diamonds and he knew that but every year he got me that same shit. Bastard. He just did it to get on my nerves, too. And I never got to wear the damn things anyway. Not that I would, but they have to be "stored" and "cleaned" and "put away." What good was having something if you have to ask for a key to get it out when you want it? I mean, *shit!*

I told myself to stay calm. It's okay, it would be over soon. I stuck around for a good thirty minutes so no one would get "suspicious" and then I disappeared back on the veranda so I could scope out my birthday fuck. This was my favorite birthday ritual. I would wait until about midnight when people are starting to think about leaving, but knowing they'll stay at least another hour. I used this hour to scope out the man I want to take to the pool house. Sometimes, I just liked to get pounded. That's what I wanted tonight. It was my birthday, after all.

I finally spotted him. He was a young guy, probably in his mid-twenties. Those were the best. They were eager to please, but not so much that they didn't take their time to get you off. He was a waiter for the same catering service that I had worked for. He was tall and he was dark and he was quite handsome. I'd had my eye on him all night.

"Hello, Kara," someone said behind me.

I turned around to see Todd, my old lover. I glared at him, realizing he was the reason I was in this mess to begin with. If he had treated me decently and never cheated on me, I would have never met Grant.

But he had. Nothing I could do about it, either. But, oh, good God, why was he here? Mainly because Grant insisted on staying friends with him. I figured he would kick him out of his life once we married, but lo and behold, he couldn't part with his friendship. I knew it was mostly Todd that kept the friendship alive because his family didn't have near the money that Grant's did. Todd needed Grant to get him in to places and to give him jobs when he needed extra cash. I had long ago given up trying to get Grant to dis-invite him to my birthday parties. Mainly because I realized the parties weren't really for me.

"I said hello," he said.

I rolled my eyes and focused back on the guy. I had to make my move soon. He was already helping to clean up and I knew he wouldn't be there much longer.

"Happy birthday," Todd said and leaned over and brushed his lips against my cheek. "You look beautiful."

I rolled my eyes at him. The nerve of this guy.

"Come on," he said. "Every year you ignore me and every—"

"I gotta go," I said and started off.

He grabbed my arm. "Listen, why don't we have lunch?"

I eyed him for a moment. "Todd, why do you even talk to me? You know there's nothing between us."

"There was once."

I groaned. "Why do we always have to go through this? We both know that I think you're an asshole and if you say one more word to me I will have you thrown out of here."

"I just wanted to wish you a happy birthday," he said.

"Thank you," I said and turned on my heel and took off. I had to play this carefully. No one could even see me look at the guy or the "talk" would start and Grant would be on my ass. I had to play it by ear.

I smiled cheerfully at a few people and made my way towards a table he was cleaning. I grabbed a napkin off a table and, as I passed him, I dropped it. I sighed loud enough for him to hear me and took my time bending down to retrieve it. The guy looked over, spotted me, smiled and bent for the napkin at the same time I bent for it. Our heads almost hit.

"Excuse—"

"Shh," I said quickly and quietly. "I need you down at the pool house in ten minutes."

He eyed me and started to say something.

I shook my head and mouthed, "Ten minutes".

He nodded that he got my meaning. I took my time going to the pool house, which was down a little hill. I stopped and spoke with a few people and acted very nice and affable. As soon as I got there, I let myself in and ran to the back of the room and turned on the light. I heard the door open. My heart began to beat wildly.

"Hello?" he called, looking around.

I grinned from ear to ear. "I'm right here."

He found me, standing in the shadows, and smiled slightly. He wasn't sure of the implication or of his good luck, for that matter. But he wasn't about to leave.

"I'm Kara," I said.

"I'm Jack."

"Nice to meet you, Jack," I said and smiled.

"What can I do for you?" he asked.

"I think you know," I said and walked over to him. I undid his bow tie and stared into his eyes. "Don't you?"

He gulped.

"I thought so," I said and grabbed his head and pulled his lips to mine. The electricity went through my body; it did with every new guy I kissed. I didn't kiss many, but that first kiss was the best.

He pulled back. "Just to be sure… Are we…?"

"Yeah," I said. "You're here to fuck me."

"Really?" he asked, his eyes wide.

"Really."

He grinned. "You're beautiful."

"Whatever," I said and grabbed him again. "We have to be quick."

We kissed all the way to the couch. I fell back on it and he began to paw at my body. I moaned and wanted him to rip my clothes off. I wanted him to see me naked so bad. He nibbled at my breasts through my fancy ball gown then grabbed the bodice and ripped it apart. I threw my head back and moaned. I loved that. He grabbed at my breasts eagerly and began to suck and eat at them. I stared down at his face, at his mouth which was sucking on my nipple. He licked it and then would clamp his mouth on it and then would suck it and run his tongue along it. It was so satisfying.

"Go down on me," I said. "Come on, do it!"

He grinned and pulled my dress off and threw it on the floor. I opened my legs and he got between them, staring at me, down there. I didn't have anything on but a pair of garters. I never wore panties.

His tongue came out and flicked against my pussy then he dove in and sucked on it. I nearly rose up off the couch and in a matter of seconds, as he stroked me, I came. Now I was ready to get to the best part.

He kissed his way back up my body, getting me more and more aroused. He was a good lover. Most guys were too enthusiastic, but he was taking his time. He'd been around the block once or twice and whoever he'd been around with had taught him well.

"I want to fuck you so bad," he said.

"So do it," I moaned and kissed him. I sucked on his tongue and helped him out of his clothes. Soon he was naked and I could fell his hard cock between my legs. I spread my legs and he put it in. I moaned. I loved that first moment of contact. All the anticipation just made me tense with pleasure.

"Harder," I told him. He gave me a hard thrust. I moaned and met him thrust for thrust. As I licked his ear, I said, "Wanna do me doggie?"

"Yeah!"

I grinned and turned over. He grabbed me by the ass and pulled me to his cock and shoved it in. I gasped and loved that feeling of being filled up. He didn't give me a minute to adjust, he just started pumping. I just stayed still and allowed him to fuck me for a few minutes.

"I'm about to come," he moaned.

"No, you're not," I said and pulled away.

"What?" he asked, flabbergasted.

"Shh…sit down."

He sat down and I climbed onto his lap. I glanced at the clock. We had been at this for a good fifteen minutes. I could get away with about five more, ten if I was lucky.

"You are so wet," he said.

A little too wet. It was hard for me to get friction being this wet. I had to find my groove, though, because I didn't have much time. I concentrated on it and began ride him slowly at first, then I sped up a little and he joined in, matching me.

I kissed him and began to ride his cock. He helped me by putting his hands on my hips and keeping me steady. I went up and down and then began to move in his lap, grinding in circles and squeezing his cock inside me for everything it was worth. I was hot and sweaty and so unbelievably turned on. I wanted to fuck him with everything I had because that's all I could do. I knew I would probably never see this guy again. Might as well enjoy him while he was here. And let him enjoy me.

He grabbed my breast and squeezed it hard just as I came. I threw my head back and wanted to scream with pleasure, but I couldn't because I didn't want someone to hear me. But it was like I had just been let out of jail. I felt such freedom in orgasms, such relief, that I just gave myself to them and allowed them to take me over.

He was coming too and soon we were bouncing on the couch. It ended with both of us pressing up against each other and sharing a kiss. We licked and sucked at each other's mouths until I moved back and stared into his eyes. I wondered what it would be like to be in love with a guy like this. A guy who seemed nice and kind. A guy who knew how to fuck. A guy who didn't like other guys. What *would* it be like? I'd never know.

"Wow," he breathed.

"Yeah, wow," I said and kissed his nose. "Thank you."

"No, thank *you*," he said.

I laughed and shook my head at him. I liked sitting on his lap like this. He kissed my chest and stared up into my eyes.

"So what else did you get for your birthday?" he asked.

I fingered the necklace and said, "Nothing much."

"Oh, that's nice," he said. "It looks good on you."

"Thanks," I said and took it off and put it in his hands. "Go buy yourself something nice."

"No, I can't."

"Please do." I winked and got up and pulled the dress back on. He got the hint and began to dress. We didn't say a word though I think both of us were dying to. But we knew this was where it ended. He was smart guy. He knew this was a casual fuck and was thankful for it, but he wouldn't push the issue, which meant he was one of the good ones. Damn, I wished I could've gotten to know him.

"I'll go first," I said. "You wait ten minutes, and then you go, okay?"

He nodded, then leaned over and kissed me. We kissed for a long moment until I pulled away and started to leave. I knew he stared after me and I glanced back once to see him standing in the doorway, watching me go. He gave me a little wave, which I returned. I turned back around and smiled with satisfaction. The smile stayed with me all the way to my bedroom where I fell asleep still dressed.

★ ★ ★ ★ ★

I awoke early the next morning to find my butler, James, pulling my shoes off. He was a great guy who looked like a...well, like a butler. He was short, a little balding and about thirty years older than me. He put up with a lot of shit from me and I loved him to death. We were good friends who laughed together, who talked a lot. But sometimes he pissed me off and when he did his elegant manners and cheerful English disposition wouldn't save him. And right now he was pissing me off.

"Good God, James!" I yelled and kicked at him.

"Mr. Grant wants to see you, Kara," he told me.

"Tell him to go to hell," I said and squinted in the light. "What are you doing?"

"You've gone to bed with your shoes on again," he said.

"I guess I did," I said and yawned. "Now go away and turn off the light."

"I told you, Mr. Grant wants to see you."

"I don't care," I said and buried my head in my pillow.

"Up now," he said and threw the covers off me.

"You're pissing me off, James!" I yelled and grabbed for the covers.

"Now, Miss," he said sternly.

I rolled my eyes and pointed at him. "That's not going to work with me."

"Oh, it might," he said. "Bend over."

I bent over and he unzipped my dress, helped me pull it off and shook his head at its condition. Such a shame that Jack had ruined such a beautiful thing. I concealed my smile.

"Do it for me," he said and pulled off my bracelet and slipped it into his pocket.

I stared at him. He'd take it back to the safe and I wouldn't see it again until next year. I said, "Go away."

He held out his hand. "Give me the earrings."

I took the earrings off and handed them to him. He slipped those in his pocket as well. He was still staring at me. *What was it?*

"Where's the necklace?" he asked.

My hand went to my throat. Oh, no. "Shit," I said and looked around the bed. "It must have fallen off or something!"

He didn't even blink. "I'll just have someone take a look on the lawn. Is that where you think you lost it?"

I considered. "I think so. I can't remember."

He nodded once and walked into my closet and came back a moment later with a pair of jeans and a t-shirt. I watched him. He didn't really think I was leaving my room, did he? Apparently he did. He brought them over to me and told me to dress.

I threw them on the floor. "No."

He bent and picked them up and said, "Now, young lady. Or I *might* have to spank you."

I couldn't help but laugh. "Really? What would your wife say about that?"

He shook his head slightly and said, "It's nothing to do with her, is it? Now get dressed."

"And what will you do for me?" I asked teasingly and stared down at my nearly naked body. He saw me like this all the time. He didn't care and neither did I. He was pretty much my best friend and that's the way we acted towards each other, though whenever we were in the presence of anyone else, we only showed our professional relationship. Neither one of us wanted anyone to know how much we talked or laughed. If they did, he might get fired and then I'd be friendless.

"I might bring you your breakfast in the morning," he said.

"I can do that myself."

"But you can't prepare your eggs the way I do."

He was right. Damn it. I pulled the clothes on and shook my head. "You owe me one."

"I always do," he said.

After I dressed, I followed him to Grant's study. I yawned and complained the whole way because the house was so cold. He ignored me and opened the door of the study and motioned me in. I sighed and walked in and then he followed me.

Grant sat behind his massive desk with his fingers in the steeple position, tucked under his chin. He was now in full control of his family's empire and acted the part. He was all business, aloof and snobbish. He really annoyed me.

"Nice to see you, Kara," he said.

I flopped down in one of the two big leather wing chairs in front of the desk and crossed my arms. "What do you want? I was asleep."

"It's not a matter of what I want," he said. "But a matter of your behavior last night."

Oh, shit. I turned to James for help. He stared straight ahead.

"Thank you, James," Grant said. "That will be all."

He backed out of the room and shut the door. He might have been my butler but he knew which side his bread was buttered on. He knew who signed his paycheck. And it sure wasn't me.

"What do you want, Grant?" I hissed. "And I really wish you would stop treating James like that."

"Kara," he said. "Don't start."

I groaned and tried to contain my anger. But I was always angry with him. He just got under my skin and drove me crazy. He had so much control over me, I hated him to the point of loathing myself for being a person who could hate so much. Before I married him, I had been a happy-go-lucky girl. I had been happy. After, I was just a miserable bitch. Marrying him had changed me so much, it's a wonder I could stand either of us.

"Kara," he said. "I've told you not to make any more trips to the pool house during your parties."

"So what are you saying, Grant?" I hissed.

"I'm saying you were seen going to the pool house," he snapped. "And we all know what goes on in the pool house, don't we?"

"Who told you that?"

"It doesn't matter."

"Matters to me," I said.

"If you're going to do things like that," he said in his patented condescending manner. "You have to be discreet."

I glared at him and said, "Like you, Grant?"

His eyebrows shot up a little. "Yes, like me. No one catches me and that's because it's not that difficult to be careful. It seems like you would make more of an effort and stop behaving like a teenaged boy with out of control hormones."

I held the anger in even though this was what really pissed me off about Grant. He was too controlling, too worried about what "everyone" else thought.

I should leave him. I should just pack a bag and hit the road. I'd get this urge to do it, an urge so strong that I could feel myself running away. The urge to be freed was so powerful that it would eat me up inside. I would fight it, sometimes I would fight with Grant and beg and plead for him to let me go. Of course, he wouldn't. *What would everyone say? It would look bad for the company, for the family.* And then the urge would go away and I'd be okay for a while. And as soon as I thought it had died once and for good, it called again, *Hey, what's up? Why are you wasting your life with this asshole? He can't love you, not like you need to be loved. You know that. Get out while you're still young!*

But I couldn't. He wouldn't let me go. He had too much invested in me.

"If you don't like the way I act," I said and put my feet up on his desk. "Then give me a divorce."

He groaned. "Not this again."

"Yes, this again," I said. "I can't handle it anymore, Grant! I feel like a prisoner! I can't do anything without someone telling on me!"

He seemed to consider my words and said, "If you're so concerned about what people are saying, stop doing things that give them a reason to gossip."

I couldn't win. I could never, ever win with this asshole. I don't know why I even tried. And I don't know why I just couldn't leave. I felt trapped. I felt like if I did get the nerve to leave, then what? What would I do? I'd have to get some shitty little job and some crummy apartment and I would never see James again. Because if I left, I would leave with the clothes on my back and nothing else, even though I had over ten years invested in this prick. He would have a pack of lawyers beating me down for the word "go." And I knew it. He'd told me as much.

I tried again. "Let me go," I cried and fell dramatically to the floor. I pretended to sob and flayed about. I figured if he thought I was crazy, he might be glad to get rid of me. But, alas, no.

"Shut up," he said. "And get up off the floor."

"You don't love me and you never will," I sobbed. "Why won't you let me go?"

"I won't tell you again," he said.

"Grant," I pleaded. "Just let me leave. What's the big deal?"

"You're my wife," he said. "For better or worse, you are my wife and that's the way it is."

"It's never been better! It's always been for worse."

"I'm not going to listen to this anymore," he said.

"Grant, please! Just listen to me."

He shook his head, got up and walked out of the room. As soon as I heard his footsteps echoing down the hall, my fake tears dried up. I got up off the floor and picked up an old vase, ready to smash it. But then I realized if I did that, there would be more hell to pay. I put it back on the shelf and went to his desk. I sat down in his chair and got a cigar out of the humidor. These were his "special" cigars, his Cubans. He would die if he knew I smoked one.

I lit it and smoked a couple of puffs before I put it out on his desk. Happy fucking birthday.

"James," I said later that day. "Tell me who told on me."

"I don't know," he muttered. "Are you finished?"

I glanced down at the tray of food and nodded. He took it and started out of the room. I yelled, "Tell me!"

He shut the door quietly. Well, if he wouldn't tell me, the cook might. I got up and went down to the kitchen and she gave it over reluctantly.

She said, "Don't tell anyone who you got it from."

I promised I wouldn't, but couldn't help but think this house was like some office or school. There was always rumors and gossip going around. Everyone knew what everyone else was up to. One of their favorite topics was who was in the pool house with me. I didn't care what they said, or thought, for that matter as long as they left me alone and let me do it. Usually they did and most time the rumors never made it to Grant, so I was sheltered in a way. And if they laid off me, I laid off them and made sure everyone got their pay raises and days off when they asked.

The culprit was Ted, the gardener. We'd been having sex on and off for about a year. It started about a week after he got the job. I eyed him for a few days before I made my move. He was around my age and so muscular and handsome I couldn't stand it.

I knew why the bastard had ratted on me. He was jealous.

I grabbed a bottle of champagne out of the wine cellar and then found him working on the hedges at the back of the house. I waved the bottle, turned and headed to the pool house. He followed me, not saying a word. As soon as I shut the door, he grabbed me and said something about missing me. We kissed all the way to the couch and tore each other's clothes off. I climbed on top of him and fucked him until I came. After I came, he was still pumping into me. I let him keep pumping and just before he came, I stopped him. I climbed off and put my pants back on.

"Are you kidding me?" he asked, obviously in pain.

"Sorry," I said and smiled at him. "I have a headache."

"Kara," he said. "Come *on*."

I shook my head and stared at his dick. It was tempting. "You know," I said and pulled my shirt on. "When I have sex with someone, it's none of your business."

He dropped his head and fell back on the couch.

"Why did you tell Grant?" I asked. "And how did you even know? You weren't even here."

"I was here. For a little while, towards the end."

I glared at him.

"You said I could come!" he wailed. "You said—"

"Shut up," I said. "Listen, I don't care that you ratted me out. It's just—"

"I didn't rat you out," he said and stared at me. "I told the cook and I guess it got around."

I sighed. "You knew it would get back to him."

He didn't respond.

"I don't like it when someone thinks they own me," I hissed. "I've already got one person who thinks that. I don't need two."

He said, "I just want to be with you."

"Not possible, Ted. You know that. You knew that the first time we did it."

"But I love you."

"Bullshit," I said. "You just want me all to yourself."

"That too."

I could have slapped him. I hated this whole ownership thing people had. We don't belong to each other. Maybe with each other, but never to! Why do these assholes always confuse that?

"What if I tell him about you?" I said. "What if I tell him about you, his gardener, fucking me, his wife?"

"You wouldn't do that."

"Watch me," I said and spun on my heel and left the house.

He called after me, "Come on, Kara!"

Without thinking twice, I had him fired. I didn't really like doing it but I couldn't have him watching my every move. I knew he'd make my life miserable, too. He'd hound me and give me puppy-dog looks whenever he saw me. He'd drop his head and be miserable over me. I didn't want to see that, much less be a part of it.

He had to go, so I made him.

Nap time.

I moped around the house for the next month. It really got on Grant's nerves, which made it worthwhile. I didn't have much to do during the day and now that I had fired Ted, I didn't have anyone to fuck.

It didn't take me long to realize I needed a fuck buddy and if I didn't get one, I would go crazy. But I couldn't do it here as I didn't want to get caught again. I should go on vacation. Miami came to mind. Oh, yes! I loved staying on South Beach. I loved the men down there, too. They're all so sexual and good looking. They buy you drinks and all you have to do is bat your eyes and pretend to listen to whatever's coming out of their mouths, as if you care. Then you ask them if they'd walk you to your room. They *always* say yes. You take them in your room, you get busy and after you're done, they disappear and you don't have to see them ever again.

I could be such a slut. It didn't bother me though, but it did bother Grant, which was probably the main reason I acted like that. Grant hated it when I acted so "trashy." He didn't like me going on vacations by myself and I dreaded even asking him because, knowing what a spoil sport he was, he was sure to say no. I finally got my courage up one night at dinner. Miraculously, he agreed. I almost fell out of my chair.

"You mean it?" I said. "I can go on vacation?"

"Better than you moping around here," he said and sipped his wine.

"This isn't some trick, is it?" I asked and eyed him suspiciously.

"No, it isn't," he said. "Go to Miami and have a good time."

"Can I take Emily?" I asked.

He eyed me. Emily was my college roommate and Grant didn't like her. Mainly because she had quit college to become a stripper and she didn't kiss his ass. She wasn't his "kind of people." So, she was never invited to the house. Only when he was out of town did I invite her over and then she usually wouldn't come. "That place is too stuffy," she'd say. "Come over to my apartment." Sometimes

I did and sometimes I didn't. We didn't see each other much but we talked on the phone and had the occasional lunch. She would always tell me to, "Leave that bastard!" and then give me pointers on how to clean him out once I got the guts to do it.

She didn't know anything. If I ever left Grant, I would leave a poor woman. His lawyers would make certain of that. That's probably why I didn't leave. I had grown too accustomed to my lifestyle.

"I suppose you can take Emily, if that's what you want to do," he replied dryly as if taking Emily anywhere was *the* last thing anyone would want to do.

"Great!" I squealed and considered hugging him.

"Or you could take Trixie."

"I'm not taking Trixie," I said and shuddered. Trixie was his cousin and a little snob. He was always trying to get us to buddy up but she didn't like me and I didn't like her so it wasn't ever going to happen.

"Well, whatever," he said. "Stay a week and then come home in a better mood."

I couldn't help but grin like a fool. If I didn't despise him so much, I would have kissed him.

"Maybe when you're down there you can drive up to Palm Beach and see mom and dad," he said. "They'd love for you to visit."

My smile disappeared. There was always a catch.

He looked over my shoulder. "What is it, James?"

I turned to see James standing in the doorway. He nodded once at me and said, "There's someone here to see you, sir."

"Oh," Grant said and got up and left the room.

I was going to Miami! I was so happy and immersed in my thoughts, I didn't realize Grant had been gone a long time. I got up and went into the front hall where he stood at the open door talking with a man. Well, he wasn't talking, he was arguing.

"I told you," he hissed. "Now leave!"

What was going on? I walked over quietly, wanting to hear everything. I loved it when people gave Grant hell.

"You'll pay for this!" the man spat with an indeterminable accent and then turned to leave. "I won't let you get away with it!"

I walked over towards them and tried to get a good look at him, but Grant saw me and blocked the man from my view, then snapped, "Get out of here, Kara!"

I frowned at him and went back into the dining room. He finally came back in and when I asked what that was all about he just said, "Nothing. Let's finish eating."

I nodded and he sat back down and picked up his fork.

★ ★ ★ ★ ★

Emily and I had a great time in Miami. We arrived on a Saturday afternoon after we'd gotten hammered on the plane. We went to our hotel, showered, put on tight sexy outfits and hit a few clubs. We boogied till dawn, crashed at the hotel, then got up and did it all over again.

This repeated itself for the entire week. Oddly enough, neither one of us seemed to find any guys to pick up. We discussed this at length, wondering if the men were less attractive then we remembered or were we just getting pickier in our "old" age.

"Maybe we're not as hot as we think we are," Emily said one night as she put on make-up.

We stared at each other, then studied ourselves in the mirror. She was a few inches taller than me and pretty beyond words with beautiful dark hair and eyes. I stared at her and she stared at me and then we cracked up. We were both so hot we were smoking.

"Hell," she said. "What does it matter?"

"Maybe we're just drinking too much," I said.

"Yeah," she replied. "But that's supposed to make the men *more* attractive."

We squealed with laughter but decided not to let it bother us. We had a good time even if we weren't enjoying the company of exotic men.

I didn't go see Grant's parents either. I just decided if he asked, I'd say, "Oh, shit, I forgot all about that! Sorry!" Like that would work with him. Besides, he knew I probably wouldn't do it anyway.

On the last day, I told Emily if we didn't get some sun, everyone would think we had lied about going to Miami. So, we baked the afternoon away, talking, drinking and dreading going home.

"You know," Emily said. "You should glue his dick to his belly."

I nearly spit out my drink. "What the hell are you talking about?"

She said, "One of the girls at the club got pissed off at her boyfriend and when he was asleep, she glued his dick to his belly."

"Why did she do that?" I asked.

"Cause it hurts."

"How does it hurt?"

She turned on her side and stared at me. "When a guy wakes up, he usually has a hard-on, right?"

"I wouldn't know," I replied dryly.

She cracked up and wiped at her eyes. "They usually do, trust me. Anyway, when he woke up and found himself attached to himself like that, it hurt like hell."

"Wow," I said. "What did he do?"

"I think he used nail polish remover to detach himself."

"No," I said and shook my head. "What did he do for her to get so pissed off?"

"He cheated," she said. "What else?"

Yeah, what else?

"Oh, wow," she said and pointed. "Look at him."

I followed her gaze to a very tall and handsome guy. He was dressed in a dark blue sweatshirt and a pair of jeans. In addition to that he was wearing a pair of work boots. He was a good looking guy, with broad shoulders, which I loved, and big biceps. He was big but not *too* big. Just perfect.

"He looks hot," I said.

"That he does," she replied wistfully.

"No," I said. "I mean, he looks hot in those jeans and sweatshirt. Like he's burning up."

"Yeah," she said.

"I mean," I said. "He's not dressed for the beach. Why is he dressed like that?"

"He looks okay to me," she sighed.

"No, I mean, he looks like he's sweating and..." I trailed off. She wasn't listening anyway. She was staring at the guy, lusting after him. "Yeah, show me how you really feel, Emily."

She grinned and turned to me. "Let's invite him to dinner."

"No," I said.

"Why not?"

"He could be a weirdo or something," I said.

"Or something," she muttered slyly. "Come on! Let's invite him! We haven't met anyone all week."

I shook my head and glanced at the guy again. He was looking towards us and as soon as he saw me look his way, his head jerked away. What was that all about? It wasn't necessarily like he was checking us out. It was like he was... No. But it was. It was like he was watching us. *Creep*. I shuddered and leaned back on the lounge chair.

"Nap time?" Emily asked.

"Nap time," I said and pulled a floppy straw hat over my eyes. "Wake me in about an hour."

"I'm not your butler," she snapped.

"Pretty please?" I begged.

"I guess," she groaned.

"Thanks," I said. "I want to make sure I don't burn, so don't forget."

"Will do," she said. "Oh, shit, he's leaving."

I nodded and closed my eyes.

"Damn it," she said. "I told you we should have invited him."

"Oh, get over it," I said and felt myself drifting off. "Don't forget to wake me."

"I won't," she said. "It's getting hot out here."

It felt so good, though.

"I think I'll go in and take a shower," she said and stood, gathering her things. "And then I'll come back out and get you."

"Okay," I said. "You don't want a nap?"

"Unlike you, I don't get to take naps that often so I don't need them. I have a job, you know?"

"Yeah, yeah, I know," I muttered.

"I'll be back later," she said and pulled a pair of shorts on over her bikini.

"Okay," I said and opened my eyes and looked to the side. The guy was standing a few feet away from me. He hadn't left. He had just moved where I couldn't see him. I began to feel a little weird and scenarios of being felt up in my sleep started running through my mind. But then I just felt sleepy and wanted a nap, so I wrote it off as paranoia and closed my eyes again.

"There he is again," she said and chuckled. "Sure we can't ask him to dinner?"

"Emily!" I said. "Just go!"

She went. I closed my eyes and listened as her footsteps swished through the sand and got fainter and fainter as she walked away. I wondered if she was going in the direction of the hotel or in the direction of that guy. I lifted my hat and stared around. He was gone. So was she. I knew it! She had probably invited him to the room for a "drink" which meant a "fuck." Well, good for her. She was big girl and if that's what she wanted to do, I certainly wouldn't stand in her way. Maybe she'd share.

I drifted off for a moment, then was awakened by a, "Miss?"

I glanced to the side to see the waitress. "Yes?"

"Would you like another drink?"

"No," I said. "But thanks anyway."

"Charge these others to your room?" she asked and began to take all the glasses.

"No," I said and got up and rummaged in my purse. I pulled out a fifty and handed it to her. "Keep the change."

"Thank you."

I nodded and she disappeared. I drifted off as the ocean lulled me into sleep. With my eyes closed I could hear people talking and laughing and the occasional clink of ice in a drink and the *swoosh* of a beer can being opened. A slight breeze came up off the ocean and made me shiver, wanting a blanket. Then I heard something different. I thought about it and realized I had heard a zipper being pulled. Wait a minute... Had someone walked by me?

I came awake and listened, my spider senses tingling. I listened intently but only heard the same sounds as I'd heard a minute earlier. I listened more closely. I was about to pull my hat off again but realized I was probably being a little paranoid.

It was nothing. Nothing, nothing, nothing. I might even be punishing myself because I hadn't seen Grant's parents. Guilt always wreaked havoc with me.

I settled back down and closed my eyes. I loved being here so much that the thought of going back home didn't even bother me. I might ask Grant for an extension and spend the rest of the week on the beach. I hadn't been this relaxed since my last vacation.

I grinned because I was so spoiled. I was spoiled beyond belief. And that's probably why I didn't have the guts to leave Grant. I didn't have to do shit. And I liked not having to do shit.

I sighed and drifted off again. I was so relaxed that sleep just overcame me. I don't know how long I was asleep, but I suddenly became aware of my surroundings again. All of a sudden, I felt cold. I shivered and felt a prick, like a needle prick, in my arm. It might have been a bug bite or a bee sting. I don't know what it was but it hurt like hell. A numbing sensation coursed through my arm. I slapped at my arm and started to get up, but I fell back down on the lounge. I pulled my hat off and stared around. Everything was out of focus. The afternoon lull was over and most people were gone from the beach. I tried to come awake but nothing would come in focus and nothing made sense.

I stared at the inside of my arm and at a little red needle prick. *What the hell?* I shook my head and squeezed my eyes shut and then popped them open. I still couldn't focus. It was like... It was like...

Oh, God! It was like I was on drugs! Someone had drugged me! I could tell because once I feel off my horse and broke my arm and they drugged me so they could set it in the cast. I had insisted on it because I had been in so much pain. The drugged out feeling felt exactly like this. Was I dreaming?

I had to get up! I had to—

"Don't even think about it," came a voice from somewhere close by. A deep masculine voice, topped with an English accent. "Just lay there and it will all be over soon."

My head flopped to the side and then I saw him sitting on Emily's lounge chair. He's the one who had done this to me. It was the good looking guy that Emily had commented on, the one she wanted to invite to dinner. I was suddenly very angry at him, and at her. I was also ashamed of that initial attraction I had for him. I didn't know I was lusting after some sort of criminal.

Why had he drugged me?

I tried to tell him to leave me alone but I couldn't even move my lips, let alone summon the power to talk. It was like Novocain and about a thousand sleeping pills combined and I was drifting off quickly. I couldn't stop it. Try as I could to stay awake, I couldn't.

"Is she okay?"

It was the waitress! She had to know he drugged me. She would save me! She could just look at me and tell something was wrong.

"A little drunk," he said and smiled. "I'll take her up to her room in a bit."

"Oh," she said and nodded. "Have a great afternoon."

You have a great fucking afternoon! Thanks, lady! *Bitch!* How could she be so stupid! How could she... She... Her... The man was there and... Oh, God, I was fading out.

What was he going to do to me? I couldn't think of any rational reason other than he wanted sex. But he could have probably had sex if he'd just approached me. I mean, he was very attractive and I'm sure he didn't have to drug girls to get them to fuck him. But what if...

Oh, God! He was a serial killer! He was going to kill me! That's why he drugged me. He would take me as soon as I was fast asleep. He would take me and slice me up and play with me and... *The bastard!* And where would he take me? And most importantly what would he do when he got there? And what if...

Who did he think he was? Who the hell did he... Think. He think... Think!

I couldn't think straight. My eyes felt like someone had sewn them shut. I couldn't keep them open for the life of me. My mind was going to sleep and as much as I tried to hold on to consciousness, there wasn't a damn thing I could do.

All of a sudden, it didn't matter. It didn't matter because it was no use, no use in fighting it. I couldn't hang on anymore. I fell asleep and the last thing I remembered was his big arms slipping around my waist and lifting me off the lounge.

Blackberries.

I awoke in a very dark room. Who...what...when...
where...how...? Did...? I didn't know where I was or really *who* I
was. It was like waking from an intense and terrifying dream and
still feeling trapped in it.

I shook my head and took a breath and tried to focus on
something. I was still drugged and felt groggy. I could barely open
my eyes and I definitely couldn't sit up.

Where was I?

I was in some type of old house because it had that musky smell
old houses usually have. It was a large house because I could feel
the spaciousness of the room. It was drafty and had high ceilings.

Where was I?

I finally got my eyes open. I couldn't see anything for a minute.
I looked around and spotted a window. The curtains were drawn. I
had a feeling the moon was out because I could see a slit of light
through them.

I looked at the bed I was on. It was an antique French bed that
had a canopy that went all the way up to the ceiling. It was solid
wood that had been hand-carved and painted. The foot of it rose
up to cocoon its inhabitants. It was almost creepy. The linens on
the bed were old but I could tell they were good quality. The
cotton of the sheet felt just right and it felt clean, as if someone
had washed it before they put it on the bed. Above the sheet, the
duvet was made of quilted silk and very heavy. It was almost
binding me to the bed. But it might have been the drugs that made
me feel that way.

Where the hell was I?

I stared at the window and shook my head. It cleared for a
moment, and then threatened to go back to sleep. I had to get to
the window to see exactly where I was. I was about to get off the
bed when I noticed the shackles on my feet. I stared at them. I
knew they were shackles because I'd once seen a prison movie and
the actors had to wear them when they were working on a chain
gang.

Why did I have shackles on?

It all came back to me. The beach, Emily, that guy with the
English accent... The waitress. As soon as I got out of here, I was

going to have her fired! How could she have been so stupid? She was the only person who saw us together!

I became enraged. I was so pissed off, I shook. I couldn't believe I was actually here, where-the-fuck-ever "here" was! Where was here?! I thought about the man who had drugged me. I thought of him doing that, like some sick pervert. I wanted to hurt him so bad.

"Motherfucker!" I screamed and threw the covers off me. "You motherfucker!"

I stopped and caught my breath and listened. No scurrying feet. No doors thrown open. No concerned or angry looks. No threats. No nothing. I would kill that bastard when I saw him. I don't know how, but I would do it. Who did he think he was kidnapping me? I was a member of one of the wealthiest families in America and...

Oh, shit. Shit shit shit shit fucking shit! I had been kidnapped. Shivers went up and down my spine and I felt slightly nauseous. I began to shake with terror, with remorse for going to Miami. Why hadn't I just stayed home? Oh, because I wanted to get away from Grant for a while. What the hell was wrong with me? Why did I have to go to Miami and get kidnapped?

But it wasn't something I thought about much, being kidnapped. Apparently, I should have invested some brain power into it. Grant occasionally sent someone with me when I shopped. He was always saying that you could never be too careful and I guess you couldn't. The asshole had probably been watching us all week. He had made his move to kidnap me as soon as Emily disappeared from my site.

Emily! What about Emily? Was she here? No. She had gone back to the room. *Phew.* She was probably okay. And when she came back out to get me, she would see I was gone and she'd call Grant and he'd put the fuzz on it and they were probably outside scoping out the place as I lay there. They were waiting for the right time to make their move.

I listened. Nothing. There wasn't a cop for miles and I knew it.

I was screwed. I began to scream even though I knew no one could hear me and the one who could didn't care. He didn't care because he was the one who had brought me here.

There was nothing else I could do. So I cried. I cried until morning came. I sat in that dark room and cried and sometimes I screamed. I screamed until I lost my voice. And after that, there wasn't much I could do. I couldn't do shit but wait and see what he wanted. Or how *much* he wanted. How much ransom was he asking? Hopefully not too much. Grant may have been rich but he could be a cheap bastard when he wanted to be. He hated to part with money.

Well, he'd better pay up quick and get me out of here. If he prolonged it, I would beat him to death. It would be just like him to do something like that. Get the best price. Rich people hated to pay the full price, that's why they were rich. They always bargained and always got what they wanted because they could wait everyone else out.

Damn him anyway.

I looked down at myself. It didn't appear that I'd been beaten or anything. The place where he had given me the injection had turned into a little bruise and was all but gone. I did have another bruise at the top of my arm and one on my leg. Oh, I had bumped into a chair in the hotel. I stared at my polka dot bikini and shook my head. He could have at *least* let me change into something else. I shivered. It was kinda cold in here.

I was about to grab the covers when my kidnapper walked in. *Who the hell was he?* I stared at him and, for a moment, I was intrigued. It might have been because he was so big. His movements were big and he had big arms. He was handsome and muscular, just the way I liked them. He had a big mouth, too, with nice lips. Did he know any big words? I doubted it. Big boots on his big feet. He also had big hands.

I looked away from him quickly.

He set a tray of food on the bedside table. The contents consisted of water and bread. *Give me a break!* How very typical. I mean, I didn't expect eggs Benedict or anything, but this? He had probably seen some movie about kidnapping and learned what to do and what to feed his victims. I curled my nose up at the food.

He started out of the room without a word.

"How much are you asking?" I said.

He stopped but didn't turn around. "Eat your breakfast."

"Go to hell," I said. "You know, after this is said and done, I will have you buried under a prison somewhere."

He shook his head a little and said, "That right?"

"You might as well let me go now," I said. "And save yourself the trouble."

"Eat your breakfast," he said and left the room.

I started to yell something at him but stopped myself. I hated his guts. But when would he be back again? It was going to be a long time and I knew it. I stared at the shackles and fell back on the bed, defeated.

I don't know how long I sat in that room on that bed but it was long time. I knew everything about it from the peeling but once very nice embossed wallpaper to the chandelier to the old wood floor. All I did was sit there and look around at it. There were three doors, one to my left and one to my right and one straight ahead. I figured the one to the right was the bathroom which I needed badly. The other one was to the closet. Oh, and of course, there was the door which led to the outside world.

I cursed that door and willed it to open and for someone to walk through it and rescue me. It didn't and no one came.

Everything in the room was French, from the bed to the gigantic mirror on the opposite wall where I could check my hair and face, if I chose to. There was an antique dresser and a small dressing table. There were two nightstands and on top, two ornate antique lamps with beading. I liked the lamps. I turned them on and left them on all day.

It had been a really nice room at one time. I wondered who had lived here, what kind of woman she was. She had taste and money, whoever she had been. Had *she* ever been shackled to the bed?

I couldn't get off the damn bed. I was chained to it. Shackled. That really pissed me off, too. I could, however, stretch my legs out but that was about it. I couldn't move my ankles and they began to cramp so badly I cried. I cried because I felt so stupid and I hated being here. I hated everything. I felt sorry for myself for the better part of the day.

Night fell again and I was still alone. I finally succumbed and ate the bread and drank the water. I was starving and even licked the plate though there wasn't anything on it. I would have given anything for a slice of pizza.

It took forever to fall asleep. I curled into a ball and closed my eyes tight. I could hear something running across the floorboard and I prayed to God it was just my imagination and not a rat. I hated rats with a passion. I was glad the bed was up high off the floor so they couldn't jump on it.

I really hated it there.

I finally fell asleep and awoke very early. I was actually very refreshed, as if I'd been on detox. I hadn't had a soda or a cigarette in a couple of days. I could feel my ribs and my stomach was so flat it looked caved in.

I lay there for a few minutes trying to stretch out my legs. I wasn't very successful and fell back on the bed cursing. All of a sudden the door slammed open. It was my kidnapper and he was carrying my tray of "food." Today there was the addition of an egg.

An egg. He really went all out, didn't he?

I eyed him. He was a thug, that's what he was. A total thug. A big, masculine thug with an English accent. I usually liked English accents. Grant had a few English friends. I flirted with them from time to time but that was about it. They weren't that cute. At least as not as cute as this guy. He wasn't just cute, he was handsome. He was so strong looking. So...*masculine*. And he had that thug appeal. That "I don't give one shit about anything" attitude that made people nervous. I could imagine him—

I stopped myself. I hated him. He eyed me with disdain and I returned his gaze.

"Thanks for the egg," I said dryly. "Looks like with the kind of money you're going to get out of my husband you could at least throw a girl a piece of bacon."

"Shut it," he muttered.

I was aghast. Who did he think he was? I sensed a danger from him, as if he could tear me from limb to limb if he chose, but I didn't let that stop me. "Listen to me, buddy—"

He held up one finger. "Shut it."

I gulped and shut it. I wouldn't have but the look on his face— this side of murderous—told me to, though it killed me to do so.

He leaned over and unlocked the shackles. It felt divine once he had them off. My feet felt light and airy. I hadn't realized how heavy those things were. It was almost as if my feet could lift up off the bed by themselves.

"Try anything and I will put these right back on," he said and pointed to a door. "There's the toilet. I suppose you need to use it."

I blushed three shades of red. Mostly because I had "used" it in the bed last night accidentally. I was so ashamed but I couldn't hold it any longer. I felt like a bedwetter.

"When you're done, strip these sheets," he said and walked over to the door, shut it and leaned against it.

I stared at the bathroom door and jumped off the bed. My ankles cracked and popped. I groaned in pain. I hadn't used them in two days. The blood flow, once restored, made my skin itch. The pain was excruciating. But the pain of needing to urinate was more so.

"Go on now," he condescended, as if he were speaking to a disobedient child.

I shot him a glare and hobbled towards the bathroom. My ankles were on fire. I almost wanted to get down on my hands and knees and crawl. I wouldn't have given him the satisfaction. I opened the door and peered in. It would have been a nice bathroom if it hadn't been so old. I peeked around the door at him and said, "Does it work?"

He nodded.

I raced inside and started to shut the door. I stopped when I saw him shaking his head at me.

"Uh uh," he called. "Leave that door open."

"I will not!"

"I wouldn't argue if I were you," he said and held up the shackles.

I shuddered and left the damn door open. I turned the faucet on before I sat down on the commode so he couldn't hear. I hated the fact that I had a shy bladder but I cannot stand for anyone to listen to me go to the bathroom. I did my business and washed my hands and came back out. As soon as I entered the room, he threw a dress at me.

"Put that on."

I glanced at him and shook the dress out. It was an old light blue calico dress, a dress someone might have worn during the

Depression or at least the eighties. I threw it back at him. "I don't think so."

He gave me a hellacious look and started towards me. I was almost scared shitless. He looked like he was going to beat the shit out of me. I started to jump and run but he had me then, by the waist. I squirmed and fought against him for a moment until he drew back his hand and slapped me square on the ass. The sound of a big *pop* filled the room and it stung like hell.

Did he just do that? Oh, yeah, he did.

I was so pissed off, I was shaking. I tried to claw at his face and pull his eyeballs out, but he grabbed my hands and put them behind my back. Oh God! I felt so helpless and so stupid and like a little girl. I wanted to kill him! I screamed, "You bastard—"

He turned me around and bent his body over mine until I was staring at the floor. I gave another jerk but he held me tight. I couldn't move. I screamed bloody murder but he held me there and let me scream until my voice cracked.

He picked up the dress, held it open and said, "Step into it."

"I'd rather die," I hissed.

"Now," he ordered and gave me another push. I screamed again. Another push. We stayed like that for a long few seconds. I could feel his heartbeat on my back. I could feel my own heart threatening to come out of my chest. I was suddenly very weak and I stared over at the food tray. My mouth watered. I was so hungry.

I stepped into the damn dress.

He pulled it up and zipped it. It was little tight in the chest and across the ass. I stared at myself in the mirror. It didn't look too bad though it was so old and ragged the seams threatened to rip if I moved too much. I actually looked pretty hot, like some barefoot country chick on her way to pick blackberries. Oh, God, I would have loved to have some blackberries.

"How much are you asking?" I asked and adjusted the dress across my breasts. His eyes were on my breasts as I did that. I stared at him, narrowing my eyes. "Huh? How much are you asking for the ransom?"

"That's none of your business," he said.

"I am the one who's been kidnapped," I hissed. "I deserve to know."

"None of your business," he said evenly. "Now eat and we'll go downstairs."

I almost crossed my arms and huffed, but I was so hungry, I didn't argue. Starvation will do that to you. I raced to the food and gobbled it up. I drank it down with the water and wiped the back of my mouth with my hand. He watched me, studied me as if he couldn't quite figure me out, as if he had never expected me to act like that, to act so lowly, so much like an animal. I was so embarrassed.

"Come on, then," he said and started out of the room.

"Where are we going?" I asked.

"Come on, then," he repeated and waited for me in the doorway.

I groaned and followed him. We made our way through the old house. I could tell it was a Mediterranean type mansion. A very old mansion with cracking plaster and falling down wallpaper. It was huge. We walked down the hall, then down a flight of stairs and then to the foyer where a no-longer functioning gigantic fountain sat. I stared at it, at the fish whose mouths no longer pumped water into the pool and at the carved marble flowers. It was beautiful even if it was so old.

He didn't say a word and led me around the fountain and down another hall and into the kitchen. *The kitchen?*

The kitchen was huge; one whole wall was lined with white cabinets with peeling paint. A big white porcelain sink with an old silver faucet sat in the middle of the counter. An old refrigerator sat by itself against the wall and directly in front of it, a huge old farmer's table with big French provincial chairs covered in blue French toile.

I glanced out the window. The yard was overgrown with weeds and Spanish moss hung from the huge trees. To the left was a gravel drive that was lined with a wrought iron fence. I knew we were still in Florida because I could smell the sea salt in the air. The ocean had to be nearby.

Where were we?

We couldn't be that far away from Miami. I was willing to bet the house had belonged to a plantation owner because that's where a lot of them had built their houses. Grant told me something about it once because he'd seen something on television about it.

"I want all these cabinets washed down, inside and out," he instructed. "After that, start on the pantry."

Did he kidnap me to be his maid or something? I glanced at the pantry door, then back at him. He was serious. I crossed my arms and told him, "Do it yourself."

"I won't give you a warning this time."

A warning? He hadn't given me a warning in the first time. He'd just slapped me on the ass. I rolled my eyes and said, "Whatever."

"You will do it," he said.

I shook my head. He took one step towards me, the same look on his face I'd seen earlier. It still scared me. I yelped and jumped and grabbed a plate off the table.

He almost grinned. I wanted to smack that look off his face. My nostrils flared as I fumed. He shook his head as if my look humored him. Then he went to the backdoor and opened it. I stared at it, at the outside and I had a sudden urge to push past him and run away. He blocked the door and turned to me.

"It should go without saying," he said. "But, if you try to run away, there'll be hell to pay."

I glared at him.

"We're in the middle of nowhere and by the time it would take you to find a road, or a telephone for that matter, I would have already caught up with you and then…"

I gulped. "Then what?"

"You don't want to find out."

"You can't keep me here," I said. "The police will be looking for me and—"

"They're not going to find you here," he told me. "No one knows about this place."

And with that he left. I stared after him and felt a sudden panic. I was really kidnapped and I was really here now. There was no one to call and no one to help. No one was coming for me, either. I was alone. I was under his power. I had to do what he said. And there was nothing I could do about it. It felt surreal, all of it. It was like I was watching it instead of being in it. I felt the walls closing in on me. I felt nauseous.

I threw the plate against the wall to stop the panic. It hit the wall, dented it and broke into a million pieces. As I stared at the pieces, a sense of hopelessness overcame me, impending doom. I didn't have a chance. I crumbled to the floor and began to sob. I cried for a good ten minutes. It felt good to get it out but at the same time I felt foolish for letting him get to me. I was stronger than this. But it was so hard to be strong right then.

I sat up and wiped at my face and stared around the kitchen. It would take forever to clean those damn cabinets. I thought about home. If I was home I'd be sleeping in. James would wake me with breakfast and a funny little story. I would take a long shower and get dressed. Maybe I'd go see my manicurist; she always had the best gossip. After that I would call Emily and we might have lunch somewhere nice. I would drive my Jaguar over to her apartment and we'd talk about what a shithead Grant was and then I'd leave and go back home and dress for dinner with Grant. Sometimes he would be in a good mood and he'd tell me a joke he'd heard. I would feel sad and tell him I wanted a divorce and he'd say, "Don't start this again," because he knew I was never going to leave.

I was suddenly so ashamed I hadn't appreciated what I had. I was such a whiner, such a bitch about it. Most people would kill to be in my position but I didn't appreciate it. I deserved this.

But I wasn't about to let that bastard treat me like shit. But then again, I didn't have much choice. Those cabinets weren't going to clean themselves. It might be good for me to do something to keep my mind off being kidnapped.

I got up and started on the cabinets. I opened all the doors and stared at the old junk in there. Old pots and plates and... Hey, those plates were nice. Nice clean white China. We had some just like this at the house. I'd eaten peanut butter and jelly sandwiches off them. They were the "old" plates, ones that were used for sandwiches.

I almost collapsed in sobs again. I told myself to get a grip and began to empty the cabinets. I used to do stuff like this all the time. I'd cleaned cabinets before. I was a good cabinet cleaner. I just didn't want to clean cabinets for *him*. I didn't want to do anything nice for him.

I found some bleach under the sink and a few old rags and spotted a bucket in the corner. I went to it and filled it up with water. I was surprised that there was hot water coming out of the tap. Did he live here or something? I shook my head and the hard worker in me came out and in a matter of hours, I had the top row of cabinets cleaned and sparkling.

After that my stomach growled. I went over to the refrigerator and opened it. It was filled with food. He had all kinds of food in there and he'd given me bread and water? What a bastard. I grabbed some ham and crammed it in my mouth, then found a soda. I ate and drank until I was full and then went back to work.

I stayed in the kitchen all day, not venturing outside of it except to go to the bathroom. The house was so old and big, it was creepy. I didn't think about what kinds of things lived in it, either. I focused on my work and that made the day pass quickly.

The sun was going down when I finished. I even mopped the floor and dusted off the top of the refrigerator. I was very proud of myself. It looked good. I sighed and sat down at the table. When was he coming back? What if he wasn't? What if he'd been caught and was in jail right now?

I stared at the door. Did I dare? Did I?

I swallowed hard and thought about it. I could leave. I didn't have any shoes. I stared at my bare feet, which were really dirty. *Ick.* I should take a bath. No, I wouldn't. If I took a bath and smelled fresh and clean, he might get a few ideas. He might want to rape me. I'd stay dirty. That way he wouldn't want anything to do with me.

I sniffed. I needed some deodorant. How long could I stay like this and not get sick of myself? As long as he held me prisoner, that's how long. He might make me stay here and clean this old house, but he couldn't make me clean myself.

I shook myself. My thoughts were bordering on the delusional. Why was that? Sensory deprivation. I was going through sensory depravation. But it all made sense, though.

I sighed and stared at the door. Did I dare? I dared. I wasn't a mouse. I was a human being and I could walk out that door. He probably wasn't coming back anyway. It was all a test. Maybe Grant had set it up because I didn't go see his parents. No, that couldn't be right. Could it?

What did it matter? I was still here, wasn't I? Yeah, but not for long.

I got up slowly and walked towards the door. I had a sudden urge to run but proceeded with caution. When I got to it, I opened it slowly and peered out. It was near dark. I wouldn't have much time to find a road. I looked around for any sign of him. I didn't see him or hear him. I noticed an old pool to the side and an old set of stables that were just about falling down. Behind the carriage house were what looked like woods. Brush.

It was now or never, so it was now. I took off running and took off in the direction of the woods and got lost almost immediately. I didn't know which way was where. Soon, the direction of the house was gone and night came in a swoosh. All of a sudden, everything was dark and dreary and damn scary. I heard animals moving around and thought about snakes and alligators. Oh, God, alligators! Why had I run this way? Why didn't I take the driveway?

I didn't know. I wasn't myself. I wasn't thinking straight. The only thing on my mind was freedom and I was drunk with it, with the thought of getting away.

I took a breath and looked around. *Okay*, I told myself, *just go slow*. I began to walk cautiously but stepped on a sharp rock that tore a hole into my foot anyway. I let out a scream and it echoed up and into the trees, then was gone. Pain shot through my foot but I stifled my next scream, sure my kidnapper would hear me.

I wanted to cry, break down. I couldn't. The pain in my foot was excruciating but I forced myself to keep walking. After a while I had the mild impression that I might just be walking in circles. I cursed myself for leaving, cursed myself for getting kidnapped, for being a bitch. I felt like I had brought all of this on myself for some reason. Maybe it was just Karma.

I felt tears on my face and realized I was crying, bordering on sobbing. I sat down by a tree, pulled my knees up to my chest and began to sob, loudly enough that the animals scurried away and left me alone. I don't know how long I sat there, but all of a sudden I heard footsteps and then a bright light was shined in my eyes. I squinted and held my hand over the light. It was him. I was almost happy to see him.

"Get up," he ordered.

"I can't," I whimpered. "I hurt my foot."

He stared at me for half a second before bending over and sweeping me up like a sack of potatoes. He threw me across his shoulder and carried me all the way back to the house. I didn't fight; I just hung on and was glad he carried me because my foot was throbbing with pain.

When we got back to the house, he took me into the kitchen and literally threw me on the floor. I landed with a loud thump. *Ouch.*

I just lay there and waited for him to do something. What was he going to do? He just stood there and stared at me, cursed under his breath and left the room. He came back a minute later with rubbing alcohol and some cotton balls. He grabbed my foot and poured the alcohol straight onto my wound. It burned like fire. I let out a scream and my entire leg shook with stinging pain. Once he was done cleaning it, he bandaged it.

"Now take off your dress," he said.

I stared up at him. "What?"

He was taking off his belt. No, he wasn't. Yes, he was. *No!* There was no way I was going to let him beat me.

"I told you not to leave the house, didn't I?" he said.

"But…" I said and considered my words. "I just wanted to go for a walk."

He almost smiled. "Do it."

"No," I said. "I didn't do anything wrong. I just went for a walk and got lost."

"You're not a very good liar."

I didn't know how to respond to that. I don't think he meant it as a compliment.

He bent down and stared into my eyes. I tried to look away once, but I couldn't. His eyes were blue and they sparkled a little. They were very nice eyes. I shook myself. What the hell was wrong with me?

"I told you not to leave the house, didn't I?" he said. "And you did so anyway, didn't you?"

I nodded like a bad girl.

"Now you have to be punished."

I stared him dead in the eye and spat, "I don't think so."

"I think so," he said and grabbed my arm and pulled me up off the floor. I struggled against him but he was a lot bigger and stronger than me. Besides that, he didn't have a hole in his foot. He pulled me over to the table, sat down and pulled me across his lap.

He didn't use the belt, which he had dropped on the way over to the table. He used his hand.

I wriggled but he still managed to push the dress up over my hips and then he managed to spank me, like I was some little girl. He kept at it and though it didn't hurt as much as it embarrassed me, I screamed bloody murder. He didn't stop until my ass was as red as my face.

He pushed me off his lap and said, "Now go to bed."

I glared at him and pulled the dress down. I turned on my heel, changed my mind and turned back around with my hand on my hip. "I just want you to know that that didn't hurt."

Oh, my God. I was such a dumbass! I realized that as soon as the words were out of my mouth. His face took on a slight look of slight shock, then humor. But just before I could congratulate myself on my snappy comeback, I realized my mistake of being a smartass. The humor part only lasted a split second before it was replaced with rage.

He had to be crazy. *Had* to be.

He leapt up from his chair, grabbed the belt off the floor and ran at me. I ran/limped out of the room as quickly as I could. He was hot on my heels and chased me through the house. I kept thinking I should try to get into one of the rooms but none of the doors would open. *Great!* Why hadn't I gone through the house and found a safe place where I could hide? You know, just in case some maniac was chasing me. I was idiot, that's why!

He caught me near the fountain. He grabbed the back of the dress and it ripped in two. I wriggled out of it and took off again, but he grabbed me and pulled me down. I screamed and punched at him, but then he was over me and the belt was licking my legs and ass. And it hurt a lot worse than his hands. He swatted at my legs until I begged him to please *stop!* He swatted at me until I gave up and just laid there. He swatted at me until he had my ass officially whipped.

I hated him so much. I would kill him one day. I would! He couldn't treat me like this! I wasn't a disobedient child! I was a grown woman! I didn't deserve this! I seethed as I stared at him and screamed in his face, "How could you do that? That how could you do that to me?"

"That'll be all now," he said as if I were his maid or something.

"Oh, I don't think that's all," I hissed and waited for him to do something so I could slap him.

"Now go to your room," he hissed and turned on his heel.

I jumped up and, with tears streaming down my face, screamed, "I'll go to my room, you son of a bitch!"

He gave a wave and disappeared. I wished I had a gun. I cried for a minute or so and told myself I would get out of here someday. I was about to head to the front door when I realized how tired I was. I was so tired I could have fallen over. I should just go to bed and worry about escaping tomorrow.

I turned and looked around. Where the hell was my room?

Sourpuss.

I slept in. He didn't wake me as he had the day before. I woke up early but went back to sleep and when I woke up again and didn't see my tray of food, I went back to sleep. I think I slept the better part of the day away.

There was no sign of him.

Like I gave a shit. I never wanted to see him again. I finally got up and checked my ass out in the mirror. No bruises or welts or anything but my legs were slightly red. Maybe I had thought it hurt more than it actually did. Still, what a bastard. When Grant found out about this he would kill him. I had to laugh at that one. Grant would probably want to fuck him. I'm sure a lot of people did. But I didn't. I shuddered, thinking of him touching me, but then... No, I hated him and the thought just made me cringe.

I stopped moving for a second and heard footsteps. It was him. I was almost relieved. I shook myself. What the hell was that about? I ran back to the bed and jumped in, covered myself and pretended to be asleep.

He stomped into the room and went to the window where he threw open the curtains. The sun blinded me for a moment and I buried my head in my pillow and ignored him. I wasn't about to let him know I knew he was in the room.

He came over to the bed and said, "Get up."

I still pretended to be asleep.

"I said get up."

I ignored him, though I was dying to tell him to fuck off.

"Now."

I didn't move.

"Do you want another row?" he asked.

Another *row?* Why would I want to fight with him when I knew I couldn't win? And that's what killed me. I couldn't win. I never won any fights, not with him or with my sisters or with Grant. I was a bad fighter because I was weak. And, unlike him, *I* didn't like hurting other people. Maybe that's what made me weak.

"Now," he ordered.

"I'm not getting up," I said calmly.

"You will," he said and reached down to take the covers. But I was already ahead of him and moved just before he got his chance to snatch them away. I jumped up and pulled them under my body and dared him to take them. He dared and jerked them out from under me and, as a result, I rolled off the bed and landed on the floor. It was long way down from that big bed and my ass bounced on the floor before landing with a thump. *Ow!* My ass literally ached. As if I wasn't already sore from yesterday.

I was as mad as a wet hen. But I didn't move or cry out from the pain. I just sat on the other side of the bed and waited, noticing all I had on was my bikini, which I was sick of wearing. Damn, what I wouldn't have given for a pair of pajamas.

He came around and, when he saw me sitting there, he almost smiled. But of course, he didn't. I don't think he *could* smile. I couldn't imagine this guy ever smiling. He never smiled. It was doubtful he even smiled when he was little kid. All the other kids probably called him sourpuss.

"You've got work to do," he said.

I shook my head and glared at the wall. "I'm not doing anything else for you."

"You will," he said and grabbed my arm.

I jerked it back just before he got his grip on it. "No, I won't. You tore my dress and I don't have anything to wear."

"I'll get you another one."

"Oh, really?" I said. "Are you going to make another trip to the Salvation Army?"

Again, he almost smiled but he wouldn't let himself. That's how much of a bastard he was. He bent down in front of me and said, "You did a fantastic job on the kitchen yesterday. It looks brilliant."

Was that a compliment or something? Wow, gee, you're welcome. Did he think that little compliment would make me do his bidding or something? What an asshole! If he ever got a woman, he'd probably give her a frying pan for Valentine's. Hopefully, she would bash him over the head with it. I stared at him, still bent down in front of me. I wanted to kick him over.

"I thought you might like to know that," he said, obviously proud of himself for being able to say something nice.

What a prick! That just flew all over me and before I could stop myself, I pushed at him. He lost his balance and fell back on his ass. The look on his face was priceless. He couldn't believe I'd just done that. I tried to contain my laughter but couldn't and was almost squealing with it. He hadn't expected that, had he? Served him right. But then, I immediately regretted pushing him over and then laughing about it. He was really pissed off now and that meant I was going to have to pay for my insubordination.

He jumped up, pulled me up by the wrist and then out of the room. We didn't say a word and he didn't stop until we got to the kitchen, where he pushed me into the room. I looked around, crossed my arms and prepared for the fight. But then I felt so tired and I still wanted to laugh about pushing him over. I decided to just let it go. It's hard to stay mad for that long. It takes too much energy. And I was hungry.

He left the room momentarily and came back with two cans of paint and what looked like a pair of shorts and a top.

"What's that for?" I asked and pointed at the cans.

"You're going to paint the cabinets," he informed me and threw the clothes at me.

"Like hell I am," I said. "You know, I'm not a slave here. I deserve better treatment."

He glared at me, still pissed off. I glared back before looking at the clothes. Yesterday I had a calico dress and today I had a gingham shirt that *might* cover my tits if I was lucky and a pair of pedal pusher jeans that had be as old as my mother. Where did he get this crap?

"You're a criminal," I said and stared at the clothes. "And you've got terrible taste."

He just stared at me.

"I'm not wearing this shit," I said. "And I deserve better treatment. You have no right to do this to me and—"

"You've got no choice but to do as I tell you," he said. "Now shut up and do as you're told."

I bit my lip to keep from yelling something terrible at him. I bit it because I knew I'd pushed him far enough.

He started out the back door. "I suppose I don't have to tell you to stay put, do I?"

"You don't have to," I said smartly. "But you should."

He almost smiled again. One day, I'd get to see his teeth but this was not the day. He covered the smile with a scowl. His teeth were probably rotten and that's why he never smiled. The poor bastard.

"By the way," I said. "What's your name?"

He was about to shut the door when I asked that. He stopped and stared at me for a moment, as if he couldn't believe I would even want to know. A spark of interest came to his eyes. He looked at me a little differently, too.

"Not that I care or anything," I said.

"Why do you want to know?" he asked softly.

"Well, we haven't been properly introduced."

He kept staring at me like that, with that different look. Then he replied a little awkwardly, "It's Nate."

Nate? Short for Nathaniel, right? What was his last name? I didn't ask. I just said dryly, "Well, I'm Kara. It's nice to meet you."

Again, the almost smile. Again, he stopped before it could come to fruition. "Oh, and take a bath," he said before he slammed the door shut. "You're getting ripe."

"Fuck you!" I yelled, though it didn't do me any good. I sighed and picked up the clothes and started to pull them on. But I still had my bikini on. It needed to be washed or something. I looked around to make sure he wasn't peeking through the window, then stripped it off and pulled the clothes on. I washed it out in the sink and hung it over the back of a chair to dry.

After I found a rubber band in one of the drawers and pulled my hair back, I got to work. I actually liked to paint. I hadn't done it in a while but it didn't take long for me to get back into the groove.

I stopped in the afternoon and ate some of the food out of the refrigerator. After I ate, I decided to go on a tour of the house as it didn't scare me as much as it had yesterday. I supposed it was becoming familiar and I should get acquainted with it, just in case he decided to chase me again. I needed a place to hide.

I took off out of the kitchen and went down the hall. I opened the first door I came to. It was a maid's room, very small with a tiny closet, bed and dresser. The next door was an also a maid's room and the next. I finally made it down the hall and to the right was the large sitting room. It had a vaulted ceiling and several large wool rugs scattered over the oak floor, which didn't look to be in too bad of shape. There was a long red velvet couch and several wing chairs and bunches of tables scattered here and there, all topped with neat looking knickknacks and books and ashtrays and lamps. All old and collectible.

Whose house was this? Who had lived here? And why the hell was it being used to hold me prisoner? Why not find a cave or something?

None of it made sense. But I did remember Grant saying once that a lot of wealthy people who lost their money just let their houses go. When they couldn't afford the upkeep, they just moved out or rented them. They couldn't bear selling them, especially if they had been in the family for a long time.

I kept walking and found more sitting rooms and upstairs more bedrooms. All the rooms were filled with antique furniture. I even saw some Louis XIV chairs as well as some Chippendales.

I went out the front door and took in the enormous lawn. There was yet another fountain that no longer worked. I walked over to the stables and noticed they were relatively clean and in good condition as they were made of stone. In the back I found the pool and the carriage house. It was all in bad shape but I could tell that it had once been beautiful.

Why would someone walk away from this?

I didn't know. But I did know I had to get back to work, as much as I hated doing it. I worked all day and have to admit, the kitchen looked a helluva lot better when I was done.

He didn't come back until it was dark. I had found a radio in one of the rooms and plugged it in and was listening to oldies when he came through the door. He was carrying a bag of groceries. We didn't speak.

He put up the groceries then proceeded to cook supper. I was amazed at how well he did it and even more so when he prepared me a plate of steaming food and sat it down in front of me. It was loaded down with a big steak and mashed potatoes and steamed vegetables. He poured me a glass of red wine, sat down opposite me and we ate. I tried to take my time but I was so hungry I was almost grunting as I ate. The food was delicious.

He ignored me and finished first, pushed his plate back and said, "After you finish the dishes, you need to take a bath."

I didn't reply.

"I said," he said. "You need a bath. You're rank."

"I'm not taking a bath," I snapped.

"Clean the dishes," he said and stood.

"*You* clean the dishes," I said and stared him dead in the eye.

A smile flickered in his eyes. *Come on!* Do it, damn it! *Smile!* For the love of God, let me see that you have teeth. I would have to wait. The "smile" or whatever it had been was gone almost instantaneously.

"You heard me," he said and left the room.

I'd clean the damn dishes, all right! I grabbed a dish, ran to the backdoor, opened it and started to hurl it. I stopped. I was acting really irrational. It wasn't the dish's fault he was an asshole. Besides, if I threw the dishes out in the yard, he'd probably beat my ass again.

I washed the dishes and then I swept the floor, wiped off the counter and then the table. I hated to admit it, but I actually liked cleaning. *God!* What a woman I was. I had missed doing it, too. For over ten years I had people picking up and cleaning after me. Whenever I tried to help, they'd shake their heads and say, "Oh, no, let me." So I let 'em.

After I was finished, he came back into the room and said, "I've drawn you a bath."

"What?" I asked, flabbergasted.

"You heard me," he said. "Now go clean yourself."

"Why are you so fascinated with this bath business?" I asked.

"You know why."

"So you can take advantage of me? I don't think so."

He seemed a little embarrassed. "Got a lip on you, don't you?"

"Yeah, as a matter of fact," I said and held up a couple of fingers. "I got two."

He was going to do it! He was going to crack up! I waited in anticipation. It was in vain.

"You heard me," he said. "Now go."

"Whatever," I said and tossed the dish towel I'd been holding to the side. "I think I'll go outside for a few minutes."

"No, you won't," he growled. "You'll take a bath."

I don't know why I was so against taking a bath. I usually can't go a day without one. And here I was almost... How long had I been here? I counted. At least four days? Five? Three? I didn't know but it seemed like an eternity.

"Go on," he said.

"I'll do it later," I replied and started towards the back door.

"Don't do this," he said.

"Do what?" I said and whirled around. "I don't want a bath! Okay? I'm not a little kid you can push around. I am grown woman who does what she damn well pleases and if you and your..." I shook my head at him. "Head can't understand that, then fuck you both."

"My *head?*"

"I couldn't think of anything else," I snapped. "Sometimes I'm like that. I get flustered."

He stared at me as if trying to figure me out. He'd be a long time on that. I couldn't even figure myself out.

"I'm telling you again," he said slowly. "Take a bloody bath!"

"*I don't want a bath!*" I screamed at the top of my lungs and shook my fists.

His nostrils flared. Oh, shit. He was pissed off but so was I. This battle of wills was getting a little out of control. I knew I was in for some shit. His face told me as much.

He walked over to me, grabbed my arm and pulled me through the house and into "my" room. I screamed bloody murder all the way there. Once in the bathroom, he picked me up and put me into the bathtub. Water and bubbles went everywhere. I tried to get back up but he held me in there, not letting me move.

Oh, God. I was so going to kill him. Now my clothes were soaking wet. I swatted at him. He grabbed both of my wrists and held me tight. I moved this way and that but it was no use. He was a strong son of a bitch.

Finally, his grip loosened. I took my chance and tried to slap him. His grip tightened again and I fought with him until I got tired and he let go of me. We stared at each other for a long time, neither one of us moving. Something moved inside of me. It moved so swiftly and then disappeared but I had felt it. I felt it then. I felt something. I didn't know what it was, but it was so strong I almost choked. It was strong and it was magnetic and it was forceful. It had as much energy as a steam engine. Maybe it was hatred.

I pushed bubbles off my face and screamed, "You bastard! Why did you do that?"

He got in my face and yelled, "Because you stink!"

"You should have thought about that before you kidnapped me!"

"Now get to cleaning," he said and started out of the room.

"That's all you think about!" I yelled. "Cleaning, cleaning, cleaning! You're obsessed!"

He turned back to me and shook his head in confusion. But he knew what I was talking about. He was a typical type-A personality. Everything had to be just so, didn't it? And if wasn't, he would go mad. Talk about anal-retentive.

Maybe I did stink, though. But still, fuck him. I huffed and crossed my arms. He shot me one look before stomping over to the tub. What the hell was he going to do?

"Are you going to do it?" he asked.

"What?"

"Clean yourself."

"I'd rather," I said and screamed, "Die!"

In one swift motion, his hand came down and yanked my shirt off. Before I could blink, he did the same to my pants, which had been glued to my body. This guy was strong.

I suddenly realized I was naked.

He didn't seem to notice. He took a washcloth and began to clean me, first my face and neck. I fought against him but finally gave up and let him do it, feeling so silly and stupid I couldn't stand myself. He put the washcloth down and washed my hair, soaping it up. I just sat there and fumed, wishing I had something to hit him over the head with.

The room got very quiet as he washed me. So quiet I began to feel embarrassed. I felt my nakedness, too. I slid deeper into the tub. I wasn't a prude. I didn't mind nudity but I just didn't want him to see me like that. I was afraid he would see my flaws. I could pick out every one of my flaws; things I hated about myself, things that I had yet to accept. Like the deep scar on my belly from appendicitis. Like the freckles on my face I tried to hide with make-up. Like my earlobes. I hated my earlobes. Like the...

The room was really quiet.

I started to say something, but then I didn't. His movements slowed, and then stopped. He glanced at me, then at my body. I felt a nervous shudder come over me. Something was going to happen. What, I didn't know. But it was going to be big and it would change my life and maybe even my opinion of him.

I wanted it to happen.

He took his time looking me over good and then began to wash me again. The washcloth glided smoothly along my skin. He rinsed it out and began to clean my neck, then down to my breasts. He hesitated there and cupped them with the washcloth before he rinsed it again and brought it to my stomach. I watched his hand move along it and then down towards my legs, which were clenched together. He moved it slowly down and then back up, then down to my legs and there he stopped, hesitating before he pushed it between them. I couldn't help but let out a moan. He began to wash me there, down there, taking his time to explore it before he pulled my legs apart so he could see what he was doing. I was so turned on I could have died.

He kept the washcloth there and began to move it up and down. I moaned again and my hips raised a little. He kept washing and then he turned and pressed his lips against mine. My lips parted and an electric shock went through my body when our tongues touched. It was almost painful.

He began to kiss me softly, making me yearn for it. His hand moved up and down and then he dropped the washcloth and began to slide his finger into me. I moaned and licked at his lips, ate at them until I began to feel the orgasm. And I felt it; it came at me strong, like a thunderball. I shivered and grabbed his hand and rode it. I rode it out then grabbed onto his shoulders and pulled him into the tub.

He kicked his boots and socks off and got out of his jeans. I ripped the shirt off his back and sucked on his nipples before he pulled my legs apart. His hard cock went right into me. I moaned and opened my legs wider and he began to fuck me, pulling my head back and sucking on my neck. I began to ride him, his hard cock. He pumped into me and I felt the second orgasm almost instantaneously. I could tell he was coming, too, and he was coming hard. The rest of the water in the tub splattered out and onto the floor. He kept at until he came and then he collapsed on my chest and laid still for a moment.

Wow.

He didn't stay still for very long. He got up and found a towel and held it open for me. I didn't say a word. I got out of the tub and he dried me off, rubbing the towel between my legs. I moaned and wanted it again, wanted it so bad I could taste it. He bent down and began to dry my legs off before he came back up and licked at my pussy. I draped my leg across his shoulder and he held onto it and began to eat me, lick at me, suck at me. I humped his face and, as I came, I moaned loudly. It was so intense, the moan just ripped out of my throat. I wanted it so much I couldn't stop myself. I grabbed his head and pulled him up to me and we began to kiss again, feverishly. Passionately. I don't think I'd ever felt that kind of passion for someone as I did him. It was as if his lips left me, I would feel physically ill.

We didn't say a word to each other. We made noises, sounds of our bodies coming together. We fucked each other because it seemed as though we were meant to do it, that we were made to do it. We didn't have a choice. Something came over us and we gave into it.

He threw me down on the floor, turned me over until I was on all fours and then he mounted me. He stuck his cock in and began to ride me. I gasped and held on. Soon we were bucking up against each other and he stopped for a moment and let me grind against him before he resumed his pace. We began to fuck then, fuck each other. We didn't stop until we both came again, panting as we did so.

We fell against the floor. We laid there for a while not moving. I wanted to roll over and hug him or something but I couldn't. I'd never been close to any man, not really, and I normally don't do that cuddly thing. But for some reason now I wanted to.

I started to make my move but then he moved. He got up and wrapped a towel around his hips. I noticed that he was in great shape. A big guy with big arms and a flat, muscled stomach. Not an inch of fat to be found anywhere on his body. He looked better than damn good and then there was the matter of his dick, which was beyond excellent.

He found his clothes. I watched as he wadded them up and tucked them under his arm. Was he leaving? Yes, he was. He was headed to the door without a second glance at me. I pulled my knees to my chest and shivered. It was cold in that room.

Before he left the room, he stopped and said, "This doesn't change anything."

Embarrassment stung my face and before I could help myself, I yelled, "You bastard!"

He didn't respond. That hurt worse than his hatful words. I found a shampoo bottle and hurled it at the door. But he was gone and it didn't hit him. Like I expected it to change anything anyway.

Green apples.

I didn't really expect him to kiss me good morning—or even say it for that matter—especially since he didn't even sleep in my bed. I didn't really expect anything but I wanted something and that something was him.

He had to be the best lover I'd ever had and that was saying something because most of the guys I'd slept with were pretty damn good. But he was different. I don't how he was different or why I felt that he was, but he was—*very* much so. The way he just took control took my breath away. I loved it; I loved succumbing to him and to my desires. I hated myself for feeling that way because he had kidnapped me. But why shouldn't I feel what I was feeling? Why should I deny it?

I didn't wait for him to come and get me from my room. I got up and found a new calico dress draped across the chair and put i on, washed my face and went downstairs. He was nowhere to be found. I felt disappointment for a moment until I saw a note on the table: *The sitting room needs to be cleaned. I expect it to be done when I get back.*

He didn't even sign his name, but who else could it have been from? I grabbed an apple out of a bowl on the table and ate it on my way to the sitting room, which was dusty and dirty as it hadn't been cleaned in decades. I found an old vacuum cleaner and some dust rags and got to work, working diligently, trying to get done.

I worked until morning turned to afternoon and I would find myself stopping ever so often to think about last night and the way he had touched me, the intensity in his eyes. I felt myself grow warm and my breasts ached for his touch and his lips. I stared down at them. My nipples were hard.

This was wrong.

I shook myself. It was. It was wrong. It was wrong to be thinking of him in any sort of amorous way. But I felt it, I knew I felt it and though I couldn't call it by name, the feeling was right.

Oh, good God. What was wrong with me? I shouldn't like this guy, even if he had been the best lover I'd ever had. He was a kidnapper and that meant there was something wrong with him. Maybe there was something wrong with me for liking him.

I felt a surge of panic again, like the one I'd had the other day in the kitchen. I got up from the fireplace and shook myself. I had to get out of here. I had to leave before something happened. But what would happen? More sex? I wanted that, but at the same time knew it would be the worst thing for me. Sure, I wanted a repeat of last night. Wasn't that why I was cleaning like a good little girl? Wasn't that why I was thinking of what I could do to please him? I knew I'd do whatever it took to get it again. I knew I'd be more than willing to do whatever he wanted to get what I wanted.

It was still wasn't right. It would never, ever, be right. But that didn't keep me from wanting him. And that's why I needed to leave before it got out of control. What was stopping me from leaving? He was gone all day. He shouldn't expect me to stick around when it was his job to stick around and make sure I didn't run off.

What was wrong with me? I went from one extreme of wanting to stay to the other of wanting to leave.

I forced the thoughts out of my mind and focused back on my work, spending most of the day getting it done. When I was finished, I went upstairs and took a shower. Once I was done with that, I went back into the kitchen and found a couple of steaks in the refrigerator. I put them on along with some canned vegetables and had just set the table when he came in.

He didn't say a word. He only eyed me before he looked at the table and asked, "Who told you to do that?"

"Well, no one," I said. "I just figured—"

"I didn't ask you to do that," he said. "Besides, I've already eaten."

He took off out of the kitchen leaving me stunned and very embarrassed. I burst into tears before I could stop myself. I glanced at the table and stared at the stupid fake flowers I had found in one of the rooms. I was alive with embarrassment. I ran over, grabbed the flowers and tore them apart, like a child.

I stopped and stared at the flowers, all torn and worthless. What was wrong with me? Why was I acting like this? It must have something to do with being kidnapped. I didn't know. I'd never been kidnapped before.

Before I could stop myself, I was crying, sobbing into my hands. I wanted to go home so bad I couldn't stand it. How long could it take? What was the holdup? This place wasn't that isolated, was it? Surely he wasn't asking too much for the ransom. How much was I worth anyway? What would Grant pay to get me back? I was a valuable commodity to him. I helped to keep him looking good, straight. So what was taking so long?

I stopped crying and glanced down at my foot. The bandage was dirty. I went up to my bathroom and changed it. It was healing pretty good. And it didn't hurt that much though I could tell that there would be a scar. I should have never tried to escape. I'd never been good with directions anyway.

But if I hadn't waited so long, I might have been able to escape. If I'd only... I heard something. I glanced up and saw him standing in the doorway. My pulse began to quicken and I felt a slight dread, combined with slight excitement, come over me.

He cleared his throat and said, "I see you finished the sitting room."

I nodded and forced a smile. "Let me ask you something. Why is it taking so long?"

He got my meaning. "I dunno."

I stared at him. "Listen, I don't know how much you're asking or whatever but if you let me go, I'll get it for you, one way or the other."

He stared at me, as if considering my sincerity, but then he shook his head. "No."

"Why not?" I asked, getting angry. "I have access—"

"No," he said. "That's not the way it's going to happen."

I sighed, trying to find a way to charm him into seeing my view of things and said, "I can get you money. I can—"

"It's about more than money," he said. "Don't say another word about it."

I held the anger in and said, "Okay."

"Tomorrow, I want the billiards room cleaned," he told me.

I glanced down at my foot then back up at him. *Charm him, do whatever it is you have to do to get out of here.* I thought about what we had done, the sex we had had and just thinking about it made me able to want it again. I could feel his hands all over my body, doing those things to me that I wanted done. I could feel it so much that I couldn't stop myself. If I could get him on my side, I could get him to let me go.

Before I could change my mind, I got up and went to him, grabbed his face and kissed him. He began to kiss me back. I smiled because this was the part where he would give in to me. In all logic, he should have melted and thrown me down on the floor. Instead, he pushed me away. He didn't push me away in disgust, he just pushed me away. I felt the sting of embarrassment sweep through my body and I wanted to die for an instant just so I wouldn't have to look into his eyes ever again. I felt tears well up inside me but I held them back. He could reject me but he wouldn't see me cry.

"Why don't you like me?" I asked quietly.

"What did you say?"

I stared him dead in the eye and said, "Why don't you like me?"

"This isn't about that," he said quietly.

"Then what's it about?"

"Money."

I felt my face flush but then again, what did I expect? He was just a criminal. A nobody. I knew how that felt too, to be a nobody. I still felt like that sometimes.

"You don't think I'm worth it, do you?" I asked.

"Worth it?"

"Worth...worth it. Worth anything," I said. "Worth saying hello or talking to or..." I stopped myself. A sob caught in my throat.

"What are you talking about?" he asked.

I looked away in shame. Maybe I was just PMSing but I was so distraught, I wasn't thinking right, talking straight. I couldn't put my finger on the reason. Oh, yeah. That was why. I was going crazy because he had kidnapped me. He was making me want something that wasn't worth wanting. And it wasn't worth wanting with him because it would never work. I was put in this position because of his greed. It wasn't fair. None of it was fair to me.

"I'm sorry," I said, regaining some of my dignity. "I'm just a little emotional, being kidnapped and all. Besides, this house is creepy and scary. And I know there are big rats all over the place."

"Leave the rats be," he said and left the room. "And clean the room tomorrow."

I stared after him and as soon as he disappeared out the door, I burst into tears. I never felt as low as I did then. And I was so low because I knew I was falling in love with this guy and there wasn't a damn thing I could do about it. He was like green apples, so sour on the inside but so pretty on the outside. You take one because it tempts you; it looks so delicious. You have to have it. Then you bite into it and your face draws up and your taste buds get pissed off for what you've done to them. They were too much, not worth the trouble of eating them. I hated green apples, always had. But they always looked so pretty sitting in a bowl on the kitchen table.

★ ★ ★ ★ ★

The next morning I awoke later than usual and stared out the window. I found myself doing that every morning since I'd been here and I would leave the curtains open at night so I could stare at the stars and the moon before I fell asleep. In the morning, I couldn't see much, just some sky and treetops. But I liked to look, especially if the sun was already out when I awoke. I loved to watch the clouds move across the sky.

I should leave. The thought had occurred to me more than once. He wasn't there and who knew what time he'd be back. I didn't know. I was sure this place wasn't too far off the beaten path. I was sure I could make it somewhere.

He won't come after you... Nope, he wouldn't. Would he? What would he do if I just left? He deserved that. If he was stupid enough to leave me alone all day, I *should* leave.

I sighed and rolled over onto my back and stared up at the canopy. If he only knew me, knew where I came from, he might grow to like me. I didn't grow up in abject poverty but pretty damn close. We probably had the similar backgrounds and if he would just let me tell him about mine, he might allow himself to like me.

I shook myself. *What the hell was I doing?* Falling in love? It wouldn't be hard; he had everything a girl wanted, minus the criminal mentality. Oh, shit. He wasn't a good guy and I shouldn't try to make him into one. He didn't even have feelings and if he showed any emotion to someone, he would probably threaten their lives if they told anyone.

I cracked up. *That* would be funny. But in a way it was sad because it was more than likely right on the money. What was sadder was the fact that he and I were more alike than I was willing to admit. I hid my feelings most of the time. I couldn't remember the last time I hugged someone or felt love for another person. I was so bundled up in my pain and in my own misery that I didn't allow myself to feel much of anything.

But, no, I couldn't allow myself to feel anything for him. I had to do something about my situation before something bad happened and I was stuck there forever.

I groaned and thought about getting out of bed. He'd want that damn room cleaned. I didn't want to clean the damn room. I continued to lay there and think. The time kept slipping away. I lay there and convinced myself it was really time to go. I lay there for a long time, until morning passed into afternoon. I lay there and thought about the whole situation. There was something oddly off about it. I hadn't been locked up or really beaten or mishandled in any way.

But why hadn't the cops come for me yet? How long had I been there? I figured about a week and a half to two weeks. Why was I still here? Why hadn't he moved me? It seems like they did that a lot in the movies—moved their victims from place to place and the police would always keep the trail hot.

And why did he leave everyday? Maybe he wanted to get rid of me. Maybe he hadn't thought this whole kidnapping business through and decided it was a bad idea. But if that was the case, why did he come back every day?

On the other hand, if he was stupid enough to think I was just some imbecile that he could tell what to do and I'd stay put, then I should leave on general principal.

I *should* leave. I should get up and just leave. I didn't have any shoes. I didn't have any money or any identification. My beach bag... I had my beach bag with me that day. Had he taken it and if so where had he stashed it?

I didn't even know what room he slept in. I would find out.

I got out of bed and took a quick shower, pulled on my shorts and gingham top and tiptoed out of the room. I stopped in the hall and listened. No sounds. Nothing. He wasn't here. What was I afraid of?

I got a move on and checked all the upstairs bedrooms for signs of inhabitation. It didn't look like they had been touched in decades. There was a coating of dust on everything.

He had to sleep somewhere. Where did he sleep?

I made my way downstairs and looked through all the rooms. I didn't find anything. I was about to give up when I remembered something. In a paneled room at my house, there was a secret door. But you had to lean on it to get it to open and if you didn't know about it, then you'd never know it was there. And, of course, behind the door was a room. Ours was a library for some old books they didn't want anyone to touch.

This old house had to have a secret door. Where was the secret door? All the rooms downstairs were paneled in dark, heavy wood. I started leaning on the walls. None of them gave. I went through all the rooms and the one in the billiards room finally gave. I grinned. I should have been a detective or something.

I pushed the door open and sure, enough it was his room. It was huge and windowless. The air was stale and seemed to hang heavily. There was no bed, just an old leather couch and a fireplace. There was a duffle bag on the floor and on one of the tables was a laptop, plugged in. *Yes!*

I ran to it and before I could stop myself I shook the mouse. The computer clicked on and the screensaver came up. I was about to try and hook up to the internet when I stopped. What was I going to do? Check my email?

I looked around for a phone. I didn't see one. I hadn't seen one, not even an old one, since I'd been here. I had a cell phone in my beach bag. There was a closet door on either side of the fireplace. I opened the first one to find a bunch of old junk, nothing of any use to anyone, not even the person who had put it in there. The other closet had some of his clothes and shoes. And in the back of it was my beach bag!

I laughed with delight and grabbed it and emptied it on the floor. All my stuff fell out. My flip-flops, my cell phone, my wallet which was stuffed with money! Yes! Jackpot! The cell phone battery was dead so it was of no use. There were a few candy bars in there that Emily had stuck in because she hadn't carried a bag to the beach. I tore into one and my taste buds jumped with joy. I have never tasted anything so delicious.

And my cigarettes! Ah, yes! I decided to wait and light one outside, in case he didn't smoke. That way he wouldn't smell anything and know I had been in there. Couldn't be too careful.

It was time to leave. I decided I couldn't take the beach bag with me, mainly because it weighed a ton and I didn't want to lug it around. I took out my wallet and flip-flops and pushed the bag back into the closet.

I just then noticed a huge bag of clothes on the floor of the closet which, I assumed, was more stuff from the Salvation Army. And, I was right. The bag was full of used women's clothing. Why did he do that? Oh. He must have realized after he kidnapped me that I would need something to wear. But the Salvation Army? Why not go to the mall? Well, I guess it would look weird to a salesclerk to see this big guy buying women's clothing. Or it might look funny. I laughed, thinking of Nate being a cross-dresser, then

I stared at the clothes. I guess no one would give a shit at the Salvation Army.

I looked though the bag until I found a pair of black Capri pants—too big—and a white t-shirt—too small. But they'd do and with my flip-flops, I'd look like I was on my way to the beach.

I pulled the clothes on and shoved the bag back into the closet. I was about to shut the door when I found myself touching his clothes. I stepped in and breathed their scent in. They smelled freshly laundered. I couldn't help but go through this stuff. I wanted to know what he had. He didn't have much. He just had some clothes and the laptop. The laptop…

I tried to force myself not to go through his files but the snoop in me wouldn't let me. I didn't want to, in part, because I wanted him to remain a mystery. If I found out he belonged to some boy band fan club…well, that wouldn't be very cool.

Still… Wasn't it odd that a criminal had a laptop? And it was a nice laptop, top of the line, one used for businesses. I had one similar to this at home and spent most of my time on it as I had nothing better to do. I was good at working on the computer. I could probably find out some stuff on him.

I went over to it and opened up "my documents" and went though his files, pausing on a few. One file was labeled "ideas/inventions." Inventions? He was an inventor? I opened it up and sure enough, there was a detailed description of a product that would improve some machine on a manufacturing line. It would cut work time in half, the description said. Huh. He was smart, real smart. For an instant, I felt admiration for him, the reverted back to the uncertainty. These files could belong to someone else for all I knew. He might have stolen the computer.

I found another file which was a business proposal and at the bottom, it listed all of his credentials, which included his PhD Wait a minute. That meant Nate was a Dr. *Dr. Nate?* That boggled my mind and I read on to find that he'd worked for some of the biggest companies in the world. Who was this guy? Had I misread him? Why would he—an inventor—kidnap me? Maybe he needed start-up money.

I heard a noise and jumped. I listened for a moment and realized it was the big grandfather clock in the next room. *Shit.*

stared at the computer screen, wanting to keep going through his files but knowing it was getting late and it was time to go.

I turned the computer off and got up. Oddly enough, I felt sad. But I had to leave. I wasn't a prisoner. He'd probably realized his blunder soon after kidnapping me and that's why he left me alone during the day. He was smart enough to know when he'd made a mistake. In fact, he'd probably called Grant and told him where to find me and Grant had decided to let me sit and stew. He'd probably think it was pretty funny to leave me here for a while. More than likely it would have been his idea to make me clean the damn place.

I could hear him now, "Make her get dirty. She hasn't done anything in years. You'll have to make her do it; she doesn't like to be told. If she misbehaves, you have my permission to spank her. But don't touch her face. We have a party to attend next week and she needs to look good for it."

I cracked up. As soon as I saw Grant again, I was going to slap him.

Maybe I wouldn't go back. Maybe I would start a new life. I had enough money to get me through the next few weeks. I regretted giving the waitress at the beach that fifty. That had been over a thirty dollar tip and that thirty bucks would have come in handy now.

But she probably needed it more than me. Even so, I couldn't waste money like that anymore. It would be like the good old days, days that really sucked because I didn't know how I was going to come up with the rent.

Big deal. I had done it once and I could do it again. I would make my own way and never again depend on anyone else for anything. I would go around under an assumed name and live a mysterious life. I would have lovers and I would have fun. Maybe I would go to Mexico. I heard you could live down there on a little of nothing. And that's what I had—a little of nothing.

I left the room exactly as I found it and made my way out of the house and to the driveway. I didn't stop and look over my shoulder. I wasn't into all that nostalgic crap. When something's over, it's over and I don't cry about it. Besides, if he had wanted me to stick around, he should have stuck around to guard me and make sure I didn't run off.

I stuck to the edge of the driveway next to the trees to stay out of sight just in case he was in the house and looked out. I knew he wasn't but I was feeling paranoid, thinking at any minute he'd jump out of the bushes and grab me. I quickened my pace and wondered how long it would take to get to the end of the drive.

It took a long time. The driveway had to be over a mile long. I kept walking and walking and thinking I might just be going in a circle and would eventually end back up at the house. But I didn't. It wasn't long before I spotted the gates.

I got a tingle of excitement. I had been held for so long, I couldn't wait to see what the real world looked like again. Had anything changed? Had anything happened while I had been away? I couldn't wait to find out.

The gates were tall, wrought iron and ornate. They fit the house well, but one was hanging off its hinges and threatening to fall to the ground. They were rusted. Like everything else in that house, the gates were suffering from years of neglect.

Neglect. Then it suddenly occurred to me. That's why I had responded to Nate in the way I had. I didn't love him. I was simply suffering from neglect. Years of neglect, years of wanting something—love—and knowing I'd never get it. But does anyone ever really "get" it? And was it really worth having when you got right down to it? What was so great about love anyway?

I didn't need it and I certainly didn't need it from someone like Nate. I thought about his files, about his inventions. None of it made any sense to me. But it didn't matter anymore.

I walked through the gates and after a few more steps, I came onto an old highway, probably the highway that was used before they built a bigger and better one somewhere close by. I didn't hear or see any traffic.

I stopped next to the asphalt and looked around. I sniffed. I could smell the sea breeze. I was somewhere near the ocean. I stared back in the direction of the house and then around a bit more. I spied a little trail on the other side of the road. I felt a little anxious. Should I? Why not?

The trail led onto the beach. The beach was deserted, maybe because it was still winter. There weren't any houses built on this side of the beach, nor were there any hotels. I walked to the water and took off my flip-flops and put a toe in it. It was ice cold. I shivered and backed away from it.

Maybe we were further up north than I'd suspected. I looked around but didn't see anything. So, I started walking. It seemed like I walked forever and was about to get back on the highway when I saw something ahead. It looked like a bar. It might have been a mirage. Even so, I quickened my pace.

Once inside, I told myself, I'd make a few calls and get out of this mess. But who was I going to call? Not Grant. Let him worry for a little while longer. I should call my mom. She was probably worried sick. I'd call James after I got done with mom, definitely. And Emily, I needed to call Emily and ease her mind. I'd have to assure her she didn't do anything wrong by leaving me by myself. But then I thought about that and almost laughed. Emily would never think she was at fault for anything, even my kidnapping.

Oh, and maybe, just maybe, I should call the police. Shit, I wasn't thinking straight. They should be called first.

Then it hit me. I was free! I was free to do anything I wanted. I didn't have to call anybody or do anything. The thought of running away occurred to me again. I stopped walking and thought about that. Mexico or home? Mexico or home?

I groaned and realized I was near the bar. It was called Nelly's. It looked like the kind of place the locals hung out and ate oysters. Without thinking, I walked in. Inside, a few people were drinking the afternoon away. It was old, with a plank floor and a jukebox in the corner. *What now?* I looked around for a phone but didn't see one.

No one noticed me standing in the doorway. I looked at all the other people and wondered why they were acting so nonchalant. But then again, they didn't know me. They didn't know I had just escaped. I was almost disappointed with the situation. I had half-expected someone to jump up, point their finger in my face and yell, "It's her! That girl who's been kidnapped!" I had expected something, but then realized I was dressed down, my hair wasn't done and I didn't have on any make-up. Any picture they might have seen of me wouldn't have resembled me, the person in this bar, looking a little shabby and poor.

Maybe they hadn't released a picture of me to the press. Maybe the press didn't know anything about my kidnapping.

I walked up to the bar, which was full, and waited. The bartender had his back to me. I started to say something when I felt someone staring at me. I looked to my right and saw Nate, who was standing at the end of the bar. My heart dropped to my knees. *Stupid, stupid, stupid!* Nate's eyes were spitting fire. He was so pissed off, he looked like he wanted to strangle me. I stared at the bartender, realizing my mistake, my idiocy. I felt like throwing up. I felt like kicking my own ass for being so stupid and foolish. What was wrong with me? Why had I come in here? I had the good sense to leave yet I didn't have the good sense to keep going.

Nate walked over to me just as the bartender turned around, saw me and said, "What can I get you?"

"She's with me," Nate said. "What do I owe you?"

"Four-fifty," he said.

Nate threw a bill down on the bar and then grabbed my arm and pulled me towards the door. I didn't fight him but I did look around. I could do something. I *should* do something. I couldn't go back with him. There was no telling what he'd do.

"Don't even think about it," he hissed under his breath.

I hung my head and allowed him to pull me out of the bar. He put me into an old Ford pick-up and we drove back to the house. Neither of us said a word, but what do you say in a situation like that? "Sorry I ran away?" It wouldn't have made a difference what I said. No matter what I said wouldn't make anything right with him.

When we got back, he still didn't say a word. We went into the house and still nothing. I was dying for him to say something so I could explain my situation and maybe ask him a few questions, like *When the hell are they going to pay up?*

I was about to go up to my room when he mumbled something. I whirled around and snapped, "What did you say?"

"You heard me."

"I did not."

"If you leave again," he said. "You better stay gone."

"What the *fuck* does that mean?" I hissed. "And who the *fuck* do you think you are?"

He just stared at me.

I was suddenly livid. I felt cooped up and suffocated and just violent. I wanted to hit him so bad I could feel my fist slamming into his face. I refrained and thought about all the stuff I'd found out on him. I wanted to call him on it. I wanted to know why he had kidnapped me. I wanted to call him Dr. Nate. But then, I just wanted to make him pay for making me feel so bad. I snapped, "It's your own fault. You leave me alone day in and day out and don't expect me to leave?"

"Would you rather I tie you up?"

I screamed, "No, I would rather you let me go!"

He didn't respond, which infuriated me even more.

"And to think..." I stopped. "Why did you come after me?"

"Who says I did?" he asked. "I might have just stopped in for a drink. Isn't that what you did?"

"What the hell does that mean?"

"It means," he said. "I don't care."

For some reason, those words hurt. Those hateful words were the story of my life. No one cared about me and neither did he and I had been a fool to misjudge the situation, to have any hope that it might be more than what it was. I had wanted something from him and I felt stupid for wanting it in the first place.

Before I knew what I was doing, I went after him, clawing at his face. I wanted to rip his skin off. He had struck a nerve in me and he was going to pay. He grabbed my hands and shoved me off him. I fell on the floor, but I was back up and at him again in seconds. He shoved me off again and I went right back at him. He lost his balance and we fell to the floor, with me on top. I began to beat at him, screaming at the top of my lungs like a child who's been wounded and hurt and just can't take it anymore. He lay there and took it for a while, until I was exhausted and sobbing. I was crying so hard I couldn't breathe. I began to gasp. He got up, pulled me up and forced me to bend down, telling me to "Breathe." My breathing soon came back.

I fell back to the floor and curled into a ball and cried. I knew it was years of bent-up frustration that was coming out of me but I couldn't help myself. I knew I looked pathetic, but I didn't care. I had to do it. I only wished he hadn't been there.

Without a word, he picked me up and carried me to my room and lay me down on the bed. I almost reached out for him but stopped myself just in time. He saw me do it and his head fell to his chest, then his eyes fell on me and he climbed on the bed.

"I don't know what to say to you," he muttered.

I stared at him and again felt that connection. Why did I feel a connection to him? I didn't know, but I did. I felt a kindred sprit. I knew I was just lonely. I knew that I was so hungry for love—anyone's love—that I was willing to do almost anything to get it. I'd plead, I'd grovel, I'd beg. It didn't matter. I'd just do it because I needed it so badly.

"Just…" I began, though I hated myself for saying it. "Could you just hold me?"

"I don't know how."

I began to cry again and shake my head. He was telling the truth. He was like me. He didn't know how to connect. We were both like that, two people who weren't close to anyone.

I put my hand on his face and he almost smiled at me. I couldn't help but laugh a little. I asked, "Am I ever going to get to see your teeth?"

"What do you mean?"

"You've never smiled," I said.

"Neither have you."

I smiled widely and said, "There. Now show me."

He ducked his head and smiled. I smiled back. He had nice teeth, straight and white. His eyes even sparkled a little.

"Wasn't so bad, was it?" I asked.

He shook his head. I moved my face towards his and he did the same. Our lips met and we pressed them together and began to kiss. It was a slow, nice kiss.

He began to make love to me. I'd always thought making love was boring; I preferred fucking. But as he made his way around my body and I began to respond, I knew that I'd just never really been made love to before. I'd been fucked and that was pretty much it.

He started with soft caresses; he didn't rip my clothes off. He did everything gently and without effort. He kept it up until I responded and began to kiss him. He kissed me back, gently pushing his tongue inside my mouth. We were on a different plane then, somewhere neither of us had ever been before. We were in it together and there was no place I'd rather have been.

I pulled him down on me and held him there as he kissed my breasts, as he pulled my shirt off and began to suck at my neck running his tongue along it. I began to arch and want him as he stroked my entire body, as he pulled my pants off and began to stroke me there.

I opened my legs wider and he slid in. We moved together, in sync, against one another. We moaned and got lost inside each other and as we came, we came together and I have never in my life felt so close to someone yet so distant. I wanted him. I wanted to know everything about him and yet I was afraid to ask one single question. He stayed with me until I fell asleep. When I awoke the next morning, he was gone.

Little masochist.

The next morning, I found another note on the bedside table telling me to clean the billiards room. I made a point *not* to do it.

In fact, I slept in, then took a long shower. I found another dress lying across the arm of the chair in my room. It was polka dot dress that buttoned down in the front. I slipped it on and went downstairs. I fried myself an egg and some bacon, ate and then and went outside and walked around a little staring at the decaying mansion. I stepped back from it and took it all in. Why the hell did he bring me here?

I didn't know.

Next, I did a little sunbathing and, as I lay there, dozed. It was almost like I was back home, living with Grant. All I needed was James. I imagined him standing beside me with a silver tray in his hand held up by three fingers.

"What will it be today, Miss?" he'd ask.

"Oh, James," I'd tease in my haughty socialite voice. "I would simply *love* some flapjacks."

He would inquire as to what, precisely, flapjacks were.

"Darling," I'd reply, yawning. "*Do* we have to have this discussion again?"

"Afraid so, Miss," he'd tell me. "Might flapjacks be pancakes?"

"Don't be so thick, James. Of *course* they are."

He would nod. "And would the young Miss fancy some bacon to go along with those flapjacks?"

"Yes, and some freshly squeezed orange juice. *Do* be sure to remove all the pulp. I *loathe* the pulp."

"Of course," he'd say. "Anything else?"

"Just one more thing."

He'd cocked his head to the side.

"When *are* you going to leave your wife for me?"

He'd smile, give his head that slight shake that told me I was getting *this* close to being too naughty and if I didn't stop it, I could fix my own breakfast.

I realized I missed the hell out of old James. I wondered if he missed me. I laughed, thinking he was probably kicked back with his feet up on some table.

"James," I said aloud to the sun. "I hope they're treating you alright, buddy."

And they better be, too, or there would be hell to pay when I got back. When I got back... But when would I get back?

★ ★ ★ ★ ★

Later on, I was in the billiards room playing pool by myself when Nate came in. It was the most fun I had since I'd been there. Besides doing the sex thing, that is.

He came into the room and didn't speak. Neither did I and we pretended to ignore one another for the longest time. I kept playing pool. He looked around and the look came onto his face, the look of anger and sheer annoyance. There was frustration there too.

"What happened?" he asked, looking around the room, then back at me.

"Eight-ball, corner pocket," I said and hit it, sending it on its way. I had won the game. Of course, the competition was weak.

"Kara?" he said. "What happened?"

"Don't know what you mean," I said and threw the pool cue on the table.

"You know bloody well what I—"

Before he could finish, I turned on my heel and left the room. I went into the kitchen and made myself another sandwich. He didn't come in there for a long time but I could tell he was dying to.

I was almost finished eating when he came into the kitchen. I hid my smile and didn't say a word as he stared at me, arms crossed. The room shook with silence and the faint ticking of the clock on the wall.

Finally he said, "This isn't working."

"You're right," I said and leaned back in the chair. "It's time you realized that."

His nostrils flared. "Don't fuck around with me. You don't know who you're dealing with."

"No," I said. "*You* don't who you're dealing with. You might have kidnapped me but that doesn't mean I'm your slave."

He didn't like that, I could just tell. He probably thought that fucking me last night would pacify me and I'd do whatever he wanted. He liked the fucking but would rather die than admit it. I wasn't going to admit it, either.

I went on, "What are you gonna do when they catch you? Ever been to jail before?"

"Shut up," he hissed.

"I bet you have," I said. "I bet you broke out 'cause once they got a guy like you, they're gonna keep him for good."

He stared at me as if he couldn't believe I was saying these things to him. After all, he was an educated man. I knew it got to him, just implying someone like him would have ever been to jail. He thought he had me all figured out and here I was, all of a sudden, acting like a supreme bitch again.

"Shut it," he muttered dangerously. "You will do it tomorrow."

"No, you're wrong," I said.

The danger in his voice was now across his face. He was very angry. Big deal. He liked being angry, it's probably all that he knew, that one emotion that came from a deep rooted hostility at the entire world. I almost stopped myself from pushing him even more, but for some reason I didn't. Or couldn't. Maybe I liked seeing how pissed off I could get him.

"I'm not doing anything," I said and put my feet up on the table. "You can leave now."

"Why don't you leave?" he asked.

"You know," I said. "I think I might."

I got up and started out of the room. He grabbed my arm and hook his head.

"You're not going anywhere," he said.

"But you told me to leave," I said and wriggled out of his grasp. "Isn't that what you want?"

"No," he said. "But you need to be taught a lesson."

"Huh?" I asked.

He didn't respond. He only grabbed my arm and dragged me through the house. I yelled at him that this was getting a little old but he wouldn't let me go. So, I just let myself be dragged and then he took me into my bedroom and threw me on the bed.

I jumped up. "Oh, no, buddy, we're not doing this again."

Not one word came out of his mouth. He just turned on his heel and left the room. He came back in with a rope. I blinked. Uh oh.

"No!" I screeched and jumped up off the bed.

He grabbed me and wrestled me back to the bed. I slapped at him and tried to claw his face but the held me down and in no time had my arms and legs tied. I hadn't expected this. I was almost scared. But something inside me told me that no matter how far we went, he would never really hurt me. I prayed that instinct was correct.

After he had secured the ropes, he turned and started out of the room. *Bastard!* I tried to get the ropes free but it was no use. He must have taken a rope-tying class or something.

He glanced over his shoulder then stopped, standing stock still for a moment. My heart, which was already racing, sped up. His hesitation made me realize he wasn't finished. What was he going to do? But then I knew and knowing made me want it.

His eyes were all over my body making me feel—and want to be—naked. My nipples hardened under his intense gaze. I felt myself grow warm, wet. Just because he *looked* at me like that. He couldn't deny his desire for me. That look told on him. He wanted me as much as I denied wanting him, maybe even more so. I could be wrong but I had a feeling I was right.

Suddenly, the ropes didn't matter. It didn't matter that I was tied up, almost enslaved. Nothing mattered but the look on his face. I stopped struggling, stopped trying to get the ropes free. I just stared at him and waited.

He came over to the bed and continued to stare at me. Then he began to unbutton the dress until it came apart and fell away from my body. I didn't have any underwear on. I hadn't worn any since I'd gotten here mainly because I hadn't packed a bag.

I was uncovered, naked. He didn't look away from me, or my nakedness. He just stared. He wasn't looking at me so much as a human but as a woman. He was a man and this was the way he was supposed to look at me, with lust, pure unadulterated lust and desire. It wasn't something a person could fake.

The lust was building inside of me. I had to have him do something. I moaned, arching away from the bed, wanting his hands badly. I wanted him to paw at me and to use me because, in turn, I'd get to use him.

It took a long time before he began to play with me. One finger came down and I tensed. Before it reached my skin, I trembled and shivered. The anticipation was too much. His finger went to my belly and he traced a line from it down, where he traced another line through it until he was at pussy. I couldn't move my legs or arms. I had to lay there and enjoy the torture. I moaned again, this time more intensely. The finger came back up and lightly touched my nipples. He switched back and forth between them until I moaned for his lips to be on them.

He bent over and his tongue came out and he licked my nipple, sucked it into his mouth and bit down gently on it. I moaned more loudly. It was too much. I couldn't contain myself. He began to nibble on my breast and his hand was between my legs sideways, going up and down and it felt so good I couldn't control myself. All I had to do was lay there and let it happen. I didn't force the orgasm to come; it came on its own. It came quickly and sporadically until I was spent and trembling.

He didn't stop there. He began to kiss my body, all of it, my face and my legs, everywhere he kissed and explored before he kissed me, his tongue forcing its way into my wet mouth. I moaned and sucked at his tongue and his hands kept moving. His dick was hard and I could feel it pressing against my leg. I wanted it inside me, filling me up, fucking me hard, fucking me like it didn't give a damn what or where as long as I stayed there until it got its satisfaction. Until it was finished with me.

The feeling of the ropes, the constriction swept over me. But then came a feeling of freedom, of release combined with beautiful pain. I wanted out but I wanted to stay put, to stay secure. There was so much security in being tied up. It was all up to him, what to do and how to do it. I was just the willing vessel.

He didn't untie my legs. He slid his cock between them and pulled them open just enough so he could get in. He took his time and eased into me before he gave a good hard push and forced me to take it all.

He kissed me hard as he began to fuck me, grabbing my head and holding it still as he forced his tongue into my mouth. I kissed back but couldn't move. I had to take it; so I lay there all tied up and took it as he fucked me, as he brought the best out in me. It was getting to be too much; it was too good. I was panting and the orgasm inside me was building. Soon, it erupted and exploded.

I shuddered as it hit me and then stared into his eyes as I came. He stared back and I could tell he was about to come, too. He might have been using me, but it was me he wanted beneath him. It was him I wanted on top of me. No one else would do. It was like I had found my place in the world and my place was with him.

The orgasm held on and intensified, which made me pant more. He pulled back and began to pump into me harder. As the good feelings washed all over me, I watched his face. I loved to watch his face as he came. His face had such a look of concentration. I loved that look.

Once we were done, he fell beside me, breathing heavily. Then he turned and looked at me. I turned and looked back, wondering what he was thinking, but then realizing I knew. The look he had was almost hopeless, like he had lost something and, while it made him sad, he was glad to have lost it. In its place, something better had come along.

I knew exactly how he felt.

✱ ✱ ✱ ✱ ✱

I didn't understand what was going on. I didn't realize what was doing. But the next morning, I found a note that told me to clean the billiards room. I stared at the note, at his handwriting and wondered why I was feeling something for this man. What was that something? I didn't know.

I didn't clean the room. In fact, I was lying on my stomach in the sitting room reading an old book when he came in.

"Just who do you think you are?" he snapped, eying me. Then he shook his head and said, "Oh, no, not this again."

I glanced over my shoulder at him. I turned back to the book.

"Why are you doing this?" he asked quietly.

I ignored him and sat up. "I think I'll go take a bath now."

Just before I took my first step out of the room, he came at me, grabbed me by the shoulders, staring into my eyes. I felt breathless, weak. Strong. But then he released me and almost looked ashamed for a split second. He started out of the room.

"It won't happen again," he said.

"You…" I began, not really knowing what to say. "What do you mean?"

"I don't want to…" He stopped, not knowing what to say either. "I'll try to do better."

He really felt bad about all that stuff. He really did. I didn't. I didn't feel bad about it. Did it make me some kind of pervert?

"Nate," I said. "You did nothing wrong."

He dropped his head. I took the initiative and walked over to him and took his hand. I placed it on my breast and stared up at him. He stared down at me and looked so sad. I hated that, hated what it meant. I had to take that look off his face, so I tiptoed and kissed his cheek, then his neck, then his lips. He stood there and allowed me to kiss him like that, gently and without reservation. He knew I wanted to kiss him. He should have known it anyway.

I stepped back from him and said, "You did nothing wrong, Nate."

He nodded.

I stepped back to him and the words that came out of my mouth were as much of a shock to me as they were to him, "Do it again."

"Do what?"

Do what? Do what? What did I want him to do? Could I ask him for it? Would he give it to me? Why did I want it? What did it matter?

"Tie me up again," I said and licked his ear. "Tie me up and do whatever you want to me."

He moved back so he could look in my eyes, as if he wanted to make sure I wasn't joking. "But, but—"

"Shh," I said. "Let's don't talk about it. Let's just do it."

"I've never—"

I put one finger on his lips. "Just try it. Do it for me."

He stared at me. "I can't."

"You can."

"No," he said and took a step back.

"Why?" I asked, exasperated.

"It's not right."

"It is right," I said. "Do it."

"No."

I was suddenly infuriated. He always turned it around on me. My hand was up to slap him but he blocked it. I glared at him. He glared back. I hissed, "You know what I want. Now give it to me."

He stared at me for an instant before pushing me backwards until I was up against the wall. "Is this what you want?"

I groaned but didn't move away from him.

"Is it?" he asked.

I stared at him, fuming. He pushed himself up against me. I felt constricted, suddenly needing my personal space. This was a little too much. But it *was* what I'd wanted.

"Is it?" he asked, his hot breath in my ear.

"Yes," I cried.

He let my arm go and moved away from me. I was embarrassed so much I loathed myself. He reduced me to that. I couldn't win with him because he wouldn't play.

"You bastard," I said and felt the tears on my cheeks. "How could you do that to me?"

He shook his head. "To you? What about what you're doing to me?"

"And what am I doing to you?" I hissed. He didn't respond. "Tell me!"

"You're making me do things I shouldn't do."

"It's not about that," I said. "Don't you see? I trust you, Nate. That's why I want it. It's just the way things are between us."

"There is no *between us*," he said.

He could have said anything to me but not that. That made me feel so low. I had never felt so low.

"I mean…" he mumbled. "I don't what I mean. But this can't happen."

I looked down at the floor, wanting to die. I looked back up at him. "Don't think about it. Just do it."

"No."

"Why not?" I asked, getting frustrated.

"I know what you're doing and why you're doing it," he said. "I know what you are."

"What am I?" I snapped.

He came over to me, grabbed me by the back of the head and forced me to look in his eyes. I melted and everything he'd said disappeared from my mind. He wanted me and he wanted me now. I wanted him. That's all that mattered.

"This is what you like, isn't it?" he hissed.

I gasped as he pushed me back against the wall and pressed up next to me. I moaned as he began to grind against me. I grabbed his head and pulled his lips on top of mine. We kissed savagely for a moment until he lifted my dress up and shoved his hard cock into me. He began to fuck me standing up against the wall. He grabbed my ass and pulled me up so I could wrap my legs around his waist.

He slowed down and moved his hips so his cock could go in deeper and muttered, "You're a little masochist, aren't you?"

I stopped moving as the realization of his words sunk in the way only truth can. Was I? Was that what I was? A little masochist? What did it matter, though? Nothing mattered but what he was doing to me and what I was getting out of it.

"Do you like it?" I asked. "Do you like me being a little masochist?"

He gave another push but didn't respond.

"Come on," I said and bit at his neck. "Tell me you love it."

He ignored me and began to fuck me. I held on with all my might and before I could help myself, I was coming and I was coming hard. I cried out and my nails dug into his back. He was pumping furiously into me and then he came, shuddered once and released me. I fell out of his arms and slid down the wall. He left me in a heap on the floor and started out of the room.

I watched him go sadly. I felt like such a…such a…lowlife. I wanted the floor to swallow me up and make me disappear from the world.

Before I could stop myself, I screamed, "I hate you!"

"You'll get over it," he called from just outside the door.

I glared at the door and listened to his departing footsteps. Why was life so hard? Why was love or whatever this was so hard? Why was everything so complicated? And why did I put myself through it? What was the payoff? The payoff was the sex but there was more to it than that. The payoff was something I needed and that something was deep and beautiful. It was something I had to have, would give anything for. It was something I'd never get my hands on. I almost wished I hadn't experienced what I had. That way, once it was really and truly gone, I wouldn't miss it. It aroused such pain inside me, such longing. Nothing after this would seem worthwhile, nothing would be good enough. And I couldn't have it. I was better off not having even a taste in the first place.

The tears began to spill onto my cheeks. I got up, pulled the dress down and walked to my room, fell on the bed and began to sob. I didn't try to analyze why I was crying, I just did it. I don't know how long I cried but when I looked up, Nate was standing beside the bed. He looked down on me and shook his head, almost with sympathy.

"Listen," he said with a loud sigh. "You'll be leaving soon and there is no reason to—"

"Don't say that!" I exclaimed. "You have no right to tell me how to feel! If I want to feel something for you, I will! You don't have to like it or give it back to me, but you can't keep me from feeling it!"

"It's not that I don't want to," he said. "But what good would it do either of us?"

That just made me cry harder. "I don't know but I feel it with you and I can't deny it. I *want* to feel it."

He looked so sad then, like a little boy who's just been told there's no Santa Claus and he's finally accepted it. He was just a person, a man, sitting there beside me, wondering what to do next, wondering who this woman was beside him. Probably wondering how he'd gotten here and what he'd do next.

"You don't know me," I said. "You just think I'm some rich bitch. I wasn't always rich, you know? And it's not even my money. It's my husband's."

He sighed and looked away from me.

"He's gay," I said. "My husband is gay and he never loved me. And—get this—he never wanted anyone else to love me, either. He couldn't give it to me and now you won't give it to me so I guess I'm just a pathetic person that no one could ever love. I guess I am sick."

He stared at me, his mouth open. He clamped it shut and shook his head.

"What?" I said. "Go ahead. Tell me how disgusted you are with me and how much you hate me and all that. I could care less. No one loves me and no one ever will."

"I don't know what to say to you," he said. "I just don't know."

"You don't have to say anything," I said. "Just don't push me away."

"It would never work."

"It doesn't have to work," I said.

"What do you mean?"

"I mean," I said. "We're here, aren't we? Why can't we just… Why can't we just *be* here? Right now?"

"Because you'll be gone soon."

I fell back on the bed and turned away from him. I couldn't win and neither could he. He was just a realist and I had been overly optimistic. It would be over soon and he was right. We shouldn't start something we wouldn't be able to finish. But when is love ever finished? Even if you fall out of love with someone, they're still out there somewhere, aren't they? Breathing the same air and staring up at the same stars? You shared something once, something brilliant and magical and what was so wrong with sharing it? What was so wrong with letting it go when it was time?

I turned back to him and took his hand even though he didn't want to give it to me. I took it and held it, then gave it a squeeze.

"I don't care," I told him, not caring what I was saying, just needing to say it. "I don't care who you are or who you've been with or what you've done. I like you, and if that pisses you off, fine. I don't care. But I'm not going to lie to myself and say I don't feel what I feel right now. And I feel love, Nate, I feel love and I've never felt it like this. It's so strong inside of me and it hurts. It hurts me."

I gasped after the words were out of my mouth. But it did hurt to love like this. It hurt like hell. I'd never felt anything close to this. And I'd never felt it because I'd turned myself off for so many years, just to get through the hell of a loveless marriage. Just to get through the day.

He turned back to me. "Is this how you really feel?"

"I don't know," I said. "But I've never felt it before. And if I don't tell you and do something about it, I'll never forgive myself."

He bit his bottom lip and sucked it into his mouth. I craved that lip; I wanted to kiss it so bad.

"But why?" he asked. "Why would you feel like that about me?"

Because he had stirred something deep down inside me that had been asleep for a long time. He had forced me into feeling something I had forgotten. He had reminded me why love songs were written and why I had always felt that something was missing in my life. He was the reason I felt this way. He was why I was here, why I was still here. I was crafty and smart enough to escape from this house if I had wanted to. But I stayed because of him.

"I don't know," I said. "But I do."

He nodded. "I can't give you what you want."

"It doesn't matter," I said and stared at him. He wasn't that hard. He wasn't that mean. He just didn't know what to do with me. He'd never met anyone like me. He was just a man and that meant he didn't know what to do with women, not really. For the first time, I saw through the hard shell and into his true being and what I saw was so much like me. We wanted the same thing, he and I, but we were both too afraid to take it, even when it was being readily offered up like it was right then.

Just then, he turned to me and pulled me gently into his arms. found my arms slipping around his neck and pulling him in close to me. We didn't speak, we didn't kiss. We just held each other and I felt something deep within me stir and finally release.

I stared into his eyes and wondered how he saw me. What did he *see* when he looked at me? Did he see me as I saw myself or did he see someone else entirely? Did he like what he saw or was h just trying to figure out a way to keep me at a distance? Did he see the purity of my soul, the eagerness of my heart? And what did I see when I looked into his eyes? Did I just see myself reflected back?

He stared at me and nodded slightly, confirming my suspicions. He felt what I felt but he felt wrong about it. He'd done something bad, he'd kidnapped me and it tormented him. This wasn't the way it was supposed to work, he knew. But that was just the way it was.

He said, "I think I understand now."

That's all I needed to hear.

Trouble brewing.

The sex didn't stop but there was no longer a need for formalities. We just went right at it, into it. We played the games and afterwards, we would laugh at ourselves. He'd sometimes "punish" me by giving me a spanking and sometimes he just took what he wanted. Once he came into a room I was cleaning and, without a word, bent me over an old couch and fucked me. I was so turned on I was shaking. After it was over, he zipped his pants and disappeared out the door.

The sex just kept getting hotter and hotter. It was addicting, not only to me, but to him as well. It was like we couldn't get enough of each other and, really, we couldn't. When we weren't having sex, we were talking, laughing, bringing out the best in each other. It was odd to me how quickly it changed, how we went from enemies to lovers within days. There is a thin line between love and hate and we'd crossed it in the right direction.

I'd never felt so alive, so wanted, needed. Feeling like that was, in a way, better than the sex, though the sex was the best. Sometimes it was rough and sometimes he tied me up and sometimes he just made love to me. He'd start slow, giving me deep, long kisses that lasted for minutes at a time. He'd hold me tight, like he didn't want me to get away, and he'd caress me and touch me in a way that no man ever had. I would surrender to him, especially when he was gentle, though I liked it when he was rough, too.

"I wouldn't have you any other way," he said one day and climbed on top of me. "I love the way you are."

"I love the way you are too," I said and wrapped my arms around his neck.

He bent down and began to kiss my chest before he went to my breasts and then he began to tell me how he loved my body, "I love your breasts...I love your skin...your hair, your face, your eyes...I love..."

I waited breathlessly, knowing what he was going to say and wanting him to say it.

"You," he moaned and came back to my mouth, kissing me and then my chin, cheeks and earlobes. "I love you and you and you."

I shivered with delight at his words. *He loved me!* I didn't ask him if he really meant it. I knew he meant it. He didn't say things he didn't mean. I couldn't help but grin. I had him then and I knew it. He had me, too.

"I love you, too," I moaned, not missing a beat and held him still so I could kiss him more deeply.

"I love to be with you," he moaned.

"I love to be with you, too," I moaned back. "I love for you to take me."

He began to ride me harder, making me gasp and moan and want more. He kept it up until I was nearly bucking off the bed and so was he. We slammed against each other and it took every single ounce of energy we had to sustain it. Then we were coming and we were coming hard. It was one of those tingling orgasms, tickling its way around my body. I couldn't stop moving though I was beginning to tire. I had to keep it up until it came to me, until it took me, until it went away.

He was right behind me, coming so hard he gasped. When he was finished, he lay down beside me and stared at me. I turned to him and stared back. He smiled slightly and moved the hair out of my eyes with one finger.

"I meant it, you know?" he said quietly.

I felt a rush of warmth swoosh through my body. I had never felt anything like what I felt for him. It almost scared me but, somehow, it felt right.

"I know," I said. "And I meant it, too."

He nodded and smiled a little. "Good."

"Let me ask you something," I said. "Whose house is this?"

"Mine," he said.

"Really?"

He nodded. "Really."

"So is that why you kidnapped me?" I asked. "To help you fix it up?"

"No," he said and laughed. "But I thought you should earn your keep. I also wanted to keep you form getting bored."

I tried not to roll my eyes. "How did you get this house?"

"I won it in a bet," he said.

"A bet?" I asked, not believing him. But he nodded. I shook my head and said, "You did not. No one would just give you a house like this in a bet."

"I've done a lot of work on it," he said. "First time I saw it I almost hunted the bastard down I won it from."

"And who was that?"

"You don't know him."

I probably didn't. Besides, there was something else I wanted to know. I asked, "Why didn't you ever tell me that you're a Dr.?"

His eyebrows shot up. "How do you know that?"

"I'm a snoop," I said.

He smiled slightly. "What else did you find out?"

"Nothing much," I said. "Why don't you tell me why you kidnapped me?"

"I told you once," he said. "Money."

But there was more to it than that, he'd said that earlier. What else was there? I stared at him, knowing he wouldn't give it up. I didn't really care, either, not enough to make him close himself off to me. And he would if pushed too hard. I'd learned that about him. I could push just enough to get what I wanted but then I had to hold back. I'd get to the bottom of it one day, but this would not be the day.

I sighed and looked around the room. "So, are you gonna live here?"

He shook his head. "No, I'm going to sell it. It's a bit too fancy for me. And too large."

"It could be a nice hotel," I said.

He shrugged. "I suppose so. Whoever wants to buy it can do whatever they like."

"When are you going to sell it?"

"Soon," he said.

It suddenly struck me. Soon, I wouldn't be here. And neither would he. Soon, probably very soon, we wouldn't be together and there was no way I could live without him. But he had committed a crime and would more than likely do jail time when it was all over. My mind began to spin and I felt like crying.

"What's wrong?" he asked.

"What about..." I began and stopped myself.

He eyed me and nodded for me to go on. But I couldn't tell him what I was thinking. I didn't want to spoil the mood. Besides that, I foolishly thought there was plenty of time for us to make plans.

"Nevermind," I said and pressed my body up next to his. "Tell me about the place you come from or your childhood or something."

"Or we could do this," he said and slapped my ass, then squeezed it.

I grinned. "Yeah, I'd rather do that, too."

★ ★ ★ ★ ★

I was so in love with Nate, it scared me. But I'd never been happier. I was a changed woman, doing what came naturally. Love had a way of making me forget about my misery and complacency in life. All I thought about was the day ahead. I didn't plan for next week or think about a vacation or a shopping trip. I also didn't think about what I was doing, falling in love with my kidnapper. Who cared what he was? Where he'd been? I had no clue and it didn't matter. All I cared about was what was in my foreseeable future and all I saw was him.

The time flew but I didn't keep track of it. I didn't even know what day it was, didn't even care. I got my orders from him, did what he wanted and at night the fun started.

The work on the house was getting done. In fact, the house was almost entirely cleaned and painted. In a way, that frightened me. What happened once the work was over? And something else was odd. I noticed that some of the furniture was disappearing from the rooms. I asked him about it but he just shrugged. I knew he was selling it to antique dealers but I didn't care. It wasn't my house. As long as he left my bed alone, they could have everything else.

But, it was obvious there was trouble brewing. The trouble would be that all of this would be over soon and no matter how far I pushed it out of my mind, there was no denying it. It wasn't going to last. I knew something was up with me being there, something was wrong with it. I should have already been "rescued." I would think about it from time to time but after a while, I didn't care and wanted them, whoever "they" might be, to never, ever find me. I could live like that for the rest of my life and wouldn't have minded one bit.

I was completely in denial. It was a perpetual state of bliss.

We had a routine. We would wake up feeling each other up. I loved those touches first thing in the morning. They brought me awake, made me want him. He was always ready, too, and his dick would be hard with want for me. It would have been a shame not to climb on top of it and ride it. The morning sex was always intense, but a little rushed. We had work to do.

When we were done, we would shower, then go down to the kitchen and help each other make breakfast. As we ate, we would stare at each other and sometimes I would tease him about what he had done the previous night. He'd usually just shake his head at me.

After breakfast, he would disappear or sometimes he would stick around to help me. Next would be lunch. If I was by myself, I would fix a sandwich. If he was around, he would sometimes go out and buy us something from a restaurant nearby. They had the best cheeseburgers I'd ever eaten.

Once lunch was over, we would nap a little, and wake up groping each other. More sex and then a long shower, and next dinner. After dinner, the games would begin and he would take over. He was very determined and I would lose myself during our games, was glad to lose myself, to give myself over to him. I specially loved it when he bent me over his knee and spanked me.

We would play half the night and wind up asleep in each other's arms. We would wake and start the whole thing over. It was better than any amusement park or vacation or concert or anything in the world. It was so good, I knew it would never last but, at the same time, the thought of it ending was unbearable.

Sometimes we took a trip to the beach and spent the afternoon sunbathing. It was like we were a real couple, though anytime anyone saw me, he would get nervous and force me to go back to the house.

One morning, as he was about to disappear out the door, I asked him, "Where do you go during the day?"

He shrugged.

"Come on," I groaned. "Give it up."

"I have business," he said. "Be back later."

"Wait, Nate," I said, sitting up taller. "What about…what about the ransom?"

He seemed a little shocked at my question and said, "Why are you asking me this now?"

"I dunno," I said. "It just seems odd to me, that's all."

"What seems odd?"

I stared at him, realizing he didn't want to hear this. Maybe he was like me, denying that the future was here and we were living on borrowed time. I suddenly felt sick about it.

"It's just that," I said. "Why hasn't the ransom been paid? Haven't you gotten it yet?"

He stared at me and swallowed hard. "Do you want to go home?"

I felt dread come over my body. I began to stammer, "Uh uh…"

"Be honest," he said. "And tell me what you want."

I shrugged and said, "I want… I mean, I just want it to be over. I want us to be able to…you know… I just want some…something. I don't know what I want, Nate. It's just an odd situation."

He kept staring at me, and then an unreadable look crossed his face. "We'll talk about it later."

I started to say something else, but he disappeared out the door. He never answered my questions.

I sighed and got up and washed the dishes. As I washed them, knew something was going on. What, I didn't know. But something was wrong. How long had I been here?

"Fuck it," I muttered and wiped my hands dry with a dishtowel and threw it on the counter. I went into his room and sat down at his computer. Now or never. It was now.

I couldn't do it. I got up and began to pace, feeling like I was about to have a panic attack. I glanced over at the desk and a stack of papers caught my eye. I went though them and pulled out a newspaper.

As I shook it open, I glanced over the paper and my mouth dropped when I saw the headline: *Millionaire's wife kidnapped from Miami hotel.*

I laid the paper over the desk and smoothed it out. The article didn't so much disturb me as did the date: February 14th. I had been here since February 14th? That was Valentine's Day.

It had to be April now. Or it might even be the around the first of May. How long had I been there? I shook my head. It didn't seem like I'd been there that long, but the warm Florida weather wasn't much of an indicator. I knew it was hotter than when I first got there but it had been warm from day one.

I stared at his laptop. I ran over and turned it on. As soon as it started, I pointed the mouse at the time and the date popped up. I was shocked beyond belief and almost fell to the floor. It was August 7th.

That night, he brought me something special. He did that sometimes. Nothing fancy, just a flower or a favorite candy bar. Sometimes, a pack of cigarettes, which I would have to ration because he wouldn't buy them for me everyday. He told me constantly that I should quit, that he'd quit after twelve years of smoking.

"Hiya, baby," he said at the kitchen door.

I smiled at him. "Hey, yourself."

He held up a bag. "Got a surprise for you."

I grinned and took the bag. Inside was my favorite ice cream, the one I'd told him about last night—pistachio. "Let's not let it go to waste," I said and got a couple of spoons.

"Thanks," he said and took the spoon.

"Nate..." I began, thinking I ought to bring up the ransom again and maybe even a game plan of some kind. Something needed to be said.

"What is it, love?"

I didn't want to spoil the mood, but this had been avoided for too long. I said, "We should do something, Nate. We can't live like this forever."

He stared at me. "What do you mean?"

"I mean, we should move," I said. "We should—"

"Wait a minute," he said. "I thought…"

"You thought what?" I asked.

He stared at me, his mouth open. "I thought you… This morning you said something about wanting it to end."

"Huh?"

He shook his head and said, "Nothing," and smiled at me. "We can talk about it later."

"Okay," I said and smiled back. "Thanks for the ice cream."

"You're very welcome."

We shared the ice cream, feeding each other spoonfuls until it was all gone. Once it was finished, he grabbed the back of my head and pulled me to him. I went with him willingly and shared the kiss, as we had the ice cream.

"Let's go upstairs," he said.

He took my hand and lead me to my bedroom and there he laid me down and started kissing me, rubbing my body though my dress. I moaned and stared at him. Suddenly nothing mattered but him and his touches and his love. It didn't matter that they were probably never going to come and rescue me. I didn't want to be rescued. I had a safe haven here. Why would I want to leave it? I couldn't believe an hour ago I was biting my nails with nervousness and wondering what I was still doing here. It was obvious I was here because I belonged here.

"Wanna play a game?" he asked and grinned wickedly.

"You know I do," I said.

"Tie you up, then?"

I nodded eagerly and he did what he did best. He tied me up, securing the ropes until I was bound so tightly I couldn't move. I began to feel pain, but the pain was immediately replaced with his lips. He was kissing me, kissing over the ropes, loving me and whispering my name.

I threw my head back and moaned.

He muttered something. I didn't hear him, but I caught something in his words. It was the word "miss".

"What did you say?" I asked.

"Shh," he said and began to kiss me, again.

I let the sensations sink in, though his muttering was beginning to bother me. I asked again, "What did you say?"

"Now be quiet," he said and tightened the ropes.

"Ow," I said as the ropes cut into my skin. He had never tied them this tightly before. "What are you doing?"

"You know what I'm doing, love," he murmured and began to trace lines down my body with his finger.

I let it go and went back into the moment and in this moment I was bound and he was in total control of me. When he would tie me up, he would touch me, bring me to the brink of orgasm and then pull away. He would do this until all of my senses were alert and ready for more. Just when I was about to go over the edge, he would untie the ropes, sometimes repositioning them, or leaving them off altogether. Tonight was different. There was something different about all of it. He was more concentrated than ever before, as if he was going to make sure I got all I wanted.

"How's that?" he whispered hotly and licked my ear. "How do you like that?"

"I love it," I breathed and turned my head to his. We kissed, licking at each other's mouths until he began to squeeze my breast. I moaned but something flickered across my mind. It was that word again, miss. Miss. He had said, "I'm going to miss you." No, he didn't. Did he? Did that mean...? No! No! Nooooooo!

I suddenly wanted out of the ropes, wanted out so much I began to scream. He looked shocked. "Take them off now!" I screamed. "*Please!*"

"Shh, shhhhhhhh," he muttered and began to caress me. "It's okay. I'm here. Shhhhh... Calm down."

He kept caressing me and I began to calm. I didn't even know where that panic came from, but it was a deep dark place.

"I'll take 'em off," he said and began to untie me.

I calmed down but my heart was still racing and I was sweating. "You're not leaving, are you?"

"Shh," he said and put a finger to his lips. "I'll untie them now."

It was true. It was so true. It was our last night together. I suddenly couldn't breathe. I couldn't move, think. I began to cry and the crying turned into sobs. He held me and told me to be quiet. I couldn't stop. The thought of being separated from him was unbearable.

He untied the ropes and held me close for a minute. We didn't speak for a long time. I couldn't have said one word. It just couldn't be happening.

"But—" I began as the tears began to spill out of my eyes.

He cut me off with a "shh" and put one finger to my lips and told me to lie back on the bed and open my legs. I was about to argue with him, but then I thought I should do what he wanted because it was what I wanted, too.

I lay back and he began to devour me with his eyes, the way he always did. The intensity of the situation was what I liked best. I loved the way his eyes ate me up and savored me. He loved the way I looked, the curves of my body, the flatness of my stomach, the roundness of my hips.

He got between my legs and began to caress me with his mouth, just pressing it against my pussy at first before he began to lick and suck on it. I began to come almost instantaneously and I tried to pull him on top of me.

He shook his head and told me to get up on all fours. I couldn't help but smile and I got up. He ran his hand over my ass and slapped it. I shivered and trembled. He did it again and again until my ass was red as an apple and once it was, he bent down and kissed it before shoving his hard cock into me and riding me hard, like he wasn't going to stop until he fucked me raw.

I moaned as began to fuck me even harder. I had to hold onto the bed. Thoughts kept trying to come into my mind, thoughts about him leaving me, about me going back home. I pushed them away and enjoyed it, enjoyed what he was giving. No matter what happened, I wasn't going to let him go. I would figure out a way to keep him. I don't know how, but I would.

He began to ride me even harder and he pushed his hand between my legs and pressed it against my clit. I began to rub against his hand and loved the feeling of his hand and of his hard cock and of him.

It didn't take long before we were both coming. I threw my head back as it hit me, and it hit me hard. He gave a hard thrust and pulled out and came all over my back. His hot cum dripped all along my back and down between my cheeks. I ground up against him and moaned with delight.

"I love you," he said and pulled me down on him.

"I love you, too," I murmured and kissed his earlobe. "Nate, you know, we can—"

"Shh," he said and put a finger to my lips. "Let's sleep."

"We have to talk about this," I said.

"In the morning," he muttered. "Goodnight."

It was no use. What was the use in all this? It was all going to be over no matter what I said or did. But I knew what I was going to do. I was going to convince him to stay with me. We could run away together.

We lay down and held each other and we fell asleep and of course, when I awoke he was gone. That's when I realized my mistake. I had told him I wanted it to be over and he'd misunderstood me, thinking I meant us. Oh, God, why did I do that? Did I really want to be unhappy? I had inadvertently self-sabotaged myself. As usual? I was my own worst enemy.

Before I could chastise myself too much, Grant came into the room. When he saw me crying, he wasn't too happy. But then again, I wasn't too happy, either.

Home again.

I asked Grant what took so long. He shrugged and said, "America's a big place, Kara, you know?"

I let it go. I let it go because it didn't really matter. I knew there was nothing I could do to get Nate back. I knew I would have to resume my life. I knew I would never fall for anyone the way I had fallen for him. I shouldn't have slept that night. I should have said something. I should have told him I wanted to be with him. But I was an idiot, thinking it went without saying.

I was in so much pain from missing Nate, I literally ached. I would think about him and want to die from not having him near me. I would pray for him, pray to have him return to me but I knew that would never happen. And that killed me.

I cried a lot but kept it to myself. I didn't want anyone to know what had happened. I didn't want them to taint it. No one would understand. I didn't understand it myself.

I took my emotions, my love for him, and I buried it. I buried it beneath all the other good stuff I had felt in my life. It took up most of the room. I ignored it and hoped it would stop tormenting me one day. But I was afraid of that day. I was afraid to stop loving him. I knew once I did, I would lose the one thing in my life that had meant the most to me. The one thing I had had in my life that I never thought I would. I had never felt deserving of love but with him, *because* of him, I knew I did deserve it. And then as soon as I accepted it, it was snatched away from me.

This went on for six months or so.

Finally, it broke. It had to. The misery couldn't go on forever and one morning I awoke feeling a little better. After I showered, I ran down to Grant's office and started going through his CDs. He had an excellent collection and sometimes I would go into his office and play some music. I was dying to listen to some Smiths. I finally found the one I wanted, popped it in and grinned when *There Is a Light That Never Goes Out* came on. It was one of my favorite songs just because it was so simple. It just said so much without putting the listener through a lot of pretentious bullshit.

I sat down in Grant's chair and was about to get lost in the music when someone knocked on the door.

"Come in!" I called and turned the stereo down.

James stuck his head in and said, "There's someone to see you, Miss."

"Oh?" I asked and peered over his shoulder. Maybe it was Nate. I almost smiled but then stopped because it wasn't Ned. It was Todd.

"Hello, Kara," he said and entered the room.

James closed the door softly.

I knew the disappointment showed on my face. I would fantasize about Nate showing up one day and every day I'd be disappointed. I turned away from Todd and said, "What do you want?"

He sighed, sat down in one of the chairs in front of the desk and said, "Listen, I'll cut to the chase."

"What chase?" I asked and picked up my cigarettes.

"Here," he said and flipped a disc at me.

I eyed it but didn't pick it up. "What is it?"

"Why don't you find out?" he said and stood, ready to leave the room.

"What kind of game are you playing?" I asked him.

"I'm not playing a game, Kara."

"Oh, come on, Todd," I said. "You've been playing me since the day I met you, in one way or another."

"Yeah," he said, tuning back to me. "And I'm sorry about that."

I swallowed hard and looked at the cigarette between my fingers. I'd forgotten to light it.

He said, "Let me tell you something, okay? I've needed to say this to you for a long time but every time I get close, you shut me down. I have to say it now."

"Okay," I replied, feeling a little uneasy.

He took a breath and said, "When we first met, I was blown away by you but I was an asshole and I hurt you. I didn't know what I was doing back then, Kara, all I know is that what we had scared me. And, of course, I couldn't marry you. I had to marry someone my parents wanted me to."

I stared at him realizing that was the predicament a lot of rich kids found themselves in. They were raised with every conceivable advantage but the one thing they needed and wanted—love—was kept away from them. He was like Grant, in a way. Grant couldn't be what he was because of his wealth and Todd couldn't love who he wanted for the same reason. It was the trappings of the elite and they trapped themselves in it. I was suddenly glad I'd grown up poor. I didn't have all this bullshit to deal with. I could love whomever I wanted. There were no guidelines set forth for me. But for them, they didn't have a chance at real love. It was all about connecting, marrying the "right" kind of people. Grant had just married me, someone of lower class, to get back at his parents because they wouldn't let him be who he was.

It didn't do me much good. I just got caught up in it. But it didn't matter anymore.

Todd went on, "I've always regretted doing that to you because you're a good person and I screwed it up. You don't know how many nights I've spent awake thinking of you. I stayed friends with Grant just to be nearer to you. But you hate me now and there's nothing I can do about it."

I was almost touched but then I got suspicious again. "Yeah, that sounds good but what's in it for you?"

"Nothing," he said. "I just want to make things right between us again."

"Todd, there will never be—"

"I know that," he said, cutting me off. "I know we had something special once, when we were kids. We're not kids anymore but I always regretted acting like that to you. I'll regret it forever, Kara. Don't think I won't."

"Okay..." I said, not understanding what he was getting at.

"It's just that," he said, then stopped. He cleared his throat and continued, "It's just that I thought you should know what happened."

"What are you talking about?"

"Why you were kidnapped," he said.

I sat up taller and picked up the disc. "What are talking about, Todd?"

"Go through those files," he said. "And you'll know."

"Wait a minute," I said. "Are you saying...? What are saying?"

"You're a smart girl, Kara," he said. "You'll figure it out."

With that, he left the room. What the hell had just happened? I stared at the disc and then into space for a moment and was about to pop it into Grant's computer when I thought that might not be the best idea. So, I ran back to my room, turned on my computer and inserted it. There weren't any files on it. The disc was empty. But why...? Damn Todd anyway. What was up with this? I stared at the blank computer screen.

Wait a minute.

I worked until I finally uncovered a hidden file on it. Good thing I'd been bored for the last ten years and the computer was my only boredom relief, otherwise I might not have ever figured out what was going on. I was almost excited. What could it be? Family secrets? God, I would love to get something on those bastards.

As soon as I opened the file, I knew that I had something on them. But not something I wanted to have. What I found out shocked me. It also made me a little sick to my stomach.

★ ★ ★ ★ ★

Grant just stared at me. God, I wanted to slap him so bad. I waved the disc in his face. "I know what you did."

"How did you find that?" he asked.

"What does it matter how?" I asked. "It's all in here."

He nodded.

"Aren't you going to say anything?" I asked.

"What were you doing in my office?"

"You bastard!" I yelled. "You stole his idea!"

He shrugged. He was so smug I should have beaten him on general principal.

"I can't believe this," I said, shaking my head.

"Who gave you that?"

"Shut up," I hissed. "Just tell me how you could have done something like this. Just tell me how you could have stolen Nate's idea. He had a great idea and you stole it. He worked so hard and you *took* it all from him. You destroyed his life, didn't you? He was nothing after you were done with him."

"'Nate'?' he said. "Are you on a first-name basis with this guy?"

If he only knew... He never would, I'd make sure of that. I said, "Don't try to turn this around on me. Just tell how you could have destroyed him."

"I didn't destroy him," he replied dryly. "Stop being so dramatic."

I rolled my eyes.

"How did you get the disc?" he asked.

"I found it," I lied. I wasn't about to tell him his best friend had sold him down the river. Especially since it worked to my advantage so well.

He shrugged. "What's it to you?"

"To me?" I snapped. "It's everything, that's what it is. You took his idea and you didn't give him shit for it. *That's* why he kidnapped me."

He sighed. "That's crazy."

"No, it isn't," I said. "I wasn't kidnapped for money. I was kidnapped for revenge."

He sighed again but didn't say anything.

"He was the guy that came here last year, wasn't he?" I asked. "He was the guy who yelled at you at the front door, wasn't he? He threatened you but you let it slide, didn't you?"

He nodded.

"Why did you do it?"

"Our stock was down," he said. "It was a good idea but he couldn't execute it. We just took it and improved it. The product—"

"You sacrificed me—your own wife—for the business!" I yelled. "How could you?"

"Well, it wasn't like that, you see—"

"God!" I yelled and shook my fists in the air. "What is wrong with you?"

"With me?"

"Yes, with you," I hissed, seething. "You've given up your life for this bullshit and you don't have anything to show for it. You're just a miserable bastard."

"Shut up," he said and sighed again.

"You don't have anyone who loves you…" I stopped. I was getting mean and I didn't want to be mean. Not anymore. I didn't have to. I, for once, had the upper hand. But it was true. No one loved him. They used him, his money. I tried to love him, and maybe I did, at first. But that was a long time ago. I could have loved him if he could have loved me, which he couldn't. It was over before it ever began.

I calmed down and said, "Is this why you left me there for so long? Is that why you didn't pay up?"

His eyes narrowed at me. "I *did* pay up."

"When?"

"After a few weeks," he said. "I kept the police out of it, just like he wanted. He told me he'd leave you alone so you could leave on your own. I kept waiting for you to materialize."

"What are you saying?" I mumbled, almost shocked at what he was insinuating. And what he was insinuating was true. I had kept myself prisoner. But even more importantly, Nate had kept me there, he'd even brought me back from that bar. Why? But I knew why now. He'd brought me back because he didn't want me to leave so soon. For the same reason, I hadn't protested and had gone back with him. We both knew we had some unfinished business.

"Yeah, that's right, Kara," he said. "He left you alone, didn't he?"

I gulped.

"I thought so," he said. "He left so you could leave but the thing is, you didn't leave, did you?"

I looked away from him.

"Why didn't you leave?" he asked. "I gave him what he asked for and I thought I'd have my wife back. Why didn't you leave, Kara?"

"Because he gave me something I needed," I said and stared back at him.

"No, because you're a whore."

I didn't take the bait. He wanted a fight but I wasn't going there.

"So," he said. "I waited and waited and waited some more. Before long, I had a pretty good idea of what the two of you were doing."

"You don't know anything."

"You act like a whore, I know that," he snarled. "What's wrong with you?"

"Don't you dare judge me," I hissed. "Who the hell do you think you are?"

He glared at me. "But you didn't leave, did you? I mean...I didn't know where you were. I hired private detectives to find you but they couldn't. And he didn't tell me, either. He only promised to let you go. You stayed there with him even after you were allowed to go. I expected more of you."

"More of me?" I hissed. "You've got to be kidding! You are not going to turn this thing around on me! You're the one at fault!"

"I'm at fault?" he spat. "Oh, yeah, me. And you're out there spreading your legs for anyone who looks twice at you. You're the one who stayed with that guy for months on end doing God knows what."

He eyed me with contempt. Sex. Sex was so bad, wasn't it? He just couldn't stand the thought of it. Then I got it. He was jealous of me, of my sexuality. He seethed knowing I was out doing what I wanted, doing what my body told me to do. He couldn't allow himself to do anything like that. He was too prim and proper, too uptight. He didn't want me to do it because he, himself, couldn't do it. He thought we should both be miserable. I was done with that.

"Yeah, sit there and judge," I told him. "Sit there and not feel one thing, don't even think about taking responsibility for yourself, Grant. Look what you did to me. I might have been kidnapped, but I won't be your prisoner anymore."

"If you think—"

I cut him off, "I think. You did all of this because… Hell, I didn't even care why! You're just a greedy son of a bitch who got caught! Who gives a shit? I don't."

"Then why are you in here bitching about it?"

"I'm not bitching," I said. "I'm done with it, Grant."

"So?"

"So, you know what I want," I said. "It's time for you to let me go."

He shook his head and stared at the wall.

"It's time for you to tell your parents who you really are and stop being such a miserable bastard."

He didn't say a word.

"I want to know where he is," I said. "And I want a divorce with a big settlement and if I don't get it, I will go to your parents and tell them how you're running the business."

"You think my old man hasn't ever done anything like that?" he asked. "Everyone does it."

"I don't care, Grant," I said. "But I won't go along with it anymore. If you don't let me go, I'm going to tell the world you're gay and that our marriage is a sham."

"Well," he muttered.

"I'm going to do what I have to do and this time you can't stop me." I threw the disc on the desk and started out of the room but stopped and turned back to him. "And don't screw me. And I want this divorce to be short and sweet, got it?"

"You're ruining everything," he said.

"No," I said and reached to shut the door. "That was you."

He just stared at me. But I had a feeling I was going to get what I wanted. All thanks to Todd, who had, ironically, brought Grant and me together in the first place. And now he helped tear us apart. I was going to send him a big basket of fruit.

Goodbye, I'm going home.

Try as I could, I couldn't find Nate. I looked everywhere and under every rock. I hired private investigators but they came up with nothing. All I knew was his first name and that he was from somewhere in England. Grant wouldn't tell me anything, either. He told me, "If you want that son of a bitch, you can find him yourself."

But I had nothing to go on and it soon became apparent that nothing was all I would ever have. I didn't stop my search for months. I longed and ached for him. But he was nowhere to be found.

With all my money from the divorce—plus alimony—I moved to Miami, bought a beach house and set up a new life as a rich divorcée. I brought James along with me and his wife, who became my housekeeper. It was just the three of us most nights and we all dined together. We were this nice little family. Sometimes their kids or grandkids would visit and I would give them the house to themselves and go to a hotel. Sometimes Emily would come to visit and she and I would hang out together on the beach.

It was during one of those visits that I was staying in the same hotel where I'd been kidnapped. Just as the sun was about to set, I went outside to the beach, kicked off my shoes and took a long stroll. I still missed Nate desperately but one day, I rationalized, I would wake up and it wouldn't hurt so badly. That day was a long way off but it would come and he and I would both just be memories to each other. Fond ones, but just memories.

I dreaded that day.

As I made my way down the beach, I thought about James. He would sometimes ask me what happened to me when I was kidnapped. He wanted to know why I had all of a sudden left Grant. I didn't tell him, of course. But he knew something was up. He knew something had happened and he figured it was something remarkable.

"What happened?" he asked one day. "Come on, tell me."

I stared at him and sighed. "You really want to know?"

He nodded.

I went over the details quickly, not revealing too much, and told him I think I fell in love with Nate.

He didn't seem surprised. "Sounds like a classic case of Stockholm Syndrome."

"What's that?"

"It's when the abducted party starts sympathizing with their kidnapper."

Was that what I had? I tried to think back to the time when I started sympathizing with Nate. I couldn't pinpoint a specific time. I decided it didn't matter. Whatever had happened, happened. There was nothing I could do about it and I shouldn't feel bad because I did love him. If came out of trauma, then it came out of trauma.

"I don't know, James," I said. "But I know I'll never see him again."

He stared at me sadly and said, "Maybe you will."

We smiled at each other and I was so glad to have a friend as good as him. I didn't tell him that, it would be too corny, but I felt it. I hoped he felt the same way about me.

They say things happen for a reason. They're right. They do. If Grant hadn't stolen Nate's idea, I would have never met Nate. It's possible but unlikely that we might have crossed paths in London or wherever he was from. We might have had a drink together. I might have had sex with him, but he wouldn't have ever been allowed to strip me the way he had, down to the bare bones. He would have never been able to show me myself like he did. I wouldn't have let him near me in that way. I would have used him and his body and then ran away before he could get close.

I would have been a bitch.

I sighed and turned around and started back to the hotel. It was getting dark and I had plans to see a guy I'd met a few days ago for dinner. I didn't want to meet him but I knew it was time to move on. I knew that I might not ever love anyone as much as I loved Nate, but I did have the capacity. I had always been afraid of being unlovable. Now I knew I wasn't. And I had love to give, even if I couldn't give it to the person I wanted.

Just before I got back to the hotel, I sat a few feet away from the water and watched it. I sat there and felt tears on my cheeks though I didn't feel like crying. I felt the ache, the old familiar ache in my heart that I longed to be rid of. I felt that enormous lump in my throat that always came up whenever I was sad.

I was moving on. I was moving on from Nate. I had given it plenty of time, but I didn't have anymore time to waste.

All of a sudden, I felt nauseous. My eyes blinked and I realized that there was hand in front of my face, on my mouth and nose. The hand was holding a white handkerchief that had something strong and odorous on it and I was breathing that smell in.

I realized, with regret, that I should have hired a bodyguard like Grant had told me to, especially since I insisted on moving to Miami. "Once you've been kidnapped," he said. "You're an even bigger target. I know you don't like to listen to me, but do it this time."

Oh, well. Hindsight is twenty-twenty.

★ ★ ★ ★ ★

I awoke with a start lying on a bed. I was blindfolded. I could tell I was in some sort of cheap hotel. I could hear the traffic on the nearby interstate and I could feel the cheap, scratchy bedspread beneath me. Oh, shit, this was just great.

I reached up to untie the blindfold when I heard the voice.

"Don't."

My heart began to race and it began to swell with love. I whispered, "Don't what?"

"Don't take it off."

I couldn't help but smile. "Why? Why not take it off?"

"You know why," he said.

I pulled the blindfold off and there he was, larger than life, grinning at me from across the room. I had dreamed of this moment for so long, I didn't know how to react. You never react in the way you plan, it comes out all wrong. And it comes out wrong because you don't realize how happy you'll be when you see the one person in the world that you've longed to see.

"How have you been, Nate?" I asked.

He smiled deeply at me. "Terrible. And you?"

"The same," I said. "You're a hard person to track down, you know?"

He nodded. "I had to lay low for a while, being a kidnapper and all. I couldn't make any sudden moves."

I nodded that I understood. And I did finally understand. I said, "That's all over now. We don't have to worry about it."

"No," he said. "We don't. Not anymore."

And we didn't. He came to me then. He was at the bed and then he was by my side, with me. As soon as he touched me, I felt whole again. I was where I was always meant to be. He was my home, my security. I was never leaving home again.

He started to kiss me, but then pulled back and said, "This time, let's do it right."

I smiled at him. "Yes, let's."

And we did. We did it right, right from the start. It was just me and him and for once in my life, the right thing had found me. And it never felt so good.

Lightning Source UK Ltd.
Milton Keynes UK
UKOW052148270612

195166UK00001B/39/P